HEIR APPARENTLY

by

AVÉ

Stork Street Entertainment

Original. Artistic. Independent.

To MILLICENT KELLY
for supporting and
believing in me
when no one else would.

October

Chapter 1

RRRRRRRRIIIIIINNNNNGGGGG!!!

The mallet on top of the old-fashioned alarm clock sitting on the nightstand violently attacked the two bells flanking it, filling the room with the most putrid sound. A hand peeked out from under the thick, white duvet, silenced the alarm, and retreated. A young man reluctantly peeled his head off the comfortable pillow, flung his legs off of the side of the bed, and sat rubbing his eyes. Slowly, he began to doze off when another putrid sound assaulted his eardrums, only this time it was less mechanical and more annoying.

"Victoooor! Victor, wake up! Breakfast ends in twenty minutes," a voice yelled from the intercom speaker across the room. Victor groaned and shuffled to his bathroom to start his day. A quick washcloth to his face, soap to his body, and toothpaste to his mouth was all that was needed to wake him completely. He then went to his closet and put on a white button up shirt, black slim pants, black loafers, and a black belt with a silver buckle. He left his closet and walked over to his dresser where he slid on his favorite silver watch that his grandmother bought him for Christmas last year. Lastly, he clipped a sterling silver necklace with a cross around his neck and placed a white fedora on his head. After a quick look in the full-length mirror on the other side of the room, he nodded with a smile of approval and headed to the dining room.

He walked down the long corridor with centuries-old paintings crowding the walls. He addressed every maid, cleaner, and guard that he passed by name. Most members of the royal family never bothered learning the names of the "help" other than himself and his grandmother, which earned him great respect and loyalty from those around him.

Finally, he entered the private dining room, ready to eat. The antique wooden table was decorated with two vases of flowers and the china, silverware, and glassware of his ancestors. Around the table sat the members of his immediate family. At the head of the table sat the newest member of the family, his stepfather, Christopher Duke of Spiti or affectionately known as "The Duke." He was formerly known as Special Agent Christopher Schaeffer, a handsome 35-year-old agent with the National Investigation Bureau. Adjacent to him was his mischievous little brother, Prince Seth - a tall, stocky 19-year-old with a deep disdain for obedience. Across from him was the eldest of the three children, Princess Jacqueline "Jackie" — a tall, intelligent 24-year-old beauty who loved "gracing the cover" of the trendiest magazines. And finally, at the other head of the table sat Princess Mary, aged 51 years and the heir apparent to the throne of The Kingdom of Iakos.

"You're late," Mary reprimanded, without even looking up. Though everyone else at the table had an almost empty plate of food in front of them, Mary had a black folder and official papers spread out across her placemat.

"Good morning to you too," Victor snapped back pulling out the seat next to Seth.

"Oh no!" Mary said, "Breakfast is over."

"What?"

"I called you down thirty minutes ago. I sent your plate back. We must go," Mary said as she began sliding her papers into a pile and placing them into the leather folder.

"Why would you do that?" Victor replied, trying in vain to remain respectful.

"Because I called you and you didn't come. You could have gotten dressed after."

"Whatever," Victor mumbled.

Mary stood, "I have a busy day before Chris and I go off to the coast for the week. The Queen has summoned us so you will not make me late. Let's go!"

Victor looked at Mary, lost. "Us? Grandmother summoned us?"

"Yes. You and me. What about that simple word are you missing?"

"Wow, mum! Are you two starting already?" Jackie interjected, as she got up with her plate and glass and placed it on the cart by the window for the cleaners to take away.

"Did she summon us as her daughter and grandson? Or did she summon us, her two heirs?"

"What does it matter?" Mary hissed, giving her new husband a kiss goodbye that lasted a little too long.

"Ewww, that's my cue to leave," Seth cringed, clearing his spot as well.

"The car is in the courtyard already. Let's go!" Mary said, marching out of the room and up the corridor. Victor kissed Seth and Jackie on the cheek and then followed Mary, power walking like a suburban mother. He really wasn't looking forward to this car ride.

It usually takes about 40 minutes by motorcade to get from the Rousel Palace in the country province of Spiti, to the State Palace located in the exact center of the capital city, Parados. By chopper, it's about 15-20 minutes but the helicopter is reserved mainly for the Crown.

Victor got in the large black SUV to find Mary already inside typing on her iPhone. She leaned forward keeping her eyes locked on her phone and ordered, "State Palace" to the driver. He nodded and repeated the destination into his wrist. Then, the five-car motorcade began to move. The first car was a local police car that usually lights up once they are off the grounds. Next were three identical black SUVs: one with security, one with Victor and Mary, and the third doubling as a decoy for security purposes and a spare just in case one of the other SUVs stops working. Lastly, another patrol police car that ensures no one can drive up from behind and hit anyone.

They drove for miles quietly until Victor tried to break the silence. "Mother?"

"What?" She replied. Completely turned off by her lack of interest in his conversation, he gave up and pulled out his phone to play a game. "What?" Mary repeated.

"I just wanted to know why we are being summoned?"

"Victor, your guess is as good as mine."

"Right." Victor put on his headphones and isolated himself.

As they made their way through the countryside, they sat in silence. The hands on Victor's watch danced gracefully from diamond to diamond. As the minute hand came almost full circle, the foliage and endless timber became asphalt and concrete. They made their way through the streets as Victor watched the array of lives he rarely got to see. All of them fantasize about being a primary member of the royal family — the fortune, power, fame, and palaces — but they never get to see the seclusion, the constant security, and heaviest of all, the limitations. Duty always prevails in this family and Victor knew all too well of the sacrifices this family has made in the name of "duty". Heads turned and watched the motorcade run lights and make up its own road laws with their faces lit up with excitement. If only they knew that the grass on this side was greener because it was artificial.

Finally, they slowed as they approached the center of the capital city: the largest residence in the island country emerged — a long white palace with a grand black and gold gate spanning the perimeter of the almost 1000 acres of sculpted gardens and parks, tree-lined walkways, and helipad at the center of a circular maze garden at the rear of the palace.

The motorcade stopped at the gate, a military guard whispered to the security guard in the first SUV and — viola — entrance to the home of the Crown. They drove along the road that circles the palace and came to the private entrance secluded by large trees and a camouflaged doorway that matched the two-story windows lining each floor of the 4-floor building, not including the tower. Victor and Mary stepped out of the SUV and shuffled quickly through the doors held open by two bowing military men. The first corridor Prince Victor and Princess Mary entered was lined with large portraits of former Iakon monarchs.

After a few more turns they arrived at two tall, burgundy-stained wooden doors with gold trimming and handles, and two guards standing in front. They both bowed, "Your Royal Highnesses!" and opened both doors revealing the internal residential foyer. The walls were painted a pale peach, which complemented the perfectly buffed white marble floor. Their shoes sang of their presence louder than anywhere else in the palace.

Golden light fixtures were mounted along the walls both downstairs and upstairs. And of course, the hall was complete with two marble staircases covered with a burgundy carpet, held down by golden stair rods. The stairs semi-circled to meet and form a landing above another door, which led to the private dining room. Along the stairs stood a gold painted banister with a regal design featuring crowns, crosses, and national symbols. And finally, an enormous chandelier hung from the second floor, almost reaching the first, and featured well over 100 dangling glass pieces.

Victor stood with his hands behind his back, confused. "Why are we just standing here?"

"Her Majesty told me to wait here for her," Mary replied. "So that's what we're going to do."

"Well, where is she?"

"Did I give birth to you without a patience bone or something?" Mary spat, unwarranted.

"No, but maybe the doctor could have rubbed off some anatomy knowledge onto you so you wouldn't say things like 'patience bone,'" Victor retorted, his calm voice dripping with sarcasm.

"How dare you speak to me in that manner?"

"Oh, and in what manner would you like me to speak to you? Oh wait, you wouldn't! You want me to stand here and take your attacks with no reply, whatsoever."

"No, you disrespectful child," Mary snarled, articulating every word clearly. She advanced toward him, with her posture never faltering. "You will speak to me with respect!"

"Then, respectfully, learn how to give it for once," Victor spat back. Neither of their voices was raised, but the tension in the air rose exponentially. Victor tried not to make a habit of going tit-for-tat with his mother because he was raised to always respect his elders, especially in the Royal Family. But ever since his mother remarried, she loved crossing lines with Victor, so much so that even when she wasn't, the line appeared obliterated.

Mother and son stood at the same height, in a staring contest that mirrored a game of Say Uncle. Finally, a voice filled the room, echoing from the walls and floor. "Alright you two, stop this now!" Victor turned to the stairs to find Queen Margaret I slowly making her way down the stairs. Her white knuckles clutched the banister. She wore a pale yellow half-calf dress and a matching woolen coat and hat.

Victor shuffled to the stairs and leapt up them to meet her. He offered his arm for her to hold as she descended. Margaret sweetly rejected the offer with an extended hand and a slight head shake. Victor nodded and followed alongside her to make sure she was safe until they reached the floor. At the bottom, Margaret continued, "What has gotten into you both? You bicker like children rather than mother-and-son."

"Well, he's always disrespecting me and I'm tired of it," Mary whined.

Margaret gently, but authoritatively extended her hand to stop Mary. "You are not a child, Mary. Don't give me that *he started it* defense like a toddler." Mary fixed to respond but immediately stopped herself. Back and forth would work with Victor, but would never work with *her* mother. Victor smirked slightly externally and laughed hysterically internally. Without looking to him, Margaret continued, "And you, Victor, need to stop talking back to your mother. I know she pushes your buttons — "

"I do not!" Mary retorted, echoing across the foyer.

"But sometimes a simple 'Yes ma'am' is enough to stop a tantrum." Margaret and Victor chuckled. Mary grunted, turned, and began to storm out of the residential suite. "Mary, you go ahead to the gardens. We'll catch up with you so we can talk," Margaret called out, then turned to her grandson. "I'm so sorry, Victor. Sometimes she acts like she hasn't aged past 5 years, but she means well."

"I'm not sure that she does, sometimes," Victor replied, as they walked into the corridors. They turned the corner and made their way through the rear entrance and into the vast State Palace gardens. As they walked, they caught up on their lives. Victor shared with his grandmother the loneliness that had been seeping into him, especially lately. He also shared the growing tension at the Rousel Palace, since the wedding. Margaret reciprocated with her frustrations and pressures with life as the monarch. These conversations were a common occurrence for them as they shared a bond that seemed unbreakable.

They caught up with Mary on a bench in the circular maze garden. She sat still sulking until she noticed the Queen and prince advancing toward her. She reluctantly stood and turned her body toward them without looking in their direction. As they arrived, Victor helped Margaret to sit on the stone bench and took a seat at her right side. Mary heavily flopped on the left side of the Queen as Victor began to chuckle at the immaturity. Margaret popped both Mary and Victor on the leg and they both sat up straight.

"I need someone to give a speech in my name at an elementary school next week," Margaret spoke coldly.

"I will go," Mary quickly replied. "I'll clear my schedule and give the speech for you."

"Thank you."

"So, Grandma, why did you summon us?" Victor finally asked.

Margaret paused for a moment and then began, "I have some rather distressing news to share with you."

"Are you ok?" Mary leaned in, her tone having dramatically changed to one of concern.

"Well, my dear, I've been having these horrible headaches for some time now, along with some nausea and vomiting. And, of course, you've seen how movement has become…difficult. About a month ago, I summoned the doctor who came here to the palace to examine me. He was concerned. So, they completed further tests and the conclusion… was not so good."

"Mummy, stop beating around the bush. What is going on?"

There was a long pause, as Margaret simply stared across the garden for a few moments. Finally, she spoke, "It's cancer."

Mary gasped, literally clutching her pearls, while Victor sat stunned. "What kind?" Victor spoke, swallowing hard.

"Brain cancer. A grade IV glioblastoma."

Mary's mind reeled, with tears building up in her eyes, which were fixed on the Queen. "So, what are the doctors doing about it? Surgery?"

"It's inoperable," Margaret replied, slowly.

Mary jumped to her feet. "What? How can they say that? You're the Queen; they can't just do nothing."

"Mummy, there are other possible treatments," Victor stuttered. He rested his elbows on his knees with his head slouched forward. "Chemo. Radiation. Maybe we can find a good clinical trial."

"Exactly and sit up," Margaret said tapping Victor's knee. Victor sat up straight as she continued. "I will begin chemo and radiation treatments today. I would like it if someone came to stay with me here at State Palace."

"Grandma, I think you should take some time at Rousel Palace to get away from the city and rest."

"No!" Margaret spoke. "The Crown doesn't neglect duty."

"But you're not neglecting duty," Victor continued. "You're resting and healing so that you can continue to do your duty."

"And I just got married," Mary rebutted.

"Mum, what does that have to do with anything?" Victor spat back.

"Newlyweds need their home to themselves. Mother will be perfectly fine right here."

"Are you kidding me? First," Victor began standing up, "it is a palace. You can fit our entire extended family in that place and still have rooms to spare. Two, your mother just told you that she has cancer and you're thinking about how it will affect your marriage? You can't be that selfish."

"Victor, that's your mother —" Margaret warned.

Victor turned to Margaret. "And you're *her* mother. Why can't she act like it?"

"And why can't you speak to me with respect?" Mary bellowed, grabbing Victor by the arm and turning him to face her. Victor violently ripped his arm away.

"Stop!" Margaret demanded, after which she grabbed her forehead and leaned forward. Victor sat back next to her and rubbed her back.

"Are you okay?" Victor whispered.

"I just need help. I guess I'll call Rose."

"No, I'll come and stay with you," Victor reassured her. "The Duchess doesn't have to come from 5 hours away when you have me."

"Thank you!"

"When is your first treatment, Mother?"

"Today, 1700 hours."

"Well I can't stay that long. Christopher and I are going to the coast and I have to get back to finish packing. Victor, can you stay?"

"Sure, mum. Go! I'll take care of *your* mother."

Mary rolled her eyes at Victor. "Call me and tell me how it goes, Mother."

"Sure," Margaret gave a quick half-smile without looking at her. Mary kissed her cheek, offered a small curtsy backed away a few steps and shuffled off to the Palace.

Victor watched her leave and then looked to the Queen. "Can I get you anything?"

"Yes, some ice cream." They both chuckled.

"Sure," Victor replied. "I'll go to the kitchen."

"Thank you! And bring it to my room. I need to rest." Victor helped her back to her apartments in the residential suite of the palace. Then, he made his way to the palace kitchen.

Chapter 2

Victor entered the palace kitchen, one of the only ordinary, temperately decorated rooms of the palace. The kitchen had a tan colored tile floor and a gray metal ceiling. Large metal vents and cabinets hung over the long lapis blue island with gold trimming at the center of the room. The island had a tan granite top with stove burners on the end closer to the entrance and sinks on the far end. On the back wall sat large metal doors that gave way to a large walk-in refrigerator and freezer.

The metal door opened with a hiss as a 32-year-old man came walking out of the refrigerator carrying a large wrapped fish. Assistant Chef Vincent Grant was a tall, handsome white male and the new chef at the palace. Chef Grant hadn't noticed Victor standing in the entranceway of the kitchen. He walked over to the island and placed the fish on the counter. He reached up to the cabinet above him in search of the right utensil to use.

"Hi!" Victor said, making Vincent jump which sent pots crashing down onto the counter. Chef Grant stood in shock staring at a chuckling Victor.

"Your Royal Highness," Chef Grant spoke, with a bow. "I apologize."

"Why? I startled you," Victor replied as he walked over the island counter.

"Yes, this is true," Chef Grant bashfully replied, picking up the pots and returning them to the shelf.

"How are you today?" Victor flirted, trying not to look at the raw fish head on the table.

"Oh, I'm fine. Just starting Her Majesty's lunch," Chef Grant replied. "Is there anything I can get you? Some sushi perhaps?"

"Oh, my goodness. Yes, please!" Victor realized that he had gotten too excited about the sushi. Chef Grant chuckled as he drew a large knife from the holder. Victor jumped out of his skin, but tried to keep a cool face.

"Are you ok?" Chef Grant replied.

"I'm fine, just bad nerves."

"Well, then I guess it's payback then," Chef Grant replied with a wink. Victor fought valiantly to hold back a blush but to no avail.

"So," Victor began. "Are you new here?"

"No, not really. I've been working here for about nine months now."

Victor chuckled, "That *is* new for this place. It holds onto its inhabitants, usually until death or retirement. So, what's your name?"

"Chef Nathan Vincent Grant, but *you* can call me Vince, sir."

"Does everyone call you Vince?"

"No, you can though!" Vince replied with a smile.

"Ok then, Vince. Well, I'm His Royal Highness Prince Victor II of Spiti, but you can just call me, 'Victor.'"

"No, sir! I can't," Vince replied.

"No? Why not?"

"Because it wouldn't be proper. You're the prince of the Kingdom of Iakos, second in line for the throne. I couldn't simply call you Victor."

Victor snickered and then leaned in, "How about in public I'm 'His Royal Highness', but when in private, 'Victor'. Deal?"

Vince's smile grew from ear to ear. "Okay."

"What?" Victor wondered why Vince was smiling so hard. Had he said something wrong?

"It's nothing," Vince replied while continuing to fillet the giant fish.

Victor walked around the island and stood in front of Vince, "What?"

Vince put down the knife and turned to Victor, who had now stepped so close that if his orientation were different, Vince would be uncomfortable. "You plan on seeing me in private." Vince looked right into Victor's golden brown eyes and for a moment, they both forgot where they were. Chills ran down Victor's spine and Vince had no sense of the world around them. "Are you always this forward Prince - I mean Victor?"

"Not always," Victor replied with a wink and a smile. He bit his lip and swayed with a false bashfulness that made him look so precious to Vince, and incredibly feminine. "Actually never, really."

Just by appearance, one would think that Victor would just be fashionable or even eclectic, but seeing him now screamed the truth. Vince took what breath he could catch and whispered, "So what makes today different?"

After another 30 seconds of silent staring, footsteps on the marble tile snapped them both out of their spell. Victor turned quickly to the maid entering the room with her face buried in her phone, while Vince quickly turned his attention back to the fish. He picked up a pair of culinary tweezers and began deboning the fillet. Victor walked toward the entranceway and stopped, remembering why he came down in the first place. "Um, the Queen would like some ice cream."

"This early? Lunch hasn't even been finished."

"That is what Her Majesty wants," Victor replied, throwing his hands up in a joking surrender.

"Ok, I will get it for you." Vince washed his hands and turned to the freezer. He opened the door and entered, yelling back. "Any particular kind, sir?"

"Rum raisin."

After a moment, he came out with a gallon of rum raisin ice cream and walked over to the china cabinet, where he grabbed a bowl. After filling it, he gave it to Victor and said, "I'll personally bring your lunch up to the suite with the Queen's."

Victor smiled, "That would be very kind. Thank you!"

He turned to exit, but Vince called to him, "Sir?" Victor stopped and turned. "Will you be staying here for long?"

"Yes, I'm not sure how long but yes."

"Then I'll see you around," Vince replied and returned his attention to the fish. Victor bounced through the palace to the Queen's bedroom in the residential suite, practically skipping with excitement.

He entered the grand bedroom where his grandmother slept every night. It was decorated with white and gold paint, Corinthian square pillars along the walls, and an enormous crystal chandelier hanging from a high, ribbed ceiling. Of course, the room would not be complete without antique gold trimmed wooden furniture. Queen Margaret sat at the edge of her king-sized bed with two doctors in front of her. An older European doctor was giving her what appeared to be a neurological exam and the other, the Royal Physician, stood back writing details from the exam onto a clipboard.

Victor stood at the doorway holding the freezing bowl of ice cream as worry enveloped him. He'd never seen his grandmother in such a vulnerable state. The prince walked over to her as the doctors both took a moment from what they were doing to bow to Victor with a "Your Royal Highness". Victor smiled at them and then placed the bowl on a tray at the foot of the bed.

"It's good to see you, Dr. Bennett," Victor said, smiling at the first Royal Physician to be of East Asian descent. "How is she doing?"

"Well, sir, I'm not sure how much Her Majesty has told you," Dr. Bennett replied, looking at Margaret's face for approval.

Margaret nodded. "It's all right. You can speak freely with Prince Victor, doctor."

"Thank you, Ma'am," Dr. Bennett affirmed and continued to Victor. "Her Majesty has a grade IV glioblastoma. Unfortunately, it is so large that if we operate, there is a great chance that Her Majesty will lose every important function she needs to carry out her office."

"What about saving her life, Dr. Bennett?" Victor spat, trying to lessen the venom from his voice.

"I'm sorry, sir. We will try chemotherapy and radiation, but I'm afraid at this stage, there's not much else we can do but keep her comfortable."

Victor's mind raced, searching for a solution. With his eyes turned inward, he replied, "What about clinical trials or experimental drugs?"

"None of the drugs that we have is at a safe enough stage to give to Her Majesty and have a promising impact on the condition. I'm sorry that we don't have better news."

Victor turned to the oncologist examining Margaret and asked, "How much longer does she have?"

"There's no way of knowing for sure, sir," Dr. Ryan replied.

"Your best guess then," Victor spoke with his voice breaking.

"Being generous … a year."

Victor lost his breath. He felt as if he'd been hit by a train and dragged a mile.

"Grandma, does Princess Rose know?"

"No, Victor!" Margaret replied with authority. "She knows I'm sick but no one is to know how bad it is."

"Grandma!"

"Stop please, Victor. Please don't stress my nerves anymore. That's all her being here would do. You know how protective she is of me."

"Yes, but imagine how horrible it would be if she finds out with an Iakos radio announcement."

"Oh, stop being dramatic, Victor."

"Grandma, I'm not! I'm showing you that she needs to be here. The family needs to be here."

"Fine, Victor! Fine. Call them, but only Rose and John are to know. No one else! The last thing this country needs is panic. If this is going to be the end of my life, I'd like to enjoy it with some shred of privacy."

"Yes ma'am!" Victor replied. He bowed, took a few steps back and then left the room. He slowly walked to his apartments at the State palace and pulled out his phone. This would be the hardest cell phone call he'd ever had to make. He scrolled through the phonebook and pressed call. After only a few rings, a deep voice answered the phone.

"Hey cousin."

"Hey Jack! Is your mum around?"

"Yes, she's in the study. Is everything ok?"

"I need to speak with her."

"Ok, give me a moment."

As the phone got quiet, Victor flopped onto his bed and stared at the ceiling. *And the storm begins.*

Chapter 3

"Wake up!"

All the air was knocked out of Victor as a dead weight flopped on top of him as he slept. Victor struggled under the weight, trying to gasp for air. He was entangled in his grayish blue comforter and black silk bed sheets. Once he finally got his bearings, he scrambled to his feet to find his one-year-younger cousin, Jack, stretched across his bed. Jack was the epitome of everything that is "#cool" or "#normal". The Iakos Chronicle named Prince Jack the sexiest and most eligible bachelor in town, overlooking Prince Victor's "exotic beauty". To Victor, however, Jack just looked like he belonged in a boy band, and he lovingly never let his cousin forget it.

"Do you think before you do anything?" Victor asked half-jokingly, half-annoyed, as he checked his body out to make sure there were no injuries.

Jack just laughed and teased Victor. "Jeez man! You're so sensitive."

"What are you guys doing here anyway? I thought your mum said that you all would be coming this weekend."

"Oh no," Jack replied. "We packed our bags last night right after you called." Jack walked over to Victor, who had picked up his phone to check the time. "Are you ok?"

"Um, I'm fine. I'm more concerned about Grandmother. I-I'm scared, Jack."

"Well, how bad is it?" Jack asked, putting his arm around Victor.

"Your mum didn't tell you?"

"Nope, all I know is that she's sick. She said I shouldn't worry myself. But I kind of figured it was more serious than she was leading on." Victor began toward the bathroom and Jack followed. Victor opened one of the large suitcases and began looking for something to wear.

"Grandmother made me promise not to say anything," Victor replied. Jack gently tapped Victor's shoulder with his fist to grab his attention. Victor looked up at him. "What?"

"Is she 'bad case of pneumonia' sick or 'we start preparing for a transition of power' sick?"

Victor stopped what he was doing. He hadn't realized that if the Queen were to die, his mother would become Queen, making him the crown prince — the heir apparent. He had to think of something to say that wasn't a lie but wouldn't disclose too much about the severity of the Queen's real condition. "She's somewhere in between them for right now." That wasn't the whole truth but it wasn't a lie, because he truly had faith that other treatments could be found from now to her last day. Victor picked out a trendy outfit and some jewelry to match.

"Why is your stuff here?" Jack asked, eyeing Victor's suitcases along the counter and on the floor.

"Because," Victor started with a sigh. "I'm moving here indefinitely to take care of Her Majesty."

"Wow, it's *that* serious then? Wait, why would you be moving here if my mum is going to be here?"

"How long is she planning to stay?" Victor asked.

"I don't know, she didn't say, but she packed 4 suitcases so I'm assuming it will be a long visit."

"Oh, great!" Victor muttered. He quickly checked himself in the mirror and they left the suite. Jack and Victor walked down the hall to the Crown Suite. It was a centuries old tradition that when the heir ascended to the throne, he or she would be living in the Crown Suite, even if the dowager consort was still alive. The Royal House of Rousel was filled with these archaic traditions that tended to over complicate the lives of the Royal Family.

Victor and Jack walked into Margaret's bedroom to find the younger of the two living daughters of the Queen speaking loudly into her cell phone, and Jack's 22-year-old twin sister, Princess Margaret of Makria who the family called "Margie," trying to spoon feed a still able bodied queen.

"Stop it!" Margaret protested, pushing Margie's hand away. "I can still feed myself."

"But you're *not* eating, Grandma."

"Yes, because I must take my medicine before I eat," Margaret argued.

"Well, then where is your medicine," Margie replied, clearly getting frustrated.

"It's in the bathroom," the Queen said, trying to lift herself off the bed. She made her way to her feet, and began to walk toward the bathroom but she stumbled as she realized that she couldn't feel her left leg very well. Her leg buckled under her weight and she began to fall. Victor and Jack sprinted across the room, reflexively pushed Princess Margie out of the way, and grabbed the Queen just as her knees hit the rug.

"Grandma, are you ok?" Victor asked, checking her knees.

"Yes, Victor. I am fine. Just pass me my walker."

Victor looked around the room from the floor, but couldn't see it in plain sight. "Where is it?" he said.

"It is folded behind that dressing table," Margaret indicated to the antique dresser across the room.

Jack walked over to the dressing table, pulled out the walker from behind it, and opened it in front of Margaret. She lifted herself, putting all her weight on the contraption in front of her as she began shuffling off to the bathroom. Victor followed her keeping about a one-foot distance behind her. After taking care of her during previous illnesses, he had come to learn a lot about the Queen's character as a person rather than a political figurehead or even a loving grandmother. He found many shared traits that reach every branch of the Rousel family tree, including a strong sense of duty, love of family, and protectiveness of the Crown, God, and country.

Once finished, Victor walked Margaret back to the bed, where she sat and took some deep breaths. "Are you ok? Do you need some water or something?" Margie asked.

Margaret shook her head. "I just need to catch my breath dear. I've had a busy morning."

"What do you mean? It's only 10 o'clock," Victor asked the Queen.

Margie jumped in to explain, "Well, she had a secure briefing and wanted to go down for breakfast."

"Go down?" Victor looked at Margie realizing that the Queen still hadn't told the family the severity of it. "You went down to the Breakfast Room?"

Off in the corner, Rose began to yell at someone in her typical dramatic tone. "No, I want to speak to Dr. Ryan in Oncology! Now!" She paused for a second. Victor looked up at the Queen as she punched the bed in frustration.

"Damn it, Rose! Hang up the damned phone!" Margaret exclaimed, making her three grandchildren jump before her. It was a rare moment for Her Majesty to show this much emotion, let alone outburst or even swear. As Rose immediately obeyed, Jack chuckled loudly taking pride in seeing his mother being reprimanded. Her Majesty continued, "Do you think?"

Victor looked up at Margie who had gone pale, which wasn't that far from her natural complexion. "O-o-oncology?" Margie slowly spoke, her voice cracking. "Who has cancer?"

"Calm down, Margie. Just because she said oncology doesn't mean anyone has cancer." The whole room paused and turned to Jack, utterly confused.

Margie and Victor let out a slow, "Wooooow!" as Princess Rose began to snicker to herself.

"What? It's true," Jack continued

"What are you talking about?" Margie teased, speaking slowly to intensify her mocking. "Oncology is the study of tumors."

"Now, now!" The Queen spoke, authoritatively signaling a ceasefire with one hand. Rose quickly covered her mouth to shield the humor on her face. "Don't tease the boy. He graduated with a degree in physical education, not medicine." The mood in the room began to lighten at Jack's expense. It was comforting for the family to see she hadn't lost her sense of humor at all. Margaret grabbed a blushing Jack and pulled him into a hug. "I'm sorry, baby, but your sister's right in this rare occasion," she loudly whispered, equally distributing the teasing.

Margie stopped smirking instantly and whined, "Heeeeey!" This, of course, made everyone laugh aloud now, including the Queen, for about another minute, until the comic relief subsided and the weight of the situation set in once again. "Um," Margie began, "how bad is it really?"

The Queen quietly took a slow, steady breath and considered the most easing way of stating the horrible news. "Well, I have some decisions to make, but I believe God has decided that this spring's birthday celebration will be my last." Margie began to sob quietly, but she sat up holding her core tightly to hold back the emotion. Margaret tapped her on the leg and spoke softly, "Let it out, dear." And just like that, the dam burst and the quiet sniffle exploded to a fountain of pain and fear. She laid herself onto the Queen, hugging her tightly. Rose and Jack slowly walked over and rubbed Margie's back. Jack turned back to Victor and their four tear-filled eyes met.

Victor's stone face began to crack under the pressure and emotion formed on his face. Jack stood up and went to hug Victor. Victor reflexively retreated a step, rejecting the offer to feel. Jack, knowing his cousin all too well, quickly advanced toward Victor tightly squeezing him into a hug with his arms pinned to his sides. Jack was at least 10 centimeters taller than Victor, but his presence would play tricks on the eye so one wouldn't notice his height until it was in direct relation to one's own. The room was filled with pain, but a comforting love emanated from each family member which greatly appeased the reality.

* * * * *

The week passed without any mention of cancer or death after that morning. Victor, Jack, Rose, and Margie spent the days taking shifts with the Queen, making sure that her spirits were lifted and doctors treated her well. That Friday evening, the Queen had summoned all her descendants and their spouses to the State Palace for dinner. By the time the dinner bell filled the halls, all but Princess Mary and The Duke were on the grounds. Dressed in evening gowns, HRH Princess Rose, Duchess of Makria and her husband, John, Duke of Makria entered the small octagonal private dining room, talking quietly to themselves. After a few minutes, the rambunctious princes, Seth and Victor, entered laughing and teasingly shifting Princess Jackie's tiara. With a fast swipe, Jackie landed a smack on Seth's cheek, who quickly grabbed Jackie by the waist and lifted her sideways.

"Come on, man. Put her down," Victor told Seth. After a few more shakes, he placed a screaming Jackie on her feet. She recoiled to swing again with a mischievous grin on her face. Foreseeing the strike about to land on Seth again, Victor grabbed Jackie and forced her into a hug, pinning her arms down at her sides. After a few moments, he asked, "Are you calm yet?" Jackie let out a playful growl and Victor held on tight. After another few moments, he asked again and this time she nodded. Victor slowly let her go and Seth resumed taunting. Victor lifted a hand, silently commanding Seth to stop. Without protest, he turned and looked for a seat around the circular table.

Just as the three sat down with Victor in between them, in walked Margie and Jack who quietly sat down next to Seth. With three seats remaining, Victor turned to Jackie and whispered, "Has Mother arrived yet?"

"I think so," Jackie whispered back. "I think Grandmother wanted to speak with her privately."

"As her mother or the Queen?" Victor inquired. Jackie shrugged and sat back, fixed her tiara that was displaced by the tussle just moments ago. Suddenly, everyone rose to their feet. Victor followed suit, deducing what was happening from past experiences. The Queen slowly entered with the help of a guard. She wore a beautiful black dress with embroidery across the breasts and a simple diamond tiara — her favorite. The family at the table all bowed or curtsied, and sat back down, except Victor. He walked around the table to the Queen's side and held out his hand. Margaret accepted the offer and held on to him as she descended into the chair.

In walked one of the butlers who announced, "Are we ready for the first course?"

"No! Just water, thank you," the Queen replied. "We'll wait for the Duke and Princess."

"Where are they?" Victor asked taking his seat, just as the couple entered. They bowed and sat at the two remaining seats. Immediately, Victor could tell that something was off. Throughout the first three courses, Mary leaned over to whisper something to the Duke and he'd just rub her arm. As everyone participated in conversation about what's going on in their lives and politics, Mary and Christopher continued to eat in silence and only converse with each other.

"So, Mary," Rose passive-aggressively called across the table. "What's new with you?"

"Rose, stop it!" John warned his wife.

"I'm just saying, she's been quiet all evening. You don't have comments to make about anything we talk about? This isn't like you."

"Wait a minute! What are you implying there, Rose?" Christopher spat. Suddenly, the room got quiet.

"I'm simply saying *to my sister* that it would be nice for her to join in the conversation rather than carrying her own over there. It's rude!"

"What if she has nothing to say?" Christopher debated.

"How would we know that when you're speaking for her? You're a *big* girl," she spat, just as John kicked her under the table. She simply kicked back and continued, "Speak for yourself."

Mary sat up, placed her fork on the table and wiped her mouth. "Uh oh," Seth commented under his breath.

"What is your problem? Why are you trying to pick a fight with me, spare?" Mary slowly spoke, every word laced with venom and eyes glaring at 100%.

"Excuse me? What did you just call me?" Rose spat back, throwing down her fork like a gauntlet. "I would be careful placing yourself higher than anyone else in the room, considering today's news."

"Shut up!" Mary threatened between her teeth.

"Or what?"

Victor looked directly across the table to see a saddened Queen, with her hands in her lap and her plate barely touched. Instantly, he'd decided that if the Queen wasn't going to stop this, he would. "ENOUGH!" Everyone stopped and looked at him, except the feuding sisters. "How dare you two bicker like this in front of the Queen - your mother — your sick mother. Have either of you looked at her to see how your words are affecting her?"

Mary turned to Victor and pointed her finger at him in an attempt to scold him. "I am your mother! You don't speak to me like that."

"Then act like it," Victor calmly retorted, deadening any rebuttal she could muster. A deafening silence filled the room, with the only sound audible being Seth shoveling food into his mouth.

With perfect timing, the butler entered. "Is everyone ready for dessert?"

"Actually, may we have the room please?" the Queen asked politely. "I will let you know when we're ready." He left with a slight head bow and backed out of the room, closing the door. "Ok," the Queen began. "It's time we all have a talk."

Everyone braced himself or herself for what the matriarch was about to say, all except Mary and Christopher who seemed already braced. "As we are all now aware, my reign is nearing its end and one of you will be taking my place as Sovereign. However,

27

it has been brought to my attention that there has been some debate within Parliament about who that next person shall be."

Victor sat up stunned, and confused. "Wait, how is that possible? Mother is the heir apparent."

"Well, not according to the laws. You see, there is a law that was enacted in 1846 which states that for a primary member of the Royal Family to marry and the marriage be legally recognized, the Sovereign must formally approve it."

"I thought that that was just tradition," said Margie.

"Obviously, so did Mary," the Queen said sipping her glass of water.

"Why is Parliament meddling into the affairs of the Executive Branch?" added John. "They have no say in such matters."

"Well," Margaret explained, "parliament voted today to send an Enforcement memo to me to rule the marriage between Mary and Christopher illegal and invalid given that they eloped without consent."

Victor looked at the Queen and asked the question that no one else at the table dared to ask given her current mood. "They want you to say that my mother and the Duke's marriage is illegal? So, what does that mean for the Crown? The monarch can't be illegally married, right?"

"In theory, that's correct," Margaret replied.

"What about in practice?" Victor cautiously debated.

"Well, according to the law, either they annul their marriage-"

"Or..." Mary promptly interrupted.

"Or?" Rose challenged.

"Respectfully, we will not do that," stated Mary.

Christopher leaned onto his forearms. "What's the other option, ma'am?"

"If you decide to continue in the marriage, then you must abdicate," the Queen spoke decisively. She started her gaze at Mary, but slowly scanned the table until her eyes locked with Victor's.

"But if Mother abdicates, then..." Victor couldn't bring himself to say it.

"...Then, yes. You would become the heir apparent." Victor fought to catch his breath. His hands became sweaty and his mouth dried. He grabbed the glass of water and began to chug it.

"Ok," Mary exclaimed. "I'm just going to ask this question since no one else will. How is Victor more qualified to be crowned than I? He's gay."

Victor's siblings and cousins gasped as Victor's face got hot. Rose looked across the counter shaking her head. "Now *that* was low, even for you."

"Mary, you know it is not against the law to be gay in this country. In fact, we do not discriminate based on sexual orientation. However, *you* broke the law," the Queen calmly retorted. "And now you must deal with the consequences. If you want me to continue to fight for you, then you both will start respecting one another. This House must stay united in the face of adversity."

"I have a question, Grandma," Jackie softly said.

"Yes, dear."

"Wouldn't it be mother's decision if she wanted to stay married or abdicate?"

"Normally, yes. However, I must decide if the marriage will remain legal. Either, I petition Parliament to change the law, or I must decide to enforce the law and rule the marriage illegal." There was a long pause as everyone digested the information. "I didn't want to make this decision, but when you decided to run off and get married; you forced my hand. Either you are single and Queen, or married and a Duchess."

Seth banged the table with his fist, startling everyone at the table. "I have a solution. Maybe you could annul the marriage for now and still have him live in the house and then when you take the throne, then you can marry the Duke again."

Victor turned to Seth, "No, Seth. Even if the marriage is willingly annulled, he will be banished, right?"

"No, Victor," the Queen replied. "That's only if I rule that the marriage is illegal. Then they would be formally banished, and Mary and Christopher would have to leave the country and renounce their titles."

"So, there are three choices then," Jackie said trying to clarify everything. "1 — They can annul the marriage and Mother would remain heir apparent, but never see each other again. 2 —

They can put it in the state's hands and take a chance on Grandma upholding the law. Or 3 — They can put it in the state's hands and have Grandma try to persuade Parliament to change the law in time, while she is fighting for her life."

"Well, what happens if we chose the third option and Parliament hasn't decided by then, Ma'am?" Christopher said.

"Christopher, that would split the Parliament about 70-30 with the greater against the marriage. Then the public learns of it, which would cause a split in the country. And *that* could be enough to cause civil unrest, possibly even revolution. So, to alleviate confusion and maintain peace in my country-"

"-You would be forced to pick me," Victor said quietly, finishing her thought. Everyone looked back and forth between the Queen and Prince Victor.

"Yes," Margaret said, as if she didn't want to say it aloud.

After several minutes of silence, Mary spoke, "So what you're telling me, mummy, is that unless I annul my marriage, then there is a great chance my natural inheritance of this great nation would be taken from me and given to my son?" For the second time in Victor's memory, he saw pain in his mother's eyes. He had always looked forward to becoming king one day, but he didn't necessarily want to take it from his mother. He thought he would inherit it in 30-40 years or something like that.

"It is up to you, Mary. Whether you choose to decide or leave it for me to decide, you don't have a lot of time."

"Mother, you're not going anywhere yet," Mary whined in full denial.

"Yes, dear. I will be going home soon and I would like to know that, when it's my time to pass on, my country is firmly in the right hands."

Chapter 4

Victor peeked around the corner, hoping that Chef - Vince - wouldn't turn around and catch him staring from the hall, again. He was so graceful in the kitchen. One could tell that Vince loved to cook - the passion behind every cut and pan flip was done with such joy, it made Victor want to learn. Just as Victor let his guard down, Vince turned toward the counter. Victor jumped back, hitting his head on something hard. He turned, startled to find a face. Nearly screaming, he reared back the opposite way trying not to go back so far that he'd be seen by his crush. Once his eyes focused and realized that it was Jack messing with him, he half-heartedly punched Jack in his left pectoral. "What are you doing here?" he whispered.

"The question is what are *you* doing? Why are you spying on the chef like a creeper?"

"I'm not spying, and keep your voice down. I'm just watching him." Victor turned back to the entranceway and peeked one eye around the corner.

"Yeah, from a distance. Again, creeper," Jack quietly sang in Victor's ear.

"Will you shut up? You can't whisper."

Jack jokingly tried to push Victor forward, but he caught himself with a large step. He quickly jumped back, pivoted around and pushed Jack back even harder. "Will you stop it?"

"You know, I can hear you," Vince called out to the royal cousins in the hall. Victor, trying to save face, sauntered into the room as if none of that had happened and Jack followed with a mischievous smirk on his face. "Respectfully, you both suck at whispering."

"Hey, I was just coming down to see if you could make some, um... sushi... for lunch," Jack pulled out of the air.

"Um... yes! Why?"

"It's his favorite," Jack teased. Victor sent his right elbow to Jack's rib, which was immediately avenged by a punch to the shoulder. Victor winced, rubbing his arm, making Vince chuckle. "So, will you make it, bro?"

Victor turned and looked at Jack, confused. "Bro? Where are you even from?"

Vince continued to chuckle at the bickering cousins. "Yes, I've made it for him before."

"Thanks, Chef Vince," the older prince replied. He was set to protest but he didn't want to miss out on the sushi.

"I told you, it's just Vince."

"It is?" Jack interjected, turning to look Victor in the face with one eyebrow flying high. Victor turned away to hide his blushing.

Vince replied, "To him it is." Jack looked back and forth between Chef Vince and his cousin; puzzled by the familiarity he didn't know already existed between the two.

"Ah, but I've found a loophole," Victor exclaimed with a nerdy finger in the air. "We agreed that I would call you that in private. Jack's here. It's not private."

Jack turned to look Victor in the face. "Private? Y'all have been gettin' busy in the kitchen? I hope not near the food."

"What?" Victor turned to Jack, giving him a look of complete embarrassment and threatening that if he didn't stop, he would suffer. "First of all, no one has said 'gettin' busy' in decades. In fact, was that phrase ever socially acceptable? Secondly," Victor lowered his voice, "you know I'm celibate."

"You're celibate?" both Jack and Vince stopped to ask at the same time.

Victor looked at the chef embarrassed, and then spoke to Jack from the side of his mouth. "Yes, I told you this like 5 months ago. Do you ever read my texts?"

"If they're interesting," Jack responded.

Vince stood, staring at Victor. "May I ask why?"

"It gives me a clear head. I can focus on my life without distractions." *Plus, it keeps away the guys who just want to say they slept with a prince,* he continued in his mind.

"If that's what works for you," Vince surrendered, returning to the meal he was preparing. Though he and the prince were beginning to develop a closeness, he felt that the subject was getting a little too personal to discuss so early. "I'll make your sushi after I finish Her Majesty's meal. What kind do you want?"

"You," Jack teased, warranting a punch to the chest by Victor, who was all too happy to oblige. "Wrapped in rice." Punch! "Dipped in soy sauce." Punch, punch. "Topped with wasabi." Punch. "And ginger to cleanse the palate."

"Will you stop?" Victor exclaimed. Both he and Vince had turned beet red.

"Ok, ok. I'll stop!" Jack surrendered laughing in this throat, which only lasted for a moment. He stood crouched like a sumo wrestler waiting to pounce.

"Hey, stop. Don't you even think about it," Victor stood with his hands stretched in front of him. He backed slowly toward the doorway ready to sprint out of the kitchen at any moment.

"I'll surprise you and have it sent up to your room," Vince called out.

Just as Victor turned to respond, Jack dove. Victor reflexively stepped to the side, leaving Jack to fall on his face. Victor chuckled and continued out the door, before he got too far, he called back to Vince, "Thank you!"

Vince continued stirring the pot on the burner and whispered longingly, "You're welcome, my Prince."

Out of breath, the two raced out across the palace gardens. Victor raced to a low tree at the far edge of the grounds. The leaves bowed at the feet of their trees across the country. Victor raced up the branches to avoid his clumsy cousin's attack. Jack attempted to climb up the tree but he lost his footing and slid out back down landing on his butt. Victor broke out in loud laughter, which, of course, Jack took as a challenge. He jumped up and tried again to climb the tree, stopping after only two branches.

"That's sad," Victor teased. Jack tried to reach up and hit him but almost lost his balance, making Victor laugh even harder.

"Oh, shut up! At least I'm the sexiest and most eligible bachelor, while you're —"

"Soon to be the next k-" Victor stopped, his smile fading. It was the first time since dinner a few weeks ago that he'd said it aloud and it nearly knocked the wind right out of him.

"Hey, are you ok, Vic?" Jack asked, affectionately. Victor always got along better with Jack than his brother, Seth. Maybe it was the closeness in age, or maybe because Seth was their mother's favorite. But in Victor's defense, he was the Queen's favorite since his birth.

"I honestly don't know. I'm worried. Grandmother is being strong but I know that she's scared."

"Scared to die?"

"No, that's just it. It's as if death doesn't scare her at all. She's scared of how this situation with Mother will affect the family, and to be very honest, I'm scared about that too. I know your mother doesn't like me."

"Eh, she doesn't like the fact that you remind her of her mom. And you don't let her say anything she wants to you without a response."

"I guess that's true."

"Well, if it means anything, I'm on Team Victor."

"Eww, please don't say it that way. It makes me feel like a popular teeny-bopper movie," Victor chuckled. "Do you know what I can't understand? Why didn't she tell me? Several months had passed since she was sick from earlier this year and I just assumed that she'd been feeling better since I'd been taking care of her since January. Why did she wait a month after her diagnosis to tell me?"

Jack thought for a moment. "Well, you know Grandmother. She likes to play things close to the chest. The only reason why she told us is because the situation with you and your mother."

"I know, I know," Victor replied. "But that still doesn't justify it. I knew something was wrong earlier this year but if I thought that she was terminal..."

"Hey," Jack said, carefully climbing up one more branch. He patted Victor's leg, "She's still here for a while. We just have to make the most of it."

Victor just sat lightly pounding his head on the tree. "Do you think Mother is mad at me?"

"What for?" Jack asked.

"Because, she may have to renounce the throne to me if she wants to stay in her marriage. I wasn't their biggest cheerleader about the whole thing, considering I found out from TV just like everyone else. But having seen what happened with her and my father..."

Jack knew what he wanted to ask next, but he also knew to tread lightly with Victor regarding his father. "Do you still speak to him?"

"Not since a few years ago," Victor said with a very slight tinge of pain and a dollop of guilt.

With extraordinary caution, Jack continued. "Well maybe you should call him. You used to talk to him about things that stressed you."

"Not as much as I talked to Grandmother. He was too busy favoring Jackie," Victor grumbled.

"Classic middle child syndrome."

"Hey," Victor warned, "I do *not* have middle-child syndrome. Even Grandmother would see it. Jackie was the first born and the only girl; Seth was the baby."

"And you were the first born male - the heir - the future king."

"I know. I just didn't expect it to happen this quickly."

Jack wanted to ask something that he'd been wondering since the dinner, but he hadn't built up the courage until that moment. "If Grandmother decides not to pardon your mother and crowns you, would you consider pardoning your mother?"

Victor thought hard, having never considered that possibility. He still loved his mother even though he couldn't stand her. She did, after all, take care of him and his siblings when his father "abandoned" him, or so it seemed at the time. "I'm really not sure. I wouldn't want to banish my mother and take the only life she's ever known away. I'm not *that* cold hearted, you know. But I will say that the next few months will determine that." Victor's phone began to buzz in his pocket. He retrieved it and swiped the touch screen with his thumb. "Hello?"

"Hello dear."

"Hi, Grandma. Is everything all right?" Victor asked with his anxiety instantly activated.

"Yes, I'm fine, but I do need to speak with you. Where are you?"

"I'm just in the gardens. I'll be in there in a few minutes."

"Thank you. Bye now," the Queen said as she disconnected the line. Victor jumped out of the tree effortlessly. Jack followed suit, stumbling a little. Determined not to be outdone, he

35

took off sprinting toward the heavily sculpted rear entrance to the palace. Victor took off after him as the never-ending war continued.

After almost knocking over 3 maids, 2 butlers, and a soldier, they reached the Queen's bedroom in record time. Both out of breath, they entered the room and neck bowed to the Queen who sat in a large, brown leather armchair. "Jack, may I speak with Victor privately?" the Queen requested. However, Jack knew that the Queen requesting attendance, or lack thereof, is more of a command. He affirmed with another neck bow, took a few steps back, and then exited the room, leaving a nervous Victor.

"Yes, Ma'am?"

"Victor, I just got off the phone with your mother," the Queen began. Victor held his breath, not sure what to expect next. "She has informed me that after long consideration and deliberation between herself and the Duke, they've decided to stay in the marriage and have asked me to petition Parliament for reconsideration of this particular law."

"Is that what you plan to do?" he asked with his hands folded behind his back as if to be standing "at ease".

"I gave her my word at that dinner that I would, if she asked me to, and the word of the Crown is bond. So, I will be summoning the Parliamentary Speaker to formally request to repeal the law."

Victor walked over and sat on the edge of the bed. "What happens then?"

"Well, Parliament will discuss and debate it and then vote. If the law is repealed, she will remain heir apparent. If it stands, then the marriage will be officially illegal, unless I pardon them."

"Why can't you pardon them now, Grandma?"

"Victor, that law was put in place to avoid a member of the royal family entering a marriage that may influence domestic or international policy."

"Has that ever happened?" Victor wondered.

"Yes,. The reason why it was passed to begin with was because the heir apparent at the time married a prince from a foreign country with whom we were nearing war."

"Why would she do that? That's just looking for trouble," Victor said.

Margaret chuckled, "She didn't know about the conflict. Just as Mary doesn't have Top Security clearance, neither did she. She didn't know that our countries were feuding as badly as we were. So, she married the boy without permission from her father, King David IV, and the countries went to war, which lasted 3 years. During this time, tension grew within the family and the country because the king grew sick."

"Oh, I see now. Her allegiances were questioned because she was married to a prince from the rival country. She never became queen, did she?"

Margaret's head sagged as she played with her fingers. "No, I'm afraid. Before he died, King David had the law passed to deny her the throne and pass it to her younger sister." She paused allowing Victor to digest the point. "You see the purpose of the law?"

"Yes, in that situation, it's for protection. But it doesn't fit this situation completely." Victor paused a moment, then a light bulb flashed on in his brain. "Can't the law be amended to say that a member of the Royal Family cannot marry a *non-citizen* without Sovereign permission? It will prevent that situation from occurring without denying Mother the throne."

Margaret paused, this time to digest his suggestion herself. She was impressed by his ability to compromise and find a solution to such a complex situation so effortlessly. "The law also is meant to ensure that the marriage will not affect any secret ongoing federal investigations, special operations, and political conflicts of interest. If the Crown is not able to verify a person who seeks to join the family, then this can pose a problem."

"Grandmother, do you want me to succeed you or Mother?" Victor stopped for a moment to gauge her immediate reaction. Her facial expressions, or lack thereof, left Victor to sweat nervously as the Queen stared into his soul.

"You know, Victor, I'm not sure at the moment. The Crown is a blessed gift from God! It's a calling and an honor to hold this position. However, it is an incredible burden. The responsibility of the fate of a country is not something for which one can fully prepare, despite the most rigorous preparations over years. I'm not sure who is more prepared, so if it's left up to me to decide, then you both would have to prove to me that you can handle the pressure."

"How do we do that?" Victor asked.

Margaret leaned forward to rise out of the chair, but as she lifted herself with her hands, her arms couldn't seem to hold her weight and she fell back into the chair. Victor shifted forward quickly and stood in front of her, offering one hand. Margaret sighed and reluctantly took his hand, allowing him to help her to her feet. Once standing, she slowly made her way to the side of the bed, and sat. "Maybe what I could do is begin with some events and responsibilities in which you both can join with me. Do you think you'd be up for it? I will need the help anyway."

"You'd have to ask Mother about her availability, but I'd be more than happy to help."

"Good," Margaret replied with a sense of relief. "Now, can you call my Private Secretary and ask her to bring me some work?" Margaret shifted herself onto the bed and grabbed the television remote.

"Are you sure you don't want to rest?"

"Yes, I'm sure. I will rest before my lunch arrives and then after I eat, I'll get some work done. I cannot just sit around stagnant and neglect my duties." Victor always admired his grandmother's work ethic, but this was amazing. Even in the face of almost certain death and the end nearing, she still put her duty to the Kingdom of Iakos first.

"Ok," Victor said. He looked at the clock, which read 14:00. He added, "And I'll go find out where's your lunch. It's getting late." With that, he left the bedroom and the Crown suite. He was all too eager to go to the kitchen again. Was it the sushi or the chef?

Just as he descended the stairs of the Residential foyer, he could hear Jack gossiping not so quietly to his sister. "You should've seen him all blushing and cheesing. I thought he was going to start drooling."

"The chef?" Margie whispered. "Really? Was he cute?"

"I don't know. Victor seemed to think so."

"Dude!" Victor exclaimed. Jack and Margie jumped and turned to Victor walking toward him ready to strike. Jack readied himself, but Margie slinked in front of him and grabbed Victor into a hug. "You can't keep a secret, can you?"

"*Dude,* you didn't tell me that the chef was a secret," Jack teased, playfully dodging Victor's strikes over Margie's shoulder.

"It doesn't matter anyway," Margie said struggling under the pressure of Victor's advance. "I want to see him."

"Well I have to go there anyway. Grandmother hasn't had her lunch yet." Victor said, ceasing his attack and fixing his shirt. He and Margie began walking into the main hallway that ran through the center of the palace. Jack followed behind them listening to them.

"So how far have you gotten with this chef guy?" Margie inquired, almost salivating for the "tea" as she loved to call it.

"Nowhere really," Victor lied. "We've just spoken once or twice."

"That's it?" Margie asked, disappointed.

"I'm afraid so."

"But he doesn't want that to be it, right Victor?" Jack interjected. Victor suddenly spun around and caught Jack off guard with a punch to the left pectoral. He yelped, stopping dead in his tracks and clenching his chest. Victor spun back around and continued walking with Margie as if nothing had happened. They continued talking about the chef. Once Jack caught his breath, he took off down the hall, the red carpet hiding his footsteps. Just as he got to about 5 feet behind Victor, Victor sidestepped hoping to see Jack fall, but he just slowed to the pace of the others and the three continued to walk and talk. A few minutes later, they entered the kitchen to find Chef Vince rolling sushi. Margie stopped at the entranceway, her jaw dropping.

"Damn," Margie whispered.

"Mmhmm," Victor quietly confirmed.

"Hi, Your Royal Highnesses," Vince spoke without breaking his concentration. "You're back. You've brought another."

"I'm sorry?" Victor spoke, confused.

"Every time you come to see me, you seem to bring someone else with you," Vince said finally standing up straight. He walked around the island, bowed at the neck. She just gawked back as he looked at Victor from the corner of his eye. He winked at Victor, making him involuntarily blush. "Are you here for the Queen's lunch?"

"Y-y-yes," Victor stammered. Jack just rolled his eyes at their behavior.

"When you two are done embarrassing yourselves," Jack said.

"Shut up," Margie warned, with her eyes never leaving the handsome chef whose eyes were locked with Victor's.

"Yes, I was going to send both your dishes up together. I've just finished yours. I just have to cut it up and then you can enjoy."

"Ooo," Jack exclaimed, as he walked over to the table.

"Hey," Victor exclaimed, finally breaking his stare with Vince. He raced over to Jack to protect his food. Vince walked over to the other side of the island and pulled a knife from the drawer. He went to the sink, ran some cold water onto the knife, and returned to the sushi rolls. Then, he began slicing the sushi while making small talk with the three HRHs. Vince took two long white plates from the cabinet above him and laid it in front of him on the counter. Just as he began plating the sushi, a butler entered the room with a large silver tray.

"Chef Grant, Her Majesty's lunch is late," the butler said, after bowing to the princes and princess.

"Yes, I'm sorry." Vince replied. "It is right here; ready for you." He indicated to the silver tray with a large plate and a metal dome over it along with a soup bowl covered with plastic and a glass of what appeared to be mango juice. The butler scoffed and replaced the empty tray for the tray with the food, then walked out, clearly upset.

"What did you do?" Jack asked, picking up on the tension between the two employees.

"I followed orders. He preferred my predecessor over me."

"That chef who didn't take the time to read the Queen's food allergies and gave her peanuts?" Margie asked.

"That would be the one," Victor replied.

Vince slid the two plates of sushi in front of the three and handed them three wrapped chopsticks. "Dig in," he replied.

They all bowed their heads and silently blessed their food, then pounced on the sushi as if they had been starved.

* * * * *

Queen Margaret sat on a large white floral couch in her office of the State Palace. She stared out of the window watching the city she'd grown to love for all these years. She remembered her late husband, Prince Victor I, and how he would make her stand at the window to remember the people for whom she worked every day. The Queen played with her thumbs as she remembered his funeral and the days that followed; how she found it nearly impossible to get out of the bed and continue to shoulder the huge responsibility she'd been carrying for 40 years. The bustle of the people earning their living, going about their days, was her sole source of inspiration in those difficult mornings. Thinking of her people drove her to push through the storm rather than be defeated by it. Now that she found herself in the current, and seemingly her last storm, her inspiration still held strong. Margaret wiped a small tear from her right cheek as she told herself, *If Parliament refuses responsibility for this historic decision, which will shape the future for generations to come, you must find the right leader for your people. You must hold on to faith and clarity to make a sound decision.* Margaret prayed every day she could remember for the last 79 years, but this morning, her words escaped her. She had knelt by the bedside and thanked the Lord for waking and granting her another day, but then it hit her that there would come a day very soon that she would be "called home" and the country would be in someone else's hands. Fear was not an opponent that Margaret wrestled with very often, so this was entirely new and didn't come easily.

Finally, a knock on the door pulled her back to the now. Margaret quickly pulled out a tiny compact mirror from the purse, which sat beside her. She cleaned her face of any sign of "weakness" and covered the humanity with powder, for duty called. After her transformation was complete, she called out an authoritative, "You may enter."

A young, handsome man entered in an average business suit. He walked with a confidence that fell just shy of arrogance. He stepped before the Queen and bowed his head. He held his head bowed, expecting the Queen to rise and extend her hand to be kissed. When he didn't hear the Queen move, he looked up to find a still seated Queen with her hand extended. Puzzled, he stepped closer and bent at the waist to kiss her hand and then stepped back. "Your Majesty."

"Mr. Speaker, how are you this morning?"

"I am very well. Thank you for asking, ma'am. This is my favorite time of year, the weather, the beauty of nature as the seasons begin to change. It's just splendid," Speaker Michaels replied.

"That it is, that it is!" the Queen half-heartedly replied.

Confused by the short reply that was uncommon for their meetings, he continued. "So how may I be of service to Your Majesty?"

"Right. Well, I have a request for you. On my desk behind you is a manila folder. Can you retrieve it for me?" the Queen requested, indicating with an open hand to her desk on the other side of the room.

"A-a-absolutely," the Speaker stammered, as he stepped backwards a few paces, then turned and walked to the desk. On top of the desk lay a large stack of manila folders and one isolated folder in the middle. He grabbed the folder and returned to the Queen, handing it to her.

"Thank you," she said, taking it from his hand. She reached into her bag and pulled out a pen and a pair of reading glasses. As the Queen placed the glasses on her face and uncapped the pen, she continued, "So Gabriel, I have a request for you."

"A request?"

"Yes, it is regarding the marriage of my daughter, the Duchess of Spiti."

"Yes, I'm aware of the situation," Speaker Michaels assured Her Majesty. He didn't know where this was going, but suddenly he felt like his job was about to get exponentially harder. "What about it, Ma'am?"

"I am formally requesting an amendment be passed to the law which currently states that the marriage of a primary member of the Royal Family must be approved by the Sovereign."

"An amendment?"

"Yes, an amendment," the Queen repeated, peering over her glasses. "I would like it amended to state that the marriage must require approval by the Sovereign only if it is a marriage in which the other party is a non-citizen."

Speaker Michaels paused, carefully deciding his words. "May I ask why?"

The Queen stopped and looked up coldly at the young politician standing before her. "Because I am the Queen and such is my right."

"Oh no, Ma'am. You've misunderstood my intention. I ask why this amendment so I may argue in your favor to Parliament. I know that some members are against the marriage since it took the form of an elopement. However, I am definitely not one of them."

"Well I appreciate your support, Speaker. This amendment will allow my daughter to remain both married and heir apparent, while protecting my country from the conflicts of interest of the past."

Speaker Michaels paused as he mulled over the proposal. "Very clever, Ma'am."

"Why thank you," she replied, signing the bottom of the document. She handed it to the Speaker, "That will be all."

"Yes, Your Majesty. I will put this at the top of the agenda for this afternoon."

"I appreciate it." The Queen extended her hand and the Speaker kissed it. He then paced backward and turned to the door. Just as the guard opened the door, she called to him one last time, "By the way, I love the suit."

"Why thank you, Ma'am," he replied, bowing to her. He then turned and exited.

Margaret leaned back on the couch and looked out of the window. *It really is a beautiful autumn day.*

November

Chapter 5

Mary sat at her desk scrolling through the emails on the monitor. Her father, Prince Victor I, designed the antique office at Rousel Palace that now belonged to her. It was complete with a floor-to-ceiling bookshelf on the right wall, a high-backed leather chair behind the antique desk, and two in front. There were potted hostas and flowers scattered throughout the room, a large wooden fireplace with an even larger painting above the mantel, and a leather seating area in the corner of the room.

Suddenly, a knock rapped at the door. "Come in," Mary called out. Someone entered the room silently and just stood in front of the desk. After a few moments, Mary finally left cyberspace and turned to see who'd entered. Immediately on guard, Mary stood up and all but yelled, "What are you doing here?"

"Stop, I come in peace. I just came to talk to you," Princess Rose replied.

"What about?" Mary asked, without softening her tone.

"I came to speak with you about the situation regarding your ascension to the throne," Rose paused for dramatic effect. "Interested?"

Mary immediately became intrigued. Her posture shifted from aggressive to perceptive. "What about it?" Mary gestured to a chair in front of the desk. They both slowly descended into their respective chairs.

"I have come across some information regarding Victor," Rose began.

"My son, Victor?"

"No, our late father Victor," Rose replied facetiously.

Mary rolled her eyes, sat back into her chair, and folded her arms. "Go on."

"It seems that Victor is cozying up to the Queen."

"What's wrong with that? Victor and Mother have always been close."

"Which would be fine if it were last year. But at this crucial time, you need to be playing the strongest game of politics you've ever played in your life. That is *if* you want to be Queen."

Mary paused and studied her sister, her face and body language, scanning for anything that would pose a threat. "*You* want me to become Queen?"

"Of course, Mary. I know we've had our differences, but you've been preparing for this ever since Mother's coronation. The country would be safer in your ... capable hands, rather than those of a child. As much as Mother denies it, she's partial to Victor. We have to do something to make it impossible for the Queen to choose him."

Mary sat up and rested her elbows on the desk with her hands clasped. "What do you propose we do?"

Rose thought for a moment and then continued, "I say we do two things. First, we need to separate Victor from the Queen."

"That's not going to happen."

"It will if I stay at the State Palace and look after her. We have to taint his image or at least make her question it."

Mary sat for a moment. "And the second?"

"We secure Parliament. We sway Parliament onto your side."

"Impossible! My sources say that they're not in my favor. All of those stuffy Conservatives policing other people's lives while they bathe in brothels..."

Rose cringed, "Ewww. Bad mental image."

"Yeah, well if you only knew."

"Hold on. Do you have evidence of this?" Rose said, sitting up.

"I know where to get some. Why?"

Rose stood up and began pacing the floor. "We can use that to make them vote in your favor. The Queen issued a request to have the law amended to say that one only needs Sovereign approval if the intended spouse is a noncitizen."

"She did? She actually *formally* issued that request?" Mary asked, shocked. Even though she had promised, Mary didn't think that the Queen would actually do what she said she'd do for her. "Wow!"

"I know! So, all we must do is make sure that the law is amended."

"So, you want me to blackmail the people who literally have my fate in their hands?" Mary asked. "No, that's too big of a gamble."

"Not blackmail, induce! And you know what they say, 'The bigger the risk, the bigger the reward'."

"And they also say, 'Don't bite the hand that feeds you'."

Rose became visibly and vocally annoyed with Mary's resistance. "Mary, we cannot just sit here and pretend that Parliament is going to vote to amend the law when the Conservatives have the majority," Rose argued.

"But the Speaker is a Liberal."

"The Speaker is just a liaison position between Parliament and the Crown. You know as well as I do that the Speaker only has one vote just like everyone else."

"Ok, stop," Mary asserted, throwing her hands up in front of her chest for clarity. "Let's be smart about this. There are 40 Members of Parliament and we need 24 yeses to pass the amendment. We can count on the 15 Liberal votes, for sure."

"Don't forget the women. There are 15 women. So that makes 30 votes. That's perfect."

"Ok, no!" Mary replied sharply. "Remember that 10 of those women are Liberals so they're already counted in the yes category. That means that that would add only 5 more. 20 votes. That isn't enough. We need three-fifths of the vote to be yes, not just 50 percent."

"Ok, so that means we only need to flip the vote of 4 members. I'm sure we can find enough dirt to sway those last 4 members."

Mary stood up, slamming her fists onto the desk. "No, Rose! I will *not* blackmail members of Parliament. That's illegal, not to mention political suicide."

"Well, then I will do it!" Rose exclaimed.

"Are you kidding me? You know that they will assume that you are doing it in my name."

"You have to win!" Rose yelled at the top of her lungs. Mary froze, surprised at her sister's conviction. "You *have* to win. It may be a cliché, but sometimes, the end *does* justify the means." Rose turned and stormed out of the room before Mary could rebut. Mary sank back down into her chair, throwing her face into her hands. As she listened to Rose's heels click down the marble hall, anxiety grew inside her. *If this goes wrong, it could ruin everything.*

* * * * *

Victor sat on the floor of his room at the State Palace, which he liked over his room at Rousel Palace. It could be his association with his grandmother there, but this building always felt more like home to him. Suddenly, a voice chirped over the intercom system.

"Victor?"

"Yes, Grandmother," Victor called toward the machine on the far wall of the room.

"Could you come here dear?"

"Yes, Ma'am. I'm coming now." He got up and walked out of his suite, down the hall, and into the Crown's Suite bedroom. "Yes, Ma'am?" Victor spoke, offering a slight bow to the woman lounging on her bed.

"I would like you to come help me today," Margaret spoke over the book on her lap.

"Sure, I'd love to. Do you need me to pick out any clothes for you?" Victor asked.

"Oh, no! Rose and my dresser picked something out for me before she left."

"Well, where did she go?" Victor asked walking over to the closet doorway. There hung a pale-blue skirt and a matching suit jacket, white blouse, white bra and white slip. On the floor below were some low heels that matched the skirt and jacket. He removed the hanger, squatted to grab the shoes, and walked back to the bed laying them across the foot. He helped Margaret out of bed and into her clothes. Luckily, she preferred to bathe at night so this process would be relatively easy. Victor was also wearing some nice fitted corduroy khaki trousers, a white button up shirt with the top button opened, and a blue blazer with matching blue suede Oxford shoes.

After he finished getting her dressed, he gave her the maple wood "walking stick" with the solid gold engraved handle (because God forbid one calls it a "cane"). They slowly made their way to the Crown Office of the State palace. Victor helped her into the chair behind the antique desk. Once settled, the Queen pushed a button on the table and a buzzer rang out, signaling permission to enter. Her private secretary entered with a large wooden box that appeared to be 12 inches by 18 inches by 6 inches. It was decorated with beautiful carvings and jewels. She placed it on the desk in front of the Queen, bowed, and then left.

The Queen pulled it towards her, unhooked the two clasps and opened it. Inside was a large stack of papers. "What is all of this?" Victor asked.

"These are briefings, legal documents, and papers that require Royal Assent," Margaret replied. "You cannot read the briefings until your clearance is raised, but you can help me sign documents."

"Ok, where do we start?" Victor asked.

The Queen pulled out a legal sized folder and opened it. Inside were papers covered in illegible legalese. At the top was the Crest of the Sovereign next to the Symbol of Parliament. "These two symbols at the top of a bill indicate the requirement of Royal Assent or royal recommendation. If the monarch approves the bill, one will then sign the bill into law. If not, the Sovereign must return the bill with recommendations. It's not necessarily a veto but a 'final approval' relationship. Amendments and revisions are approved by Parliament and are required to be signed by the Sovereign as a formality."

They discussed the mundane details of government and the responsibilities of the monarchy in detail. This content usually would bore someone to tears, but not Victor; the ins and outs of government truly intrigued him. It was refreshing for the Queen to have company while working without boring them to the point of sprinting out the door.

The phone on the desk chirped and a secretary's soft voice spoke, "Excuse me, Ma'am."

"Yes, Ms. Zhang. What is it?" the Queen replied.

"The Duchess of Makria is here to speak with you."

"Thank you, send her in." The phone chirped again, signaling the disconnection of the line.

"Go sit over there," the Queen told Victor, pointing to the empty space where Victor took the chair. He didn't question the demand and quickly obeyed, moving his chair back to the other side of the desk. Just as he settled across from the Queen, Princess Rose knocked on the door and then entered the office. She gave a small curtsy, ignoring his presence. Victor just continued to keep his eyes on the Queen.

"Mother, what are you doing down here? You're supposed to be in bed," Rose spoke.

"Rose, I'm fine. What can I do for you?" Margaret professionally asked.

"I just came to check on you before I went to the kitchen to grab some lunch. Your daughter has also told me to say 'hello,' All right" Rose hinted.

Margaret sat with her face inexpressive, "How nice." The Queen was many things, but blind was not one of them.

"All right! Well, then, I'm off." Rose turned to exit and stopped. She looked Victor up and down. He slowly turned to look up at the tall Princess. "Have you been sitting there the whole time?" Victor just stared, his face lacking expression just like his grandmother. She scoffed and chuckled as she walked off.

Victor looked at his grandmother, "Why doesn't she like me?"

"Your aunt thinks it isn't obvious with whom her allegiances lie," Her Majesty replied as she continued to flip through papers.

"May I be excused for a moment?" he asked.

The Queen nodded in affirmation and Victor sprang up. He bowed and ran off after the Princess. See made it halfway down the corridor by the time he caught up to her. "Can I speak with you?"

"Whatever about?" Rose asked with falseness in her tone.

"Ok. First, stop with the facade. I'm just trying to talk with you."

Rose shifted her weight to one side and sat in her hip, "Go ahead."

"What do you have against me?"

Rose shrugged again. "What exactly do you mean?" she asked with a fake and condescending confused look on her face.

"I mean, why are you being a b--" Victor caught himself. "- Aggressive toward me?"

"I'm not being aggressive. If you want to turn your back on your own mother for a power grab, go right ahead."

Victor stopped, realizing what was causing the contempt. "You blame me?" Rose just stood there, not confirming or denying the allegation. "You blame me for all of this? How am I to blame? I didn't ask for any of this."

Rose's soft smile melted, replaced by that of a scolding parent. She filled the gap between them and jammed her freshly manicured finger into his chest. "You are trying to steal the crown from your mother and I will *not* let you. You should be ashamed of yourself. I will not allow you to do this."

"I'm not trying to steal anything. My mother did this to herself," Victor fought back. "If her decisions have changed her path, that is on her. It has nothing to do with me."

"You could have told the Queen that you support your mother. You could have defended her. But no, you see an opportunity."

"You clearly don't know what you're talking about!" Victor threw his voice as a territorial threat, making Rose step back. "You live in Makria, 5 hours north. What do you know of it?"

"I know that you constantly disrespect your mother and are always driving a wedge between her and the Queen."

"You're insane. Did Mother tell you that? You need to stop pretending that you care about anyone but yourself."

"And you need to stop pretending that you care about your mother," Rose replied, and began to walk away.

"I do!" Victor yelled down the hall. *What the hell just happened?* Victor thought to himself as he slowly returned to the office.

The Queen, having seen that facial expression before, quickly asked, "What happened?" Victor didn't know if he should tell the Queen what had just happened in the hall. If he did, that would be doing exactly what they accused him of doing: sabotaging

51

his mother. Margaret repeated herself slowly, this time punctuating every word, "Victor, what happened?"

"It's nothing. I don't want to worry you about it." Margaret sat staring at him, waiting for him to explain. "Apparently, Mother blames me for this."

"This what?" Margaret asked.

"The conflict with her marriage and ascension to the throne," Victor explained. "The Duchess said that I'm trying to steal the crown from Mother."

Margaret paused for a moment. "She said that exactly?"

"Yes, Ma'am."

"That's nonsense. What is she thinking? How is this serving her cause at all?" Margaret said, clearly getting frustrated with the whole situation.

Victor sheepishly played with his hands between his legs, "It seems contradictory to me."

"This has nothing to do with you, my dear. This is more about your father."

"Father," Victor looked up to her, confused. "What about Father?"

"Rose never liked your father and you do have a lot of his traits," Margaret explained.

"What about him?"

She paused for a moment, thinking of a response that wouldn't hurt her grandson. "He wasn't the kind of person to allow one to treat him with disrespect. You are very much the same."

"But I thought I get that from you." Victor had the gut feeling that there was more to it than just him not allowing her to walk all over him.

"Well, let's just say you're supersaturated with it," Margaret chuckled.

Victor sat in deep thought for a moment. *Am I really to blame? No, it doesn't make sense. I told her not to elope. I was against it from the start.* "No, there has to be more to it."

Margaret reached over the table and squeezed his hand, making Victor smile. She sat up and said, "Let's get back to work."

Chapter 6

Victor had been invited to help the Queen with her daily duties throughout the whole week. As the work week began to wind down to a close, the Queen received a call from the Parliamentary Speaker requesting an audience. The Queen's private secretary called the office to inform her of the Speaker's arrival. The Queen gave Victor a letter to give to her secretary to be sent to a High Court justice. He got the message that she really didn't want him in the meeting with the Speaker. As Victor passed through the door, the Speaker bowed to him and then entered the office.

"Your Majesty," he spoke as he bowed in front of the desk.

"Hello, Mr. Speaker. Care to sit?" she offered as she gestured a seat opposite to her. "What can I do for you?"

"Well, it seems we have a problem," he took his seat. "It appears that the Princess Mary has raised some questions that has some Members of Parliament unsettled."

"What exactly do you mean?" the Queen sighed.

"Several members have brought it to my attention that they received summons to Rousel Palace."

The Queen's exterior remained stoic, but inside she began to worry where this was going. "Whatever for?"

"I believe that the princesses were making a misguided attempt to drum up support for the approval of Your Majesty's amendment request, Ma'am," the Speaker's tone grew more and more serious as he spoke. "As you know, this could be considered a violation of the Constitution-"

"Pardon? How so?"

"The Sovereign cannot do anything that may influence the vote of Parliament," recited the Speaker.

"From my view, their behavior seems to be more of foolish lobbying. I'd hardly consider it threatening, not to mention, she isn't the Sovereign yet," the Queen warned.

"Not if they are planning to threaten Members with extremely private and personal information about said Members."

"Oh, come on, Gabriel. You know that the behaviors of some Members are hardly private," the Queen spoke, chuckling at the irony.

"Ma'am, it is blackmail," the Speaker warned. "And if it is to continue-"

The Queen raised a hand, silencing the Speaker. "I'd advise you to finish your sentence with great caution, Mr. Speaker."

Speaker Michaels continued slowly, choosing each word carefully. "If it is to continue, then it may result in even Liberals voting to refuse the amendment. Yes, some will shift to support her out of fear of humiliation, but this could be severely damaging to both the image of the Crown and the Princess; worse, if she were to assume the throne. She would be creating a rift between the Parliament and the Crown and *that* could prove detrimental to both of our institutions, not to mention, the proper functioning of the government."

The Queen's face began to pulse. *How could she be so idiotic?* "Wait, did you say the 'princesses'? Both?" Speaker Michaels nodded in affirmation cautiously. "Thank you for this information, Mr. Speaker. I will have it dealt with as soon as possible." She offered her hand to him signaling the end of the conversation. He rose to his feet, leaned over, kissed her hand, bowed, and left without another word.

Margaret angrily pushed the button on her phone. "Yes, Your Majesty?" the voice spoke.

"Get both of my daughters in here now. And tell Prince Victor to have my dinner brought to my bedroom in an hour please."

"Yes, Ma'am!"

Margaret pushed herself up, leaning on her walking stick and the desk for support, and headed off to her bedroom.

* * * * *

"Good evening, Your Royal Highness!" Vince called out to a hiding prince.

Victor emerged from the hallway, pretending he hadn't been watching the chef for about 10 minutes. "Oh, hello. Is that the Queen's dinner?" Mary used to get on him about doing servants' job like cleaning his room, doing his own laundry, and going to the kitchen himself to get his food, but Victor loved the independence of doing it for himself. He didn't want to be completely dependent on the "help". It also gave him more of an excuse to visit Chef Vince.

"Yes? Will you be taking it up to her?"

Victor nodded, not removing his eyes from Vince. Vince focused as he finished loading the tray with food. He could feel a royal pair of eyes staring at him. "Is there anything I could do for you?"

"I don't know. Is there?"

Vince's eyes snapped open in shock and turned to Victor. "Wow. Are you always this forward?"

"I'm not being forward – I just asked you a question," Victor replied with a flirtatious yet mischievous grin.

"Do you like me or something?" Vince asked.

Victor squirmed internally at the bluntness of the question, but on the outside, he kept his unwavering smile. "Or something."

"Oh? And what is this something?"

"If you stick around, maybe you'll find out."

"And to where would I be going?" Vince teased.

Victor shrugged. "Guys never seem to last with me. I rarely have time to get to know people and it pushes them away. Not to mention, the whole celibacy thing."

"Well, you're going to get to know me."

"Oh really? And what makes you think that?"

Vince turned confidently back to the tray. "Because you like me." He handed the tray to Victor.

Victor took the tray and turned to the door and made it to the doorway before turning back around and saying, "We'll see about that."

"Yes. We will, handsome."

Victor blushed hard, turned, and walked off down the hall to the Residential Suite. He made his way to the Crown Suite, with his mind reeling on the best hypotheticals he'd ever experienced.

Victor walked into the bedroom grinning ear-to-ear to find the Queen walking into the bathroom. "Grandmother, what are you doing?" He rushed the tray to the bed and then swung back around to support her.

"I can walk to the bathroom myself," Margaret protested.

"I know that but I'd feel more comfortable if you had some help, you know."

Victor let her go as she entered the bathroom. As much as he wanted to support her, he didn't want to see her go to the bathroom. He just listened closely from the doorway. Once he heard the toilet seat hit the porcelain tank, he knew she'd made it to the other side.

"I need to speak with you, grandson," she called to him from the toilet.

Chuckling at the normality of toilet conversations between the two of them, he replied, "Oh? What about?"

"It seems my daughters are not as smart as one would previously have thought."

"Why would you say that?" Victor asked.

"Because they've decided to make a grievous lapse in judgment against Members of Parliament."

Victor walked over to the bed and stole an olive from the salad on the plate. "What exactly did they do?"

"Summon them to Rousel Palace and blackmail them."

"Blackmail? With what?"

"Who knows? They all have dirty skeletons that would be career-ending if brought to light," she called out, followed by a flush.

"But what else could she know," Victor sat, genuinely confused. "It's not like their mischief is all that secret."

"Victor," Margaret spoke, now washing her hands. "You will soon learn that, most of the time, what the media knows is only the small tip of an enormous iceberg." She finally emerged from the bathroom and made her way over to Victor. As he reached into the salad again for another olive, she popped his hand making him yelp. Rubbing his hand, he got up and moved to the other side of the bed to make room for her.

"What does she hope to gain?"

"Do you really have to ask?" Margaret asked, unveiling a big bowl of peppered shrimp Alfredo on the tray.

"They want to force Parliament to amend the law." He paused for a moment, bothered by this realization. *Yes, she's the heir apparent, but she gave that up when she eloped.* "Well, what do I do?"

"Victor, you know what? If I had my way right now, I'd force Princess Mary to abdicate and make you heir apparent."

"No, I don't want it that way. Despite popular belief, I don't want to hurt Mother. Honestly, I just don't think that she'd be what's best for this country."

Margaret turned to Victor with an admiring smile on her face. "Care to explain?"

"She's manipulative, not to mention borderline Conservative. And she's easily swayed and baited. Do you remember the argument with Princess Rose at the dinner table?" Victor asked.

"Which time?" Margaret joked with a muffled laugh, as she politely covered her full mouth.

"Exactly! You poke her a few times and then she comes back with a low blow. Mother doesn't play fair or fight fair and that concerns me."

Margaret's laugh slowly decrescendoed and she placed her bowl back on the tray. She turned climbed horizontally across the bed and placed a hand on Victor's. "Would it be fair to say that the root of the reason why you don't think she's right for the country is because of her opposition to your sexuality?"

It always amazed Victor at how well Margaret could read him. She was the only person on Earth who knew him. "That's definitely part of it. She can't overrule the decision of the High Court, but she can find ways to circumnavigate them."

"Victor," Margaret rested her hand on the top of his. "You have to look out for yourself at some point. When I filed that amendment request, I was trying to keep the peace and remaining neutral. But considering Mary's actions over the years, I don't think that it's wise that she be crowned."

"But then it will look like a power-grab. It will appear that I've usurped the throne," Victor argued.

"No, Victor. It will look like your mother made an irrational decision and now must deal with the consequences of that decision."

"Yes, but love is an irrational emotion. And she didn't know that a royal elopement was illegal."

"You are nobly playing devil's advocate, but Mary is not innocent. She didn't get pregnant after a late night of drinking," Margaret rebutted. Victor cringed as she continued. "She may not have intended to break the law, but she did it to spite me. She disrespected her mother, tradition, and the Crown; and *that* makes me question whether she can handle *being* Queen."

Victor needed to figure out a way to make this transition without appearing power-hungry. He stood up and began pacing the floor. Margaret struggled to get onto the bed for a moment, but managed to shift to the middle. Both of their minds reeled. *If my daughters are going to team up against Victor, then he'll need help,* Margaret thought watching her grandson.

"What is their next tactic?" Victor asked.

"How would I know?"

"Grandma, if you were in their shoes and trying to politically destroy someone, how would you do it?"

"Victor," Margaret spoke with a sternness that meant she was speaking as The Queen, "the Crown does not politically destroy anyone." Victor stopped pacing and looked at her. His face twisted indicating that he knew that was a lie. "But if I were to do such a thing, I'd attack their public image."

"So, I'll build up my public image so she can't. That way the people would be for me."

Margaret shook her head, "No. That's far too obvious."

"How so?"

"If you come out against her, then it will do exactly what I'm trying to prevent. The country will split."

Victor thought for a moment, and then he got an idea. "Well, what if I do some high-profile events with Jacqueline and Jack, and test to see how the people respond. I'll have to ask them and if they agree it would give me a separate image from Mother."

Margaret paused, playing out the different scenarios in her head. "If you do that, you have to be yourself without seeming 'pop culture.'"

"I'm not sure what you mean," Victor asked.

"Jackie and Jack have developed pop culture images which is great for members of the Royal Family who don't have great likelihood of ascending to the throne. Jackie is fourth in the line of succession as it stands right now, until you and your brother have children; Jack is sixth in line. They can have a frivolous image."

"Grandma," gently scolding Victor. "Don't say that."

"I don't mean it as a bad thing. They've made names for themselves apart from their title. But the Crown cannot be viewed as light-hearted like Jackie and Jack are: pop culture. You have to be set apart; one with the people without being one of the people." Victor always felt weird about that concept, but she was right. The Crown must maintain a certain dignity without being pompous; above everyone without looking down on anyone. It was a fine line, but he'd grown up in it, so he didn't feel like it would be a problem.

"There's a gala tonight in the city. Jackie will be attending, so I'll have you join her. There will be a red carpet but that shouldn't be a problem. I'll make an announcement."

Victor immediately began to shake. "W-w-would I have to talk to reporters? What will I say?"

"Absolutely not, Victor!" Margaret demanded. "You do not answer questions or stop to talk to reporters. You just smile graciously and thankfully as you enter and that's it."

"But Jack and Jackie sometimes answer questions."

"What did I just say, Victor? You are not them. For what I'm preparing you, you need to trust me."

*　*　*　*　*

As the secure limo made its way through the city, a knot built up in his throat. He sat on the bench facing the side. Jackie and Margie sat on the back bench facing forward, gossiping about the latest celebrity drama. On his left sat Jack and Seth, randomly bursting into laughter and cringing at videos of skateboarders falling on Seth's phone.

"I'm so excited. Victor's finally hanging out with us, in public," Margie teased, adjusting her diamond studded tiara and matching tennis bracelet that she borrowed from the Crown Jewels. She wore a petite floor-length, nude-colored gown with sequins across the breast and waist; on her feet were matching, pointed-toe stilettos.

"Hey, I go out in public with you," Victor replied.

"Uh huh, sure," yelled Seth over the ear bud blasting in his ear. "Only for state events, weddings, and funerals."

"Stop yelling!" Jack yelled back.

"Well excuse me for not being a socialite like you guys," Victor teased.

"Hey," Jack elbowed Victor in the arm. "I am *not* a socialite."

"I'm sorry, Jack." Victor teased again. "Iakos' Sexiest and Most Eligible Bachelor."

59

"Shut up," Jack replied. Margie and Jackie broke out in loud laughter.

A soft roar became audible from outside. A cold shiver ran up Victor's spine as he fidgeted in his seat. Jackie placed a comforting gloved hand on his leg. She was wearing a sleeveless mermaid evening gown with a lace bateau neckline and a sweep train. She accessorized with elbow-length black gloves, a diamond choker necklace, and a diamond and pearl and sterling silver tiara crown atop a pin up do with dangling diamond earrings.

The roar grew louder and louder as the car approached the gala until finally they were in a line of cars. Victor thought they'd be waiting in line, but as royal protocol dictates, the line of black limos and SUVs pulled over and the royal motorcade pulled up to the large red carpet between two tall buildings. The red carpet spanned at least twenty feet wide and traveled halfway down the block-long walkway and turned into the black glass convention center. Flanking the sides were bleachers; the right side was filled with press and the left side was filled with citizens screaming at the top of their lungs.

Victor leaned into Jackie and asked, "What is this gala for anyway?"

"It's an award ceremony for citizens who have done amazing things for others."

The limo stopped right in front of the passageway and a man dressed in a black suit with white gloves stood in front of the door and waited. The boys concealed their electronics in their jacket pockets. The women pulled the mirrors down from the ceilings and checked their makeup, while Victor sat twiddling his thumbs with his hands between his knees. *Why am I doing this?* Jackie and Margie closed their mirrors and picked up their clutches from their laps. Margie tapped on the window with her knuckle.

The man opened the door as another man's voice spoke over a PA system, "Presenting ... Their Royal Highnesses: Princess Jacqueline of Spiti, Princess Margaret of Makria, Prince John of Makria, Prince Seth of Spiti ... and Prince Victor II of Spiti." The crowd crescendoed with deafening screams. Margie and Jackie exited first. Jack and Seth climbed over Victor and exited next. They stood just outside the limo waving to the crowd. Finally, Victor took a deep breath and climbed out of the limo as the crowd somehow got even louder. Adoring screams flooded the courtyard as hands waved vigorously at the youngest members of the primary Royal Family. Victor began to blush and smile; he never expected to get such a reception. Jackie turned to a paralyzed Victor and winked at him, which seemed to calm him down, and reached out her hand. Victor looped his arms and Jackie hooked on to his right arm. Margie turned and hooked on to his left arm. Jack and Seth began walking down the middle of the carpet, waving to both sides. With his sister on one arm and his cousin on the other, Victor began walking down the carpet. The girls waved occasionally with their free arms as Victor nodded to the people. He turned toward the cameras and smiled. As they walked, Victor tried not to blink and squint at the overwhelming flashes of the cameras. Halfway down the carpet, all five met up in a line. Seth came around to the other side for symmetry and together they faced the cameras and posed. The photographers went crazy. Jackie called out "pose" and they all changed positions. They crowd behind them broke out in laughter. After a few seconds, she yelled, "pose" again and they shifted. Without warning, Jackie yelled "silly face" and all but Victor made their craziest face possible. Victor remembered what his grandmother said about setting himself apart, so rather than a silly face, Victor wiped the smile off his face and gave his most stoic and suave look. The photographers must have loved it because the sea of lights grew more vigorous. They turned to the other side to face the citizens and began waving back. Jack blew kisses at the crowd and they just ate it up. Finally, the five turned and made their way up the seemingly endless carpet. They turned and walked toward the entrance to the convention center. They all pivoted back and gave one last wave before entering.

*　*　*　*　*

The evening had been going on without any excitement. Victor felt so inspired by the 25 people who were honored that night: among them, the high school teacher with the highest grade improvement in the country, the part-time firefighter who saved a family of four, and the wounded veteran who raised millions for charity. He sat at his table contemplating the ceremony as everyone else took to the dance floor. Jackie danced with one of the country's most successful rappers, while Margie danced with Jack. Seth sat on the other side of the circular table from Victor.

Just as Victor got lost in his own mind, Marcus Frazier, one of Iakos' most famous entertainers, thrust him back to reality. The young, handsome singer was dressed in a black Dolce and Gabbana suit rolled up at the sleeve, and arms covered in tattoos down his wrists. He sat next to Victor, who looked back confused and bashful. "Hello?" Victor said, as if to ask *Can I help you?* Marcus didn't respond; just stared at Victor with a smoldering half-smile. "What? Something wrong?" Victor asked, through an enormous nervous smile. The night had been filled with various high profile people bowing nervously and delicate conversation, as if he were the finest piece of china that never came out of the cabinet except for the most auspicious of occasions. Finally, Victor removed the polite subtext and went straight for the gusto. "Can I help you with something, Mr. Frazier?" The tone set a warning sign to Seth who watched from above his video game.

"No, Your Highness," Marcus finally replied. "I just came to see if you were real."

"What?" Victor asked, genuinely confused.

"I'm sorry, I don't mean any disrespect. You're just like a rare bird that never pokes its head out of its perch high up above the world."

Victor didn't know if he should be flattered or insulted. "A rare bird?"

Marcus leaned in closely and whispered, "The most beautiful rare bird I've ever seen." Marcus Frazier was internationally known as a playboy, a ladies-man. So, this compliment came as a surprise to Victor, though he settled his nerves by telling himself that it could just be a platonic compliment. Marcus winked at Victor and then sat upright in his chair with his eyes never leaving Victor's. Normally, this would be a major disrespect, as a commoner should never look a member of the primary royal family in the eye directly. Most people would look at their lips or the side of their face, but Victor figured he'd let it slide considering what was happening.

"Well, thank you!" Victor blushed and began playing with his spoon to distract himself.

"So, what has compelled you to make the trip down from Mt. Olympus," Marcus asked, now clearly flirting.

"Oh, um, I just thought this event was such a positive emblem of Iakos tradition that I wanted to attend," Victor recited.

"Ok, now what's your real answer?" Marcus asked.

"What? What do you mean?"

"Not the recited answer you so eloquently practiced. Why have you really come?" he asked. Victor smiled politely and stood up. Marcus instinctively rose as well and bowed.

"It was nice to meet you," Victor plainly spoke, as he grabbed his glass of champagne and walked away. Marcus watched him walk away and got an idea. He'd practically gotten everything he wanted due to his success, fame, and social standing, so tonight would be no different. His eyes followed Victor as he walked to the dance floor and whispered something to Jack, sipped his champagne and left it on a table. Then the two cousins snuck down a long hallway with a large sign that read "WASHROOMS". Curious, Marcus made his way through the sea of tables and chairs and squeezed through the dance floor. Just as he emerged on the other side, he saw them enter the men's washroom. Quickly, he followed stopping just short of the bathroom. He pressed his ear to the door and could hear their conversation.

"Why can't I just have fun at least one night; live a little, before I have to give up my freedom to duty? I'm always hidden away."

"You hide yourself away. You should come out more and stop letting your anxiety keep you from having fun. You have to take that step yourself or it will never happen."

"Ok, well, when is the next event?"

"I don't know but I'm going to this party tonight. Come to that with me."

"Won't seem weird?"

"There you go again. We'll drop off the girls and Seth at the Palace, then switch cars and head over to the party."

* * * * *

Victor stood out on the balcony and watched the boats pass by. He loved looking at the sea at night. Listening to the ocean made him feel like with every wave crashing below, it washed his mind clear. With everything going on in his family and the country, he needed an escape and this was doing the trick. It was very like him to be in a penthouse suite at a party filled with A-Listers, and he'd be outside, by himself. Though he was enjoying himself, he began to feel overwhelmed and overstimulated by the flood of questions about himself, his family, life at the palace, etc. One socialite asked about his eating regiment. Another asked about his sex life. And of course, there was that one person to ask the forbidden, "What's the Queen really like?" He needed to get away from his getaway.

"Enjoying yourself, Sir?" A deep, familiar voice spoke from behind him. The ambient noise from the party grew quiet as the door closed. Victor turned to see Marcus standing there, with no jacket and his shirt almost completely unbuttoned exposing the GQ muscles underneath speckled with random tattoos.

"What are you doing here?" Victor asked.

"This is *my* party," Marcus laughed.

"Your party? This is your place?"

"Yes, sir. It is."

"Please don't call me 'sir.'"

"I'm sorry, Your Royal Highness."

"Just Victor, at least for tonight, please."

"Uh oh," Marcus walked over and leaned on the metal bar that spanned the length of the balcony. "Trouble in Parados?"

Victor sarcastically chuckled, "Very funny."

"I try." They both laughed for a few moments, and then Victor's energy returned to somber. "Care to share?"

"I can't talk about it with you."

"Is there something going on with the Queen and Princess Mary?"

"What? Why would you ask that?" Victor immediately raised his defenses and began examining Marcus.

"I just overheard you and Prince John talking in the bathroom."

"You were eavesdropping? And we didn't say anything about the Queen or the Princess."

"No, but you said that you will soon have to give up your freedom for duty." Victor paused for a moment, trying to figure out how not to give away too much. "Is there something happening on Mt. Olympus that us mere mortals aren't to know?"

Victor had to think of something fast to change the subject. "Is that your yacht? It's beautiful." He felt Marcus step extremely close and turned to look at him. To his surprise, their faces were only inches away from each other.

Marcus look right into Victor's eyes for a moment, then spoke, "What's bothering you?" Victor had to stop his interrogation. The only thing that he could think of was to stop him from talking, so he did - with his lips. He pressed his lips against Marcus' in what turned out to be a surprisingly enticing embrace that sent chills up his spine.

Finally grasping reality, he jumped back and turned away from Marcus, wiping his mouth with his hand. "I'm sorry. I know we both have images to protect." The balcony remained silent for a moment, and then he heard footsteps slowly get closer behind him. He thought Marcus had left the balcony until he heard words from behind him.

"I can see that something is bothering you. If you don't talk about it, it won't change," Victor felt the warmth of Marcus' breath on the back of his neck, contrasting sharply to the crisp November marine air on his face.

"I can't talk about it. And, definitely, not with you," Victor said. He turned around keeping his eyes on the tattoo etched into Marcus' pectoral muscle. "I appreciate your concern but as much as I want to, I just cannot discuss anything with you."

"You can talk to me about anything."

"Not this. I barely know you."

"Well, I'm a Sagittarius, I'm 23, born March 5th, and -"

"- And you're gay?" Victor interjected.

"If one must label it, then I'd be considered somewhere between bisexual and pansexual."

Victor looked up at Marcus' face, confused. "What?"

"Beauty is beauty. Gender doesn't really matter to me. And *you* ... are beautiful." Marcus' hand gently grazed Victor's jaw and just as he leaned in for another kiss, the door swung open with a bang. Victor and Marcus jumped to opposite sides of the balcony.

"What the hell is going on?" Prince Jack stood in the doorway. Marcus bowed at the neck and then shuffled past Jack, not

65

making eye contact. Jack stepped onto the balcony and closed the door behind him. He walked over to Victor who had begun pacing, awaiting the scolding that came with no delay. "Have you lost your mind, Victor?"

"No."

"I'd argue you have. This crowd keeps nothing to themselves. You say you want an escape and you try to find it with Marcus Frazier of all people?"

"Hey, he came onto me."

"And your legs are broken? You could have walked back into the party. You know that if anyone had seen you, it would complicate everything."

"How would it complicate things?"

Jack advanced toward him and grabbed him by the arms, "Look, I know you are under a hell of a lot of stress lately but you cannot make mistakes. Not like this. Not now. We're just beginning to test you out to the public." Jack stepped closer and whispered in his ear, "You *have* to win over the hearts of the people before Grandmother gets sick. You cannot get distracted."

"Ok, ok. I get it." Jack pulled his phone out of his pocket and walked over to the edge of the balcony. "What are you doing?" Victor asked.

"I'm calling the car to come retrieve us. We're leaving."

"What? Why?"

"Because this night is over. We attend events but we don't close them out." He turned and spoke into the phone, "Hello. Can you pull the car around? We're ready to go. Thanks." He tapped the screen and wrapped his arm around Victor. They entered the party as Victor noticed a considerable about of the guests had left and those that remained were obviously drunk. Jack and Victor made their way to the elevator.

As they waited, an arm tapped Victor's shoulder. Victor turned to find Marcus with a large glass filled with what Victor assumed to be vodka. "You guys are leaving already?"

Jack extended his arm to push Marcus back. "Yeah sorry! Great party though." Just as he spoke, the elevator doors opened and Marcus raised his glass.

"Your Royal Highnesses!"

December

Chapter 7

Rose's heels clicked violently as she stormed through Rousel Palace. She maneuvered masterfully through the maze of the layout until she reached Mary's office. Rose burst into the room, giving herself a double door entrance and causing Mary to flinch. Rose marched over to the desk and slammed a newspaper on the desk in front of Mary. "What does that *child* think he's doing?"

"What are you talking about?" Mary asked, picking up and unfolding the newspaper.

"Read the headline," Rose barked.

Mary fought the urge to tell her 'watch your tone' as she needed her help, so she just read. "IAKOS' NEW FAVORITE ROYAL FAMILY MEMBER - The normally private Prince Victor has stolen the attention from his family members who make frequent public appearances at social gatherings all over Parados. From ribbon cuttings to movie premieres, the Prince has accepted invitations for various events over the past month and Iakons are excited to see more of the handsome prince." Mary looked up at Rose. "What's the problem?"

"Do you think this is a coincidence that right when Mother gets sick, suddenly he wants to be Mr. Smile-and-Wave?"

"Rose, not everything is a conspiracy."

"I bet you she put him up to this."

"She who?"

"The Queen!" Rose exclaimed. "She told him to build a relationship with the people. We know that she found out that we were working to get Parliament to pass the amendment. So, she sends him around Parliament and right to the people."

"Do you think she would do that?"

"Someone is behind this. Victor has always hated being in the public eye. The wind blows and he breaks out in a cold sweat." Rose flopped down in the chair. "Now Jackie is bringing him to red carpets, and there's talk of him and Jack doing a spread in a magazine. We have to do something or the people will be chanting and petitioning for him to be crowned."

Mary threw her hands up. "Ok, stop! I am finally leaving this evening for our honeymoon. I need you to take care of Mother and make sure that she is taking her treatments. She keeps saying that she wants to stop them."

"Stop treatment? She wouldn't do that. That's her only chance at remission. I will deal with that, but you must do something and fast. A public appearance, sneak something to the press, anything. Just stop this!"

"I think I have a plan, Rose."

Rose stopped, "Oh?" She took a deep breath and sat back in her chair. "Let's hear it."

"If he wants to be in the public eye, fine. Then he should get the full experience: the good side of it and the bad. He has skeletons in his closet just like the rest of us. But I can guarantee he hasn't hidden them well enough before he threw himself out there." Mary sat down with a blank expression, contrasting sharply to Rose's shocked and delighted face.

"Do tell."

"Oh, come on, like you don't know," Mary hinted. "Men. Victor prefers men."

"Wait, Mary. That could backfire." Rose warned. "You know how sensitive the people are of civil rights and things. And it's not like fifty years ago when that was illegal. Now, people don't care. They even applaud those who come out."

Mary leaned forward, resting her elbows on her desk with her hands clasped professionally. "Not everyone. Like you said, Conservatives have the majority in Parliament. And if we can't move them into our corner, we might as well move them out of his."

Rose sat, stunned at the suggestion. She was genuinely surprised yet comforted at how powerful they were when she and her sister were on the same side. "That could work. But I have one question."

"What?"

"Are you willing to do that to your own son? It will humiliate him … publicly."

"And me being disowned wouldn't humiliate me?" Mary replied. "Maybe it's time he learned what the real world was like."

"Yes, but he didn't put your claim in jeopardy, you did."

"Whose side are you on?"

"Yours," Rose reassured Mary. "I'm just saying that if we're going to bring him down, we have to be smart about it. It can't have your fingerprint on it, and we shouldn't underestimate him, especially if Mother is behind him."

* * * * *

What am I doing? Victor looked at himself in the mirror. A mere 3 months ago, he would have never imagined the world around him at present. He remembered a conversation he'd had with Chef Vince over a bowl of ice cream. Vince had told him that he'd seemed different. *Am I different? Have I changed or is it just my perception of the world that has changed?* It weighed heavily on his heart that he and his mother were becoming enemies. They hadn't spoken in person in weeks; it was all reading her actions, guessing her movements, hearsay … the fog of war. And he had a feeling that it was just the beginning.

Jackie and Jack entered the room and found Victor on the floor in front of the mirror. Jackie gasped and practically yelled, "Is that Armani? You're really on the floor in Armani? Are you crazy?" Victor scrambled to his feet and turned around to a palm connecting with his forehead. He yelped and stumbled backward. "Designers don't send you clothes to wear in public all wrinkled and messed up." She began aggressively smacking out the creases on his pant legs as Jack stood behind laughing.

"You know. Something I learned when I was very young was 'Keep your hands to yourself.'" Victor swatted his sister's hands away until she finally stood up right. She wore a long black sequin dress with black scrappy heels, and of course diamonds on her neck, wrists, fingers, and head. Her extravagance was topped off with a black faux fur coat. "Someone's been dipping in the Crown Jewels again. Did you ask this time?"

Jack's muffled laughter erupted into a loud cackle at his cousin's expense. "As if!" he exclaimed.

"Shut up," she barked, playfully swinging at him. "Of course, I asked. One tongue-lashing is enough. A lecture from the Sovereign is not something one forgets."

Victor grabbed his long wool pea coat, and the three left Victor's suite and made their way to the front entrance of the State Palace. "How'd you get the jewels last time anyway?" Victor asked, fumbling with his cummerbund.

Jackie popped his hand and said, "Don't worry about it. I have connections."

"Uh oh, hide the fine china. The girl's got connections." Jack teased and then jumped out the way, barely escaping a sideswipe from his cousin. Victor laughed as they finally got to the front door. He put on his coat, wrapped a white scarf around his neck and pulled black leather gloves from his pocket. Jack saw this and laughed even harder. "Warm enough?"

"I will be," Victor replied as serious as a brain tumor. They filed into the limousine and were off for a night on the town.

The trip wasn't long because the motorcade had a police escort, since more than two members of the Royal Family were inside. Of course, when they arrived, crowds filled the sidewalk on both sides of the entrance and across the street. Women were screaming and children were jumping around. Most of the men had cameras that flickered away. Victor turned to Jackie, "Are people seriously here just to see us get out of the car? They aren't even attending the show."

Jackie leaned in closer, "We are the show." She knocked on the door and the chauffeur opened it. Jackie stepped out, then Jack, and for the grand finale, Victor. The crowd crescendoed into hysteria. The three stood smiling and waving for a few moments and then slowly entered the theater. The security guards escorted them up the marble stairs and to the third floor. After walking down a long corridor, they finally arrived at the door that read, "ROYAL BOX".

Victor's stomach began to turn and chills ran up his spine. His obsession with history heightened his paranoia. After his sister and cousin entered the box, he leaned in and whispered to the guard, "Is it safe?"

"Of course, Your Royal Highness. Why wouldn't it be?" The guard replied. "Do you have cause for concern?"

"Just a gut feeling. Historically, theaters haven't been kind to national leaders."

The guard smirked and replied, "Rest assured, Your Royal Highness isn't the nation's leader yet, sir."

Victor chuckled and entered to the box. The show sprang to life as dancers took to the stage. About an hour passed and just as the dancing snowflakes leapt across the stage, Victor's pocket began to buzz. He flinched at the sensation and looked around to make sure no one could hear it. To his luck, no one did. He slowly reached one hand into this pocket and pushed the button at the top, stopping the vibrations. He returned focus on the ballet, distracting him from the close call with humiliation.

Just a few moments later, a tap on the shoulder made him jump out of his skin, and almost his seat. His whole body tensed as the guard whispered in his ear. Immediately, he sprang from his seat and shuffled out into the hallway. "What did you say?"

"You have a call, sir," the guard said, handing him the black cell phone.

"Can't it wait?" Victor asked.

"No, sir."

Victor took the phone and pressed it to his ear, "Hello?"

"Hi, Your Royal Highness, this is Mo Li Zhang, the Queen's Private Secretary."

"Oh hello, Ms. Zhang. Is everything all right?" Victor immediately clutched the phone tightly.

"Um, no sir. Actually, it isn't." This response alone sent Victor's heart rate through the roof. Normally, her response would be, 'Yes, but ...' and then the bad news. "The Queen has had an accident."

"WHAT?" He yelled. "Where are you?"

"We're at Parados General," Mo Li replied, trying to lessen the blow of the news.

"What exactly happened?" Victor asked, as he snapped at the guard, signaling for him to get Jack and Jackie.

"From what I understand, she was trying to get to the bathroom without her walker and fell. She hit her head."

"Oh, my god, we're on our way. Thank you for calling me. We'll be in touch when we arrive." Just as he ended the call, Jackie and Jack came out of the room confused. Victor tried to collect himself, but his voice gave his panic away. "The Queen had an accident."

"What happened?" Jackie asked.

"I'm not totally sure. We have to get to the hospital." They all began trotting down the hallway. Jackie masterfully held her dress up and kept up with everyone else as they all proceeded down the stairs, through the foyer, and out the main doors. The crowd outside erupted in surprise. Ignoring the crowd, Jack and Victor piled into the cars. The security guards piled into their SUVs in the motorcade. Jackie got to the limo door and quickly waved to the cheering crowd, and then climbed in. The chauffeur slammed the door behind her and the motorcade took off.

Sirens roared, tires screeched, and engines growled as they raced through the city. Jack, Victor, and Jackie held on around turns that sent them sliding around the limo. None of them had put on their seatbelts and regretted it within seconds. After a record 10 minutes, the motorcade pulled up in front of the building that was nearly all glass. Once the cars stopped in front of the ambulance bay, two security guards and a beautiful, young East Asian woman stood in a gray slim dress and matching platform stilettos. She clutched to her phone like a life preserver. The three royal millennials filed out of the car and walked up to the young women. She gave a slight curtsy and said, "Your Royal Highnesses."

"Ms. Zhang," Victor replied.

"Mo Li, please."

"Why hello, Mo Li," Jack smoldered. Jackie punched him on the shoulder. "What?" He whined, with fake innocence.

Victor stepped in front of Jack. "Where is the Queen?"

"She's right this way." Mo Li led the group through the triage room, and down the hall. As they power-walked, the walls began closing in on Victor. His hands trembled almost as much as his heart. Every couple of rooms, someone peeked their head out of their room to catch a glimpse of members of the Royal Family. Nurses and doctors bowed and curtsied as they passed. Finally, after an eternity, they entered a secure wing of the emergency department where they stopped short of the room. Jackie, Jack, and Victor concealed their heart's fears, reverting to their familial training. Victor's stifled breath held tightly as he stepped into the room. To his surprise, she was alone in the room. *Where is everyone?*

"Grandma?"

Margaret slowly opened her eyes and smiled. "Victor, come here, baby."

The openness of his grandmother's affection was a rare occurrence and overwhelming when it happened. He valiantly fought back the tears and walked over to his grandmother who was laid on the bed. A clear tube fed her nose the oxygen she couldn't draw herself. Two clear strips held the gash on her forehead closed. "W-w-what happened?" he stammered.

"I'm okay, dear," Margaret said. Victor hadn't realized that he'd been tensing his diaphragm so tightly that he hadn't breathed in almost a minute. Air whooshed into his lungs, making him a bit lightheaded. "Don't cry, Victor. I'm ok."

"No, you're not! You're in the hospital." It all hit Victor: this was really happening. He'd done exactly what he always held against his mother. He got so caught up in the politics that he was squandering the precious time he'd had with his grandmother. "What did the doctor say?"

"He said that the weakness isn't going to get better, b-b-but I can be discharged soon."

Victor closed his eyes and took a deep breath. He needed to be strong, for everyone. He leaned in and kissed the unbandaged side of her forehead. Jack and Jackie entered the room and froze at the door.

"Grandmother, what happened?" Jackie said, with shock painted across her face. All royal protocol flew out that window; for the first time in their lives as they forgot to bow when entering.

"I'm ok. I just fell trying to walk without my walker. I thought I could make it to the bathroom."

"Grandmother, I know the walker is annoying and sometimes humiliating, but I'd rather you use it than fall." Victor sat on the stool under the doctor's table and rolled it next to the bed.

Jackie walked to the other side of the bed, slightly curtsied, and then sat in the chair. Jack saw her and realized his mistake. He bowed where he stood and then walked up to the bottom of the bed.

"Where was your daughter?" Jackie asked.

"Where *is* your daughter?" Victor asked Margaret, who shrugged and looked at Jack as if to ask him. He shrugged too.

"Mo Li?" Victor called out of the door.

The secretary entered with her phone to her ear. She curtsied, and then replied. "Yes, sir?"

"Where's Princess Rose?"

"I just spoke to her. She's on her way."

Margaret adjusted herself in the bed, then asked, "Any word from Princess Mary yet?"

"I managed to reach her. She and the Duke just checked into the hotel. She said to have Rose call her when she arrives." Mo Li immediately read the disappointment on her face. "I'm sure she just wants an update."

"She should want to be here with her mother," Victor spat.

Margaret pat his hand and looked up at her secretary. "You tell my daughter that I expect her to be here in the morning. Tell her, she's teaching me how to treat her. If my health doesn't take precedence, neither will her marriage. You tell her that!"

Victor's eyes shot open, and he looked at Jackie who shared the same expression.

Mo Li stood stuck. She didn't know if she should wait for the Queen to calm down before she sent a message to the Princess or should she pass on the threat. As uncomfortable as it would make her, the Queen's face showed no sign of softening, and she knew what she needed to do. She curtsied one more time, turned and left the room.

Jack looked around and cautiously began his request. "Grandma, you know I'm here for you, but —"

"-Jack," Margaret interjected, "go eat!"

"Thank you!" He ran out of the room and down the hall.

They all shared a quick laugh, and then Victor's smile softened. "Should we release a statement?"

"No!"

"Grandmother, at least 100 people saw us leave the theater in a rush, including press, and another 25 saw us rushing into the emergency room. Rumors are going to swirl," Jackie advised.

Margaret paused for a moment. Then she sat up and asked for a piece of paper and pencil. "Write this down." Jackie took a slip of paper from her clutch and handed it to Victor with a bedazzled pen. "Her Majesty, the Queen, was brought to the hospital tonight after a small fall on a carpet. She only suffered minor injuries including a small cut. I'm happy to share that Her Majesty is healthy and in good spirits. She will be discharged later tonight and will return to the State Palace."

"That's it?" Victor asked.

"That's it!" Margaret ordered. He immediately stood up and bowed. "Call the press now and take Jackie with you. Have her stand on your left and behind you."

"Are you sure you want me to do it and not the press secretary?" Victor asked.

"No! Only you. Y-y-you speak for me."

"Yes, ma'am!" Jackie stood, curtsied, and the two walked out of the room.

Chapter 8

Ding! The little seatbelt light illuminated on the wall above the recliner where Christopher rested with his chin in his hand, his elbows on his knees, and his eyes closed. Mary walked over to the matching champagne-colored recliner opposite him and fastened herself into her chair.

A young woman dressed in an airline uniform appeared at the doorway. "Your Royal Highnesses, we are beginning our descent into Parados."

Mary smiled back, "Thank you!" The flight attendant bowed and hustled back to the nearest chair. "Christopher!" The Duke's eyes slowly opened just enough to let some light in. "We're about to land. Put your seatbelt on." Without saying a word, he clicked on the seat belt, and returned to his previous position.

Moments inched by as Mary peered out of the window. The island nation grew closer and closer as the blue ocean gave way to the large coastal city. Swarms of people speckled the white beaches and the high-rise hotels and resorts marked the end of nature and the beginning of asphalt. The ground inched closer as the wheels of the jet rumbled underneath the floor from the wind. Finally, after floating over the runway, they touched down at Parados International Airport.

Once the plane turned and rolled off the runway, Mary pulled a little card out of her pocket with handwriting scribbled across it. Christopher looked at the pink index card and then gave Mary a disapproving expression. The plane came to a stop as a large staircase drove up to the door. Mary took off her seatbelt and rose to her feet. She walked forward through the plane, past the conference room and a full living room area to the large doorway. Mary wrapped her black scarf around her neck and tucked it into her coat. Christopher came up behind her and rested his hand on her shoulder. "You shouldn't do this."

"I know what I'm doing, Chris. Relax," Mary replied as she shrugged his hand off her shoulder. She stepped over to the window and Christopher grabbed her arm, gently but protectively, turned her to look her in the eye. She needed to know the seriousness of his warning.

"You should at least call the Queen and have her approve your remarks before you step out there. She will see it, and right now, you should be cautious," he whispered.

Mary looked right back with her poker face in full bloom, "I said I know what I'm doing." She stepped around him and nodded to the young flight attendant. With a large tug at the lever fixed to the door of the royal jet, a luxurious Boeing 787-10, she opened it and the couple de-boarded. Awaiting them at the bottom of the small metal staircase was a crowd of press, as organized by Princess Mary. Mary walked over to the center of the group of reporters and cameramen. By the time she stopped and readied herself to speak, she turned to her left but didn't see a familiar face. Mary scanned the crowd looking for Chris, and when she found him, he was climbing into the back seat of the motorcade of SUVs that awaited them.

With a security guard on either side of her, she began, "It's good to be home, although not in the best circumstances," Mary spoke into the microphones being shoved into her face. All the reporters were either recording her or scribbling down every word as to not miss anything. Without warning, she began to doubt this decision. "Last night, I received word that my mother, Her Majesty the Queen, suffered an injury to the head due to a fall. This injury was not caused by Her Majesty's other ongoing treatments. Though having suffered a mild concussion and minor scrapes, Her Majesty is doing very well. As of this morning, she's been discharged and is home now at the State Palace under the watchful eye of the Royal Physician, Dr. Arthur Bennett, for continued treatment. We thank you for your thoughts and prayers as she recovers. Thank you!"

Mary turned to the cars and she made her way through the crowd. The guards parted the sea of ravenous people in front of her and she climbed into the SUV. Christopher focused intently on his phone. The motorcade began across the tarmac and out of the large security gate. Throughout the city, people turned to see the police-escorted SUVs as their high-pitched sirens roared and lit up the streets with red and blue. Despite the excitement outside, inside was as silent as the dead. Mary and Chris sat on opposite sides of the car as both refused to relent and be the first to speak. Mary leaned forward and grabbed a bottle of water from the cup holder. She took a swig from the bottle and peered out the window at the large palace growing closer and closer. The motorcade moved through the gate without pause and stopped at the private entrance.

The deafening silence ended much to Chris' surprise, as Mary turned to her husband. "Will you support my decision to the Queen?"

Christopher turned to Mary noticing a crack in her poker face. Nervousness or maybe a twinge of regret was underlying her statement. He placed his hand on top of her leg and squeezed it. "I support you; that goes without saying. But I didn't and don't support your decision. But I will not say anything out of respect for you." Mary knew that that was the best she was going to get out of him. She was drawn to men with integrity.

* * * * *

Victor entered his grandmother's room with a medium-sized cup of tea in his hand. Margaret's gaze was fixed on the television, her eyes seeming to bulge from their sockets. She noticed Victor beside her bed. "Thank you dear. Just put it right here," she signaled to the nightstand next to her. She returned to her previous fixation. Victor spread across the foot of the bed, careful not to obstruct the Queen's view. He immediately gasped at the headline sprawling across the bottom of the screen. *"BREAKING NEWS: PRINCESS PROMISES QUEEN'S GOOD HEALTH"* Victor rolled to his side, "Um, what just happened?"

Margaret shushed him as the reporter spoke into the microphone on what appeared to be a tarmac. "After receiving some overnight backlash for not immediately returning home, Her Royal Highness, Princess Mary flew in this morning with her new husband, His Royal Highness the Duke of Spiti. The Princess de-boarded her plane just half an hour ago and told reporters that the Queen is doing much better, however hinting that there may have been another issue that, until now, wasn't previously public." The screen switched to a clip of the princess speaking, "Last night, I received word that my mother, Her Majesty the Queen, suffered an injury to the head due to a fall. This injury was not caused by Her Majesty's other ongoing treatments." Switching back to the all-too-excited reporter, she rationalized her conjecture, "Now this is in direct conflict with an

79

official statement issued by her son, His Royal Highness Prince Victor, last night, in which he said that the Queen was — quote — 'brought to the hospital ... after a small fall on a carpet' and is 'healthy and in good spirits'. This leaves all of Iakos to wonder: who's telling the truth? Is it possible that the royal household is keeping a medical secret about the Queen from her people?"

The screen suddenly went dark. He turned to his grandmother scowling as she wielded a remote in the hopes of vanquishing the betrayal on the screen. At the worst possible timing, in entered two figures in the corner of Victor's eye. Realizing who had been standing there, he rolled off the bed and stood at attention. She curtsied and her husband bowed at the neck to the Queen. Mary slowly walked over to her mother, seeing the bandage on her forehead. She bent down and gently kissed Margaret's brow. Margaret's eyes remained forward, as her scowl morphed to disgust. Mary stepped back, "Hello, Mother."

Margaret turned to Victor. "Could you give your mother and me a moment please?" she said with a yawn as she sat herself up in the bed. Victor knew what was coming so he happily bowed and left. Margaret turned to her daughter, who kept her gaze locked on the bottom of the bed, braced for the assault. To her surprise, her mother simply stared at her for what felt like an eternity. Then, she fired the first shot.

"Have you lost your mind?" the Queen began passive aggressively.

"No, ma'am!"

"Tell me, how old are you?" Margaret asked.

Confused, Mary replied, "Fifty-one ma'am."

"And of those years, how long have I been Queen?"

Mary counted in her head, "Forty."

"And of those forty years, have you ever seen anyone make a public statement about my health without my consent?" Margaret's voice uncharacteristically crescendoed to a full bellow. "Have you lost your mind? Just who do you think you are? Do you know what instability of the monarchy does to a country's economy, public market, national security, and domestic image? Did you consider any of the ramifications before you decided to stand up there and try to make up for your selfishness?"

"Selfishness? Mother, I cut my honeymoon short to fly back here and see you," Mary replied.

Margaret threw the covers off herself. "You could have taken that one-hour flight *last night* when I needed you and returned in the morning, but you didn't. The people — *my people* — saw you for whom you've become. They saw this person who I barely know and their opinion reflected that of their Queen last night. Would you have come if not for the public outcry against you?" Christopher began slowly taking steps backwards toward the door. "And you ..." the Queen fired at Christopher. "You stood there and let her make such a profoundly misguided decision."

Christopher halted his retreat, "No, ma'am. It's not my place to interfere."

"Mother, I wanted to reassure the kingdom that you are ok."

"I'm not ok!" Margaret yelled. "I'm — not — ok. I have cancer, with about nine months left on this Earth. You didn't reassure anyone. All you did was add more fuel for the conspiracy theorists and yellow journalists to escalate matters and jeopardize the state. Not to mention that we don't have an heir confirmed yet. No one should know until that is settled first."

Margaret felt the veins along her temples pulsating, along with the heat on her face, which matched the pounding in her chest. Mary paused for a moment, giving her mother's beet red face time to return to a somewhat normal shade of pink. Then she spoke, "Should we have the press secretary make a statement to clarify things? Reinforce the narrative?"

Margaret fought to calm herself further. She played out the pros and cons in her head and then came to a clear and concise, "No! We say nothing. The best way to smother this fire that you've ignited is to continue the work of running this country. Let it use up its own oxygen and smother itself." Margaret looked at her daughter and Christopher for a moment, and then shook her head. "Will you be returning to the Mediterranean for the holidays or will you be remaining in the Kingdom?"

"We'll be staying here throughout the holidays and then hopefully reschedule the trip in the new year."

"Good, then I expect you all here on the 24th for Christmas Eve service."

Mary turned to Christopher who was sporting the same puzzled look as her. "How are you going to the Christmas Service, in public, on the other side of town in your condition?"

"That's what a walking stick is for, my dear."

"And that won't make people speculate further?" Mary asked, hoping to sway her mother not to go. Ultimately, she didn't feel like going but she knew her mother would never allow that.

"And whose fault would that be?" the Queen retorted. With one authoritative hand, she motioned toward the door, "That's all." The two bowed and then left the room silently. On the other side of the door, Victor shuffled to the chair, hiding the glass he'd been using to listen through. As Mary passed her son, she simply scoffed at him and continued out of the suite. Christopher acknowledged him with a smile and a nod. Victor waved politely and waited for them to leave.

Finally, when the hall was clear, he went power walking down the adjacent hallway, and down the rear staircase. From there he made his way quickly through the palace until he got to the kitchen. He rushed in and found Margie and Chef Vince laughing hysterically. A small twinge of envy skipped up his spine, but was quelled by the understanding that she was sporting the wrong chromosomes to interest the chef; at least he'd hoped. To his pleasure, Vince turned to him with his face beaming at the sight of him.

"Hey Victor, come pull up a stool!" Margie sat on the side closer to Victor, while Vince sat on the opposite side where the cooking utensils were stored. Victor walked over the counter to see what was in the tub on the counter. Vince spooned out a pink and orange mixture and handed it to him on a freshly cleaned silver spoon. "Sorbet?"

Before he could realize what he'd done, he leaned forward and ate the sorbet right off of the spoon in Vince's hand. Margie's eyes bulged as she broke out into hysterical laughter. Mortified, he took the spoon out of a shell-shocked Vince's hand and with a full mouth, he muffled, "Sorry!"

Vince blushed, chuckling at the awkward expression on his face. "Don't be! It's ok." Vince stood up from leaning on the counter and tried to ease Victor by changing the subject. "We were just talking about your family tree."

"Yes, our enormous family tree," Margie commented, trying to stop her laughter.

"You only hear about the primary and maybe the close extended royal family. But I didn't even know that you had so many cousins."

"Mother alone has something like 23 first cousins." Victor walked over grabbed the stool and placed it next to Margie's at the counter.

Vince's eyes bugged. "Wow, now that's huge. Do you ever get together? Like, all of you?"

Margie jumped in, "No, not anymore. We haven't in years. During the holidays, it's just us. The only times we really see everyone are weddings and funerals, unfortunately."

"I wish we could at some point. Especially now, considering-" Victor stopped himself, realizing that Vince didn't know.

"Considering what?" Vince asked. Vince and Margie looked at each other telepathically trying to cook up a believable lie. However, their connection was bad and neither could think of anything. "Oh, come on. I do have a television. There's something going on. The rumor mill is in full gear."

"Well," Margie slowly began, buying herself time to think up a believable spin. "As you know, Princess Mary eloped with, now, Christopher."

"The Duke of Spiti, right?"

"Yes. Well, it has kind of put the family in a weird spot."

"Why?" Vince asked.

Margie turned to her cousin, "Victor?"

Victor looked at her with a playfully sinister glare that warned of payback to come. "Um, well, it's against the law. So that kind of throws her legitimacy into question now."

Margie looks at Vince with big eyes, shocked that he shared the truth. "Victor!"

"What? That is public record if Parliament received an amendment request. He's bound to find out." Victor turned to Vince and continued explaining, "The Sovereign's marriage cannot be illegitimate nor illegal. So, it weakens her claim to the throne exponentially."

Vince looked back and forth between the two, clearly very confused. "But she has years to find a resolution, right?"

Both Victor and his cousin tensed up, until finally Victor blurted, "Not really!" This reaction, of course, resulted an elbow to the side. "Ow! What?"

"Why not?" Vince asked, now genuinely concerned.

Margie, assuming a sudden royal air, leaned forward and folded her hands, "That's classified."

Victor looked at his cousin like she was someone else. "Yeah, that wasn't suspicious at all."

"What? He can't know anything yet!"

Vince looked confused. "Anything about what?"

"Shut up!" Victor playfully pushed his cousin to silence her from responding, but misjudged the strength of the shove and she flew off her stool. She jumped up quickly, poised for attack.

"Hey, hey. Stop!" Vince laughed holding up his hands. The two withdrew their claws and sat back down. "May I ask you this question?"

"Depends on the question," Victor quickly replied with a smirk.

"What happened to your aunt?"

"Which aunt?" Margie asked.

"The late Princess Victoria."

Both Victor and Margie paused for a moment. The energy in the room quickly changed. "We aren't sure," Victor responded, barely audible.

"What? How aren't you sure?"

Margie kept her gaze on her hands, "Our parents say she just died."

"And every time we ask Her Majesty what happened, she gets quiet and never really gives us a straight answer," Victor added.

Finally taking the temperature of the room, he realized that he'd struck a nerve in the two cousins. In desperate need to add some of the playfulness back into the room he spooned a bit of sorbet, turned it backward, recoiled the tip and launched the pink treat right at Victor. The cold sensation splattered across Victor's face. Margie gasped and jumped up from her seat. Once she fathomed what had just occurred, she broke into her usually loud laughter.

"Ok," Victor said with a menacing grin. He shoveled a handful of sorbet out of the tub with his hand and recoiled his arm facing Vince. Seeing his fate, Vince dropped to the floor. Victor grinned and launched the sorbet at the hyena to his right. Margie's laughter stopped instantly as she inspected her nice gray blouse. She scooped the remaining bit from her shirt and threw it back. Within seconds, an all-out, 3-way food fight commenced.

After what seemed like an hour, Margie went up to her guest apartments to shower. Victor and Vince stood covered in sorbet giggling and staring at each other, out of breath at the festivities. Footsteps launched them back into reality and Vince look genuinely panicked. Victor had an idea and took Vince by the hand. He ran over to the wall on the far side of the kitchen.

"Where are we going?" Vince whispered.

"Shhh. Just follow me and stay close." Victor's hand quickly scanned the wall as the footsteps got louder.

He found a crack just in time, pressed his thumb on a little square and it scanned his print. Finally a latch clicked and Victor pushed the wall. A secret door opened and Vince let out an audible, "Woah!" Victor snatched the chef's hand again and dragged him inside, closing the door behind him.

He could hear the butler who had entered the kitchen. "What in the world? What happened in here?" He ranted to himself. "Now I have to clean this up? This is going on his record."

Victor turned to Vince, "I'm sorry."

Vince smirked, "Don't worry about it. It's not your fault. Besides, he's my supervisor. Not my boss." Victor looked at him and leaned in for a kiss. After three months, he finally would get to see what kissing the chef would feel like, or so he thought.

Vince caught him by the shoulder. "Where are we?"

The prince looked irritated by the thwarted attempt. He whispered back, "What does it look like? A secret passage."

"Where does it go?"

"Everywhere in the palace. Even to places you are not to know about." Victor had an idea. He grabbed him by the hand, "Let's go."

They raced down the hall, up a flight of stairs, a series of turns, down a flight of stairs, another turn, and the up few flights of stairs until they got to a door.

"Guess where we are," the prince whispered, to which Vince shrugged. Victor opened the door and revealed the beautiful bedroom.

"Is this yours?"

Victor nodded.

"Wow! I've never been up here. It's ... it's ... beautiful."

Victor walked over to the foot of the bed and flopped down. Vince paced around the room at the lavishly decorated furniture with a twist of modernism.

"Come here," Victor spoke. Vince turned to his royal crush and sat beside him. The prince continued softly, "I hope I'm not making a mistake by bringing you up here."

"Why would it be?" Vince looked into Victor's eyes, almost concerned.

Victor kept his eyes down, "I haven't been really lucky with the trust aspect when it comes to guys."

Vince raised his hand and rested it softly on the prince's cheek. Victor leaned into his hand, as he spoke, "Look, Vic. You *never* have to worry about whether or not you can trust me. I haven't felt this way about someone in a long time."

"Really?" Victor met the eyes that were searching for his.

Vince smiled reassuringly, "Really."

"Then how come you haven't tried to kiss me yet?"

"Because I can tell that that's not what you need. You may want it, maybe even as much as I do. But affection is more important to you."

Victor chuckled, "Yes, but I am human."

Vince responded with a soft chuckle of his own, leaned in and pressed his lips softly against the prince's. He wrapped his arms around Victor and held their embrace until they both had to come up for air. Vince leaned back and smiled, "Well?"

Victor leapt up and kissed him again, playfully tackling him onto the bed.

Chapter 9

"Mother, why won't you let your dresser dress you? It is *her* job." Rose protested, as she struggled to get the shoe on her foot.

"Because I have *you* here, now. And don't rip my stockings!" Margaret argued. She held onto the bed, trying not to be pulled off by her daughter. Victor entered the bedroom with a small shoehorn. "Thank you dear," she said to him as she took it from his hand and gave it to Rose. "Here, just use this." Rose took it from her and finally slid the shoe onto her mother's foot with ease.

Victor began to leave the room, but stopped at the door and turned back to Margaret. "Is there anything else you need?"

"No, dear! Just make sure to have everyone ready."

"Yes, ma'am!" He turned and left the room. He buttoned his black suit jacket and fixed his red tie to make sure it wasn't crooked. As he descended the large stairs of the Residential Foyer, he walked over to where the Duke of Makria, Jack, and Margie stood huddled.

"Your mother and the rest of the family just arrived," John said to Victor.

"Ah, perfect! Grandmother said to be ready so I suppose we can go to the cars and wait for her." The four passed through the large doors and down the long hall to the grand state entrance. Across the extensive grounds was a crowd pressed up against the gate, waving and screaming to the Royal Family. Victor and Jack returned with waves of their own and then joined the rest of their family at the motorcade.

Christmas Eve was one of the biggest days for the Royal Family. Every year, they all piled into a motorcade and traveled to the Parados Church of Christ for a special Christmas Eve service. Queen Margaret loved this day, not only because she got to go to church as opposed to streaming sermons online from the palace as she had to do every Sunday, but because she got to celebrate it with her people. Victor always admired her love for the Iakon people and she never used these moments for her own glory, but to allow the relationship between Crown and country to shine. Though she

87

couldn't be extremely vocal and upfront about her religion and faith, she was an incredibly spiritual and faithful woman, which added to her strength.

John, Jack, and Margie climbed into the first limousine and the guard closed the door. Victor walked over to the second limousine and knocked on the window. Jackie rolled down the window, decked out in her normal extravagance. Mary sat next to her but her attention was fixed to her phone. On the side bench sat Christopher and lastly Seth.

"Hello family," Victor said.

"Hola," Jackie smiled, blowing a kiss to Victor.

"How was your ride?" Victor asked.

Jackie grunted, while Seth retorted, "Too damn long." Jackie kicked him in the leg.

"Hey," Mary barked, smacking Jackie in the leg. "Keep your feet to yourself! Only animals kick. You are too old to act so unladylike."

"Good to see we're all in the Christmas spirit," Victor laughed sarcastically.

The Duke chuckled, "Right?"

Jackie clicked the door open, but Victor stepped back. "Oh no, Grandmother asked me to escort her in because of her legs."

Mary's head shot up and her eyes pierced into Victor. "What? Why?"

"To help her walk," retorted Victor.

"Why can't Rose do it?"

"When was the last time you tried to hold the Queen up? She's too heavy for the Princess to support her."

Jackie leaned forward to block the two bickering family members. "You're riding with her?"

"Yes," Victor replied.

"Good!" Mary spat, looking back at her phone. The Duke nudged her leg in a scolding manner.

Victor simply laughed at his mother's immaturity. Jackie looked behind him and pointed at something. Victor turned to see the Queen, shuffling along with a walking stick in one hand and the other clutching onto her daughter. She struggled to get there but made it a point to keep her posture and smile as to show as little weakness as possible. Victor rushed over to her, but Rose waved him off. So, he stepped behind her and gently placed his hand on her back just to let her know that he was there. The guard strategically stood between her and the crowd at the gate so they wouldn't see her struggle. *How was she going to walk down an aisle in front of everyone?* Another guard opened the door to the high-roofed, armored Rolls Royce limousine specifically made for the Sovereign with flags on the front and back. The flags in the front waved the National Flag and the rear flags bore the Royal Standard of Queen Margaret I.

Margaret climbed into the car extremely carefully and Victor went to lean in and say something to her. Just as he stepped forward to lean in, Rose slapped the 4 inch-thick door shut, missing his head by inches. "HEY!" Victor bellowed in her face. Rose smiled and turned as if to slap him with her hair, if her hair were longer. Victor gritted his teeth and walked over to the other side of the limousine, where a guard held the door open for him.

Large leather seats faced him across from their bench. The warm air from the vent caressed his face as if to calmingly stroke him. The windows wouldn't open in the back seat, for security. Only the driver's window could open, and only 3 inches. As the motorcade began down the driveway to the grand entrance at the gate, Victor peered out the front window. The world around them warped from the thickness of the bulletproof glass. Margaret, sensing his frustration, placed a hand on Victor's leg.

"I never got to thank you," Victor spoke.

"Whatever for?"

"For supporting me, for everything!"

"Hey," Margaret kissed the back of his hand. "You had to be someone's favorite."

Victor chuckled and rested his head on his grandmother's shoulder. He closed his eyes as his heart was struck with a pang at the thought of losing her. *I'll have no one.* He took some deep breaths to clear his mind. He wanted to enjoy the little time he had with her; after all, if the doctors were right, this is her last Christmas Eve. Tears began to well in his eyes, but he had to fight them back before they got out.

The roads were blocked off and the pavement was barricaded to prevent anyone from running out into the street. They made their way through the streets as Margaret took it all in: the people waving, the street lamps wrapped in Christmas lights and wreaths, and the adoring eyes. She lifted her hand and gently waved as if they could see her, though she knew that she was just a dark silhouette in the window optically eluding passersby. The motorcade slowed as it turned down a large boulevard splitting the city down the middle. They passed coffee shops at the foot of skyscrapers, hotels, and office buildings. Victor looked up to see people in the windows with large signs that read *LONG LIVE THE QUEEN.*

Finally, at the opposite end of the city, the motorcade came to a stop in front of an enormous Gothic-styled Cathedral that was converted into a non-denominational church. It was complete with flying buttresses, towering steeples atop the west-work, and biblical figures protruding out of the stone around the west entrance.

The first limousine emptied on the curb, sending the people who flanked the pathway to the church into a frenzy. The motorcade inched forward and then Victor's mother, stepfather, and siblings exited their vehicle. Finally, it was their turn. They inched forward and then Victor climbed out of the driver side door. The crowd's cheers grew considerably at the mere sight of Victor. Mary's face turned green as she maintained her dignity and continued toward the Royal Portal on the arm of her husband. Victor stepped around the limousine and the guard opened the door, Victor stuck his hand out as if to present his grandmother. A hand joined his and out emerged The Queen. Everyone screeched in excitement. With the walking stick in her right hand, she began slowly up the stone pathway to the church. Victor diligently trailed her closely. Both waved and smiled externally, but were also concerned with her not falling. About halfway up the path, the Queen stopped to catch her breath but masked it with more intense smiles and waves at the people. After a few moments, they continued until finally they made it through the doorway.

The family gathered two by two and processed down the aisle of the sanctuary as the choir and full orchestra rang out a grandiose hymn. The congregation rose to their feet and bowed as the Queen passed up the aisle. They finally reached the front of the church and took their places at the first pew. Victor made sure to sit next to his grandmother.

The service progressed staying true to annual tradition: Christmas hymns, inspiring scripture readings, and beautiful choir songs. Finally, the pastor stepped up to the podium and began to orate on the birth of Jesus. Victor had heard the story every year of his entire life so he slowly lost focus on the speaker and began looking around the church. Large wreaths with red bows floated in front of the floor-to-ceiling stained glass windows. Long green garland traced the wall, from the rear of the church to the transept, looping through each wreath.

Queen Margaret sat attentively listening to the pastor, when suddenly something seemed different. She looked around with a blank stare. As moments passed, she grew more and more frantic, for nothing around her seemed familiar except her grandson. She took his hand and squeezed it so tightly that his fingertips began turning blue. Her thoughts swirled as she tried to make sense of her surroundings. Finally, it came back to her in bits and pieces. She remembered the motorcade, the crowd, the cathedral, and the holiday.

The congregation rose to their feet. Margaret turned to her now standing grandson who looked at her with a strange expression. "Are you ok?" She simply nodded and joined in Hark! The Herald Angels Sing while remaining in her seat.

Victor kept his ear on his grandmother, as something didn't feel right. Then it dawned on him. He listened to his grandmother sing, "Glory to the angels sing - Peace on Earth and reconciled - God and sinners mercy mild."

He turned to her and examined her expressionless face. He sat on the pew close to her and took her hand. "Grandmother?"

She turned to him, "Yes, Jack?"

"It's me, Grandma. Victor."

"I said that."

He turned to his sister who sat on his right and whispered, "Something is wrong." Jackie looked behind him at the seated Queen who was simply swaying and mouthing failed attempts at the song. She indicated for him to switch seats with her. He slid behind her and she stepped over and sat next to Margaret.

She placed a hand on her back, "Grandma, can you look at me?"

Margaret turned to her and whispered, "Of course I can. What? We're singing."

"What's my name?"

91

"What?"

"What is my name?"

"Victoria," she quickly replied and then continued to sing. Victor and Jackie looked at each other is shock, and made an executive, telepathic decision. Victor walked around to the Queen's left, and they grabbed her arms. "What are you doing?" she whispered frantically.

"Just come with us for a moment, Grandmother." They lifted her from under her arms and began walking down the aisle. The pastor, now noticing what was going on, didn't stop preaching, although all eyes were on the three at this point. Rose shuffled across the front and caught up with the Queen, Prince, and Princess now halfway up the aisle, and Margie and Mary soon followed.

In the foyer, they sat Margaret down on a bench next to the closed portal doors. "What is going on?" Rose asked.

"Grandma," Jackie whispered gently to Margaret, who simply stared off into space. "What's my name?"

"Jacqueline," she replied.

"What is this about?" Mary demanded.

Victor interjected, "In the sanctuary, she started mixing up the words to the song, her favorite Christmas hymn, and then Jackie asked her to identify her. She said, 'Victoria!'"

"So," Margie replied. "She just got confused."

"No, Margie. That's not good!" Rose replied.

Margie stopped and turned to her mother, watching as the blood flushed from her painted face. "She hasn't said Victoria's name since she died. She always refers to her relationally — your sister, my daughter, or aunt. Never by name."

Victor sat next to Margaret on the bench and began rubbing her back. "I think we should take her to the hospital."

"No!" Margaret exclaimed, seeming to snap out of a trance. "No hospital! Not on a day when all cameras are fixed on us. No!"

"Then what do we do?" Jackie replied, her voice dripping with worry.

Everyone paused, calculating their options. "We could wait here until the service is over."

"And while we wait, we summon the doctor," Victor added.

92

"No!" Margaret replied. "No doctor, no hospitals. I'm fine."

"Oh, you are seeing a doctor!" Rose snapped in frustration.

"That's not an option. And I don't want to wait and see what happens while the doctor must make his way through a virtually shut down city. You don't think that itself would be suspicious?"

Victor looked at his grandmother's blank gaze and grew frustrated. "Enough with the 'optics' talks. I'm more worried about the welfare of my grandmother."

"You know what, Victor?" Mary spat. "She's not just your *grandmother*. She's the Queen - one of the only queens left with actual governing power - so the perception of her well-being is directly correlated to the stability of our country."

"And imagine how stable our country would be if she grows sicker and sicker while the doctor is in route. She could be dying right now for all we know. SHE HAS BRAIN CANCER!" Victor bellowed at Mary. "Not the flu. She could be having a stroke."

"If she walks out that door right now, all people will see is that something's wrong. It would be a storm of speculation. But if the doctor walks in here now, that immediately screams illness."

Jackie stepped in between the two people and placed a hand on both shoulders, "This isn't helping anyone."

"No, it's him who isn't helping anyone," Mary scowled pointing a finger in his face.

Jackie swatted her finger down and screamed, "Stop, Mother!" Her voice echoed through the foyer. She immediately regretting her volume in the realization that others could hear them.

Everyone paused for a moment then Victor finally calmly came to a solution, "We will summon the doctor in the Queen's name, now, and have him meet us at the palace. Once we have confirmation that he's en route, we will then leave here. Surely, by the time we hear back, the service should be close to being over. No one out there knows when the service is truly over, but it gives us time while seeking medical attention."

Mary scoffed, "That's stupid —"

"Actually," Jackie interjected. "Victor is right. I think that plan would be the best idea."

Mary's voice grew cold. "I am the heir apparent — the acting regent in the event of the Queen's incapacity. I decide what to do."

Victor pushed Jackie out of the way and stepped forward. He looked his mother in the eye like a Beta wolf challenging an Alpha. "Then decide, while you still can."

"What does that mean?"

"If I were you, I'd make a decision before Parliament issues *their* decision on the amendment."

"Now what exactly are you implying, child?"

Jackie once again squeeze between them, "This is not helping. Victor, call Private Secretary Zhang and get the doctor on the road." Victor turned away and pulled out his phone, still seething. "Mother, stop this nonsense. No one is questioning your authority. Now let's focus on your mother."

Mary scowled, stormed off down the hall and disappeared around the corner. Margie shook her head, rubbing the Queen's back. After a few minutes of whispering on the phone, he ended the call and walked over to his family. "Mo Li said that the doctor is leaving now. Are we staying until the end of the service?" Jackie nodded, never taking her eyes off her grandmother.

Victor crouched down next to Jackie and retrieved his phone from his pocket. He pulled out his phone, turned on the flashlight. He then shined the light in one eye and then the other. The Queen flinched as Jackie softly punched his arm. "What are you doing?"

"Checking her pupils. Zhang told me to do it. They seem fine."

"Do you know what you're looking for?" Rose spat.

"Somewhat," Victor replied with laser focus. He placed two fingers in her palms. "Squeeze my fingers as hard as you can." She obeyed and Victor relaxed a bit as they were painfully even. He then made her smile hard. Both sides of her face were even, so he leaned back on his heels. Rose turned and started toward the sanctuary doors. "Where are you going?" Victor asked.

"I'm going to see how far along we are in the service," she replied. She pulled the doors open and disappeared into the sanctuary.

Victor squatted in front of the Queen, whispering, "Would you like some water?" She slowly nodded, and he walked over to the water fountain at the far end of the hall. He slid the conical cup out of the cylindrical holder and filled it with cold water. He then returned and gave it to Margie who helped her drink the water.

After a few minutes, the doors burst open as the enormous organ blared a hymn signaling the end of the annual Christmas service. Mary exited the sanctuary, slowly and reverently, followed by the rest of the family. Victor's eyes bulged as he realized what had happened. She had carried out the Royal Procession in her mother's place, while she was ill and barely conscious. He wouldn't let that treasonous act go unchecked, but for right now, he needed to get the Queen out of there. He and Jackie took Margaret's arms and helped her to her feet. Margaret instinctively put her signature gentle smile on her face. Rose placed the Queen's hat on her head and they began toward the door.

"Can you make it to the car?" Victor asked Margaret.

"Yes! I'll be f-fine," she replied.

They began out the door, carefully down the stairs, and toward the waiting limousine. It appeared that her grandchildren escorted the Queen, but they were basically holding her up. Victor and Jackie nodded and smiled at the crowd, keeping both hands on the Queen. The rest of the family smiled and waved as usual, keeping up appearances. Finally, Jackie and Victor placed her in the limousine, gave one last wave, and then climbed in. The rest of the family boarded their respective limousines, and they were off. Under instruction from the Queen via Victor, they motorcade drove faster than normal parade speed, but not enough to raise alarm. Victor, however, barely noticed the adoring men, women, and children. His only concern at that moment was his grandmother; she slowly showed signs of return to her normal self. For the first few blocks, she simply gazed out of the window, but as they moved along, she slowly began to smile and track the people that passed with her eyes.

As they made their way to the palace, Victor received a text message from the Crown personal secretary stating, "DOCTOR ARRIVED AT PALACE." Victor released a sigh in relief and shared the news with his sister. The motorcade entered the gates of the palace. As all the other cars proceeded toward the Grand State Entrance, Victor reminded the driver to drive the Queen's car to the private entrance to quickly get to the Residential Suite, as the private secretary instructed.

The car slowed to a stop as the guard flung the door open. Victor climbed out of the limo on his side and ran around the rear to find the doctor waiting with a black wheelchair. They helped the Queen out of the car and put her in the seat as she fussed the whole way down about how she could do it herself. Finally, they rushed into the palace to the Residential Suite. As they entered the Residential Foyer, the guard carried her up the stairs to her suite. Victor waited there for his sister who didn't disappoint. Without missing a beat, she ran into the foyer and Victor joined her at the top of the stairs. Even with her in 4-inch, stiletto heels, Victor had to hustle to keep up with Jackie.

They entered Margaret's bedroom as Dr. Bennett was examining her. Margaret sat on the edge of the bed following his finger with her eyes. He asked her a few basic questions, all of which she answered without hesitation or recitation. Rose entered the room and threw her purse into the chair, followed by Mary. The doctor turned around, "Her cognitive function is fine, so I say we wait for the specialist."

Rose put her hands up as if to say *STOP*, "But her cognitive function wasn't fine half an hour ago."

"Well, then it must have been a temporary episode. It can be a side effect of the medication. It is quite toxic. Some behavioral changes and memory lapses are to be expected at this stage of the disease, Your Royal Highness. Her Majesty is all there now and that's a good thing. We just need to run more tests and images to find out what's really going on at this point."

Rose grew visibly frustrated. "What about a different treatment? A more aggressive treatment?"

"Ma'am, we've been skirting around this reality for a while now. Pending verification from the tests, I think treatments are only making Her Majesty worse and aren't helping much. We need to turn our focus on preserving her quality of life at this point, so she can carry out her duties for as long as she can." As the doctor spoke, Rose clenched her fist. Victor sensed that her anger was directed more toward the reality rather than the doctor himself, though her stance told a different story.

Margaret looked up with her dignity intact and turned to Victor. "What do you think?" she asked.

"What do you mean, 'What do I think?'" he replied.

"Do you think I should stop treatment?"

Victor froze. The gravity hit him like weights in water. He couldn't even hide his expression on his face. On one level, his grandmother asking him this was a testament to how much she had grown to depend on him. On another level, Margaret didn't even attempt to placate Rose as she honored Victor's higher rank as second-in-line over Rose's fifth. And above all, her looking to him to advise on such a major decision as this was both the world's greatest compliment and the heaviest responsibility.

He blinked and quickly but efficiently weighed the benefits and risks of continuing this toxic treatment versus simply elongating the ever-hastening clock. Finally, he reluctantly spoke, "I advise that continuing treatment would do more harm than good. We should make sure that you can enjoy the time you have left with us and carry out your duties while you can, for as long as you can, rather than pumping you with poison and praying for a miracle."

The room sat in silence and Mary blinked her eyes, taking his opinion as an affront to her authority. "As Heir Apparent and Chief Advisor, I'd advise you to continue treatment, Mother. There is still a chance that the tumor could shrink."

Margaret quickly decided whether or not to remind Mary of her weak claim to that title but she decided in that moment that that was a dead horse in no need of more beating. She turned to the doctor, "And you agree with the Prince?"

He simply nodded his head. Mary scoffed and left the room. Rose turned and fired a smoldering glare into Victor's eyes and followed her sister. Victor stood confused. *Why are they mad at me if it was Grandmother who asked me for advice?*

Chapter 10

The only indication of Christmas morning to Victor was the new red and green pajamas he and the other family members traditionally received by his grandmother to wear on Christmas Eve. The night passed with his cousins, siblings, and himself drinking eggnog in the theater watching all their favorite Christmas movies. They knew every word and cackled at the same jokes for over 20 years. While the festivities normally took place at Rousel Palace, after much debate between Mary and the Queen, it was decided to have Christmas at the State Palace. Victor was growing tired of all the fighting within the family. He wanted to think of something to solve everyone's bitterness toward each other, but none of his ideas were working out in his imagination.

Victor was pulled out of his inner turmoil by a whispered, "Hey!" It came from the floor next to the bed. He slid to the edge, never lifting his head from the row of pillows. Jack was laying on the floor with a pillow and a blanket.

"Why are you on the floor?" Victor asked.

"I don't know. I fell asleep. I think I spiked the eggnog too much this year," Jack replied.

Victor wondered why he had felt so groggy, "Ya think?" He slurred. "Get up off the floor."

"No, it feels nice down here. Nice and cool."

Victor chuckled and rolled back over. "Suit yourself."

"How are you feeling?"

"I feel like my mouth is heavy," Victor grumbled.

"No, I mean about last night. The decision," Jack whispered. "It put a kind of damper on the holiday, huh?"

Victor wanted to reply, *That's the understatement of the year,* but all he could muster was, "Yeah."

They sat in silence, until a loud bang made the two hungover cousins cringe. Jack shot up into a fighting stance next to his bed, while Victor snapped to a tight fetal position as he braced for impact. He knew what was coming. "Oh, come on. Not every-" Victor's muffled voice was silenced by the sheer force of Seth, Jackie, and Margie diving on top of him.

"Merry Christmas," they yelled.

"Must you do this every year?"

"Yup!" Seth menacingly replied.

"Ha! I'm not in the bed this year," Jack said as he dove on top of the dog pile. Victor felt his previous funk begin to melt away at the joyous laughter of his family, but not enough to make him want to get up.

"Get up!" Jackie called down the dog pile.

"No!" Victor replied.

"Get up dufus!" Margie teased.

"No means no!"

"Not in Greek!" Seth replied.

"Yes, well we're not in Greece," Victor yelled, which was still muffled under the bodies.

Jackie snapped her head back and popped Seth on the forehead. "Hey, not a mindset you want to have at your age." Seth vengefully started tickling Jackie. She thrashed in the middle of the dog pile kicking and smacking at everyone else but her attacker.

Finally, Margie and Jack pushed Seth off of the bed and he landed with a thud.

"Ow," he whimpered, sending everyone into laughter.

With no warning, Margie placed one hand on Victor's side and the other under Victor's arm. He tensed up quickly. "Get up now or suffer the same fate," she threatened through an evil smile.

"You wouldn't dare," he challenged.

She began mercilessly tickling him. He thrashed under the covers until he breathlessly capitulated and struggled to climb out of the bed. He flung his legs off the side of the bed and dove off. However, his feet were tangled in the sheets and he fell head first onto the patterned carpet. His cousins laughed as they filed out of the room, while Victor scrambled to his feet joining in on the laughter.

They raced out of the room and down the hall to the Residential Foyer as if they were transported to adolescence again. They raced down the stairs and through the main palace corridor. Another family tradition was the first cousin to get to the Red Room was the first to open a gift. Jack arrived first per usual, followed by Seth, then Margie and Jackie, and finally Victor who only jogged behind them.

"Victor, you didn't even try," Jack teased.

"I wonder why," he replied rubbing his head as Jack simply laughed.

On the beautiful red couch sat their grandmother dressed in a white nightgown with white slippers and a powder blue robe. Everyone stood at the door at the sight of the Queen, shocked by her attire. She never came down to Christmas in a nightgown before. On the opposite couch sat John, while Rose crouched under the mammoth of a tree arranging gifts. Margaret fussed at her to "leave them be and sit" but Rose continued until Margaret gave up. She turned to find her stunned grandkids and her face lit up. She smiled lovingly, "Merry Christmas, darlings." They filed in, each one bowing to their grandmother, kissing her on the cheek and taking a seat on the floor around the room.

"Where are Mother and the Duke?" Seth asked.

"They were coming down last time I'd heard," Margaret replied.

"Well, they need to hurry up," Rose replied with an attitude as she turned and took her place on the couch beside her husband.

Margaret hit the mute button on the remote for the radio, silencing the American Christmas music. "Well, let's start without them." She pulled out her bible. "Let us pray." They all bowed their heads. In walked the Mary and Duke and they sat next to the Queen. She opened one eye giving her daughter a look of disappointment, and then began, "Dear Heavenly Father, how we praise your name and thank you for the blessings you granted us for the last year. But most of all, I thank you for sending us your son, Jesus Christ to save us from our sins. Lord, this holiday is particularly special considering recent developments in my health. So, I ask you this day to touch the hearts of my family with a comforting hand, guide our nation's leaders — both current and future — with wisdom and compassion, and settle the spirits of all under the sound of my voice that we may enjoy this time together. In your Son's precious name, we pray, Amen."

Everyone joined in with "Amen." Margaret continued her oration about the love of God and the miracle of God's birth. Victor tried to listen attentively and every once in a while, he looked around the room. Jack played with his fingers clearly only half listening. Jackie quickly began fidgeting, growing restless. Rose and John were cuddled on the couch, actively listening and occasionally nodding in agreement. Seth played on his phone which was half hidden between his legs. Without looking, Margaret extended her hand toward Seth, never stopping a word. He looked up and after realizing he was caught, he reluctantly gave up his phone to his grandmother. Mary and Christopher sat on the couch in their own world. They didn't talk but were poking each other, kissing each other, and teasing each other. Rose shot her sister a chastising look and Mary replied by simply rolling her eyes.

Finally, Margaret wrapped up the devotion and turned back on the radio. Rose got up and took it upon herself to hand out the gifts, which she did every year. She walked over to the tree and passed each person one gift, and on the count of three, they all unwrapped the gift; this way, everyone was included and could enjoy the moment together. After a few rounds, there sat only one round left. By request, Margaret wanted everyone to open her gifts last. Rose handed them out one by one until she took her place next to her husband back on the couch.

"All right, is everyone ready? Each of you must open your gift separately this time." Margaret said with joy beaming across her face. "Ok? Seth, you first." Seth opened his gift hastily and revealed a square box that read, SEIKO. He opened the box and his eyes burst open and his jaw dropped. They all oohed and aahed. He took the silver watch off its small white pillow and slid it onto his wrist, closing the clasp. It dangled loosely. "We have to remove a few links from the band but it looks good on you."

Rose peered over Seth's shoulder, "Mother, that's really nice! I saw that watch in a magazine."

Margaret saw the admiration on his face and that was enough for her. "Ok. Your turn, Jack." Jack ripped the paper off his thin gift. After revealing an envelope, a confused look spread across his face. He broke the official seal of Queen Margaret I and retrieved and unfolded an official looking piece of paper. Jack read for a few moments until he gasped and looked up with an enormous smile.

"What is it?" Victor asked with anticipation.

"It's a deed for land here in Parados."

Rose gasped, "Land?"

"I had it renovated with a soccer field and a clubhouse for you," Margaret replied.

"Oh, my gosh, thank you Grandma!" Jack leapt over and squeezed Margaret with a hug that pushed all the air out of her lungs. He took his place back on the floor in front of his mother, staring at the card.

"Now you two," Margaret pointed to her two sons-in-law. They opened their gifts, which revealed envelopes as well. They pulled out pieces of papers and unfolded it. They both exclaimed with excitement.

John looked at the Duke with pure excitement. "Did you get one too?"

"What?" Mary looked over at the Duke's paper. "A deed? For a cottage?"

"Yes," Margaret replied. "Each one of my sons-in-law gets a fully-furnished cottage in the mountains. John, yours has a helipad, a theater with airplane seats, and with a full screen flight simulator so you can fly in luxury."

"Wow, thank you so much, ma'am," John got up, stepped over Jack and placed a gentle kiss on Margaret's cheek.

"And for you, Christopher," she continued, "A cottage filled with top technological equipment and spy gear." The Duke's eyes slowly turned to the Queen with an expression of awe plastered across his face. "As long as you use them within the limitations of the Constitution, you can relive your 'glory years'." The whole room burst into laughter.

The Duke smiled a humbling grin and rose to his feet. He then descended into a deep bow and kissed the Queen's hand. After returning to his seat staring at the deed, Margaret continued. "Now for my two beautiful granddaughters." Jackie and Margie both ripped the wrapping paper from their presents revealing a navy-blue box with the symbol of a crown engraved on the top. They snapped open the boxes to reveal a bright light shining on their faces. Rose who sat behind Margie gasped and clutched her pearls.

"Mother," she gasped.

"What is it?" Mary asked.

Margie and Jackie turned their boxes around to show a diamond tiara in each box with a small mirror fixed to the top and a light to magnify the tiara's luster. Jackie's eyes were fixed on her tiara, absorbing every glint and shimmer.

"Mother, are those from the Crown jewels?" Mary asked.

"Yes, but I have granted them exclusive allowance so the only other person who may wear them are my granddaughters," Margaret responded to Mary. She then turned to the girls and said, "No need for my permission. Merry Christmas!" Victor knew that the gifts were just her way of telling the girls to stop "borrowing" the Crown Jewels. Margie and Jackie put their boxes on the floor next to them and dove on the Queen with aggressive and loving hugs of gratitude. Margaret chuckled as she struggled to remain upright.

"Be gentle!" Rose called out to the giggling girls. They released their grandmother, steadied her, and then returned to their seats to admire their presents.

"A-a-and now for my d-d-daughters," she stammered. "Rose, you first." Rose opened her gift and sure enough there sat a bright diamond tiara, though this one was clearly more expensive because it was gold with hundreds of small diamonds and enormous emeralds across the front.

"Oh, Mother," Rose barely spoke. Victor rarely saw her speechless; in fact, this was the first time he'd *ever* seen her speechless.

"Do you like it?" Margaret inquired, with excitement.

"Mother, this is absolutely beautiful!" Rose held it in her hand as she rose to her feet with tears in her eyes. She held Margaret in a hug that seemed to last forever. Her crying began to increase to hysteria.

"So you *do* recognize it?" Margaret asked.

"Of course. This was the tiara that Victoria used to wear all of the time."

The mood of the room grew intense. After a few more minutes, she returned to her seat wiping the tears from her eyes. John embraced his wife as she continued to stare into her box.

Margaret turned to Mary. "Your turn," she said.

Mary's box was smaller than the other boxes, so it couldn't have been a tiara. The whole room grew quiet, as she opened the box. Inside the navy-blue box was a large gold ring. In the place where a diamond would usually rest was an engraving. Mary's eyes lit up as she pulled the ring from the box and slid it onto her finger.

"A ring?" Seth asked, sarcastically.

"A ring with my official seal and standard," Mary said with excitement. Victor seemed to sink into the floor. *What does this mean? Does this mean that she will certainly be crowned queen or is this just a gesture?* Victor examined the Queen's face for a clue but to his dismay, it didn't give anything away as per usual.

The Queen slid up to the edge of the couch, "And finally, Victor!" Victor opened a flat box that didn't have the crest of the Crown Jewels on the top, but some other medallion engraved on the top. Inside rested a large golden medal hanging from a red ribbon and golden pin.

"Grandmother, you have me stumped," Victor regretfully pleaded.

She chuckled, "Read it."

"In honor of bravery, courage, and devotion to country, this medal recognizes HRH Prince Victor II of Spiti as an honorary member of the Royal Armed Forces of the Kingdom of Iakos." Victor paused for a moment trying to understand what this meant. "Does this mean that I'm in the military now?"

Margaret chuckled and repositioned herself on the couch. "No, well yes," she tried to explain. "It means that you are an honorary member of the military. It's customary for a male heir to the throne to be made an honorary member of the Armed Forces if they cannot serve themselves. This way, when it is your time, there is no question of your legitimacy as Commander-in-Chief of the Armed Forces when you're crowned king."

"Wow," Victor exclaimed, trying to mask his complete confusion. He thought to himself, *does this mean that Mother isn't going to be crowned queen?* Anxiety began to bubble inside of him, but he couldn't forget to show gratitude. So, he painted a smile on his face and walked over to his grandmother and gave her an enormous hug. He was grateful for this gift, however, considering his mother's gift, his gift didn't really reassure him with certainty either way in the matter of Princess Mary's legitimacy.

The rest of the morning remained pleasant. To everyone's surprise, there was no bickering, fighting, or arguing, just playful laughter and games. It was the best gift the Queen could have asked for. After they played a few rounds of a trivia game, Mary and the Duke went through the double doors to the balcony facing the rear gardens of the grounds. Margaret sat on the couch as before and watched her family with a joyous yet tearful grin. Victor saw this and walked over to his grandmother.

"Are you ok? Do you need any Aspirin or anything?" Victor asked rubbing her back and sitting on the arm of the chair.

"No, no, dear! I'm fine. But I do have one more present for you. Come," Margaret slapped his leg just enough to make Victor flinch. "Get off the arm of my couch and come sit next to me."

Victor obeyed rubbing his leg. "Another gift?"

"Yes, I didn't want to give it to you in front of everyone." She handed him a small ring box, unwrapped. He snapped it open and quietly gasped at a ring identical to the one that his mother received; only this ring was engraved with *his* official standard and at the bottom read, KING VICTOR I OF IAKOS. "I saw your face when your mother opened hers. I knew what d-d-drama it would cause to give this to you in front of everyone. I just wanted a pleasant C-C-Christmas."

Victor sat in shock as reality set in. This was really going to happen and there was no turning back now. He tried to find the right words, but the only thing he could think to say was, "Thank you, Grandmother!"

"You're most welcome dear. Now, I'm going to hold on to it for you in a private location. When I f-finally pass on from this life, if it is decided that you will succeed me, this ring will be brought to you immediately to sign your official ascent papers. It will remain on the palace grounds but for plausible deniability and safe keeping only myself and my Private Secretary will know where to find it, in case of a coup or security threat during the transfer of power."

"Is it really that important that I can't know where it is?" asked Victor.

"Yes!" she exclaimed in a whisper. "It's not just a symbol of power. It represents the power of the Crown to issue decrees and officialize letters, summons, documents, laws, and so much more. We are one of the last countries to still use this method, but it protects against forgeries of Crown documents and other matters. But more than that, it is fitted with a panic alarm and tracking device so in the most dangerous of times the Royal Protection Service can find you anywhere in the world. All you have to do is push all four corners of this standard down."

"Ok, now that is cool."

"I know. I was intrigued by the new technology myself when it was first brought to me. Now no one is to know about this. Normally, only the heir apparent has one but considering the circumstances, I thought it would be best if you had one also."

Victor finally breathed a sigh of relief, closed the box, and handed it back to his grandmother. Slowly, he leaned in and kissed her cheek.

"Your Majesty?" said a voice from behind Victor. Margaret shifted forward to find her Private Secretary standing at the end of the couch with a newspaper in her hand.

"Ms. Zhang, Merry Christmas," Margaret greeted with a smile.

Mo Li smiled and curtsied, "Merry Christmas, ma'am. I'm sorry to bother you this morning but we have a slight problem."

"What's the matter?" Victor said as he rose to his feet and gestured for Mo Li to take his place.

"Thank you," she said, shuffling over to the couch. She sat right next to the Queen as Victor leaned on the arm of the couch, careful not to sit.

"Is everything alright?" Margaret asked.

Mo Li lowering her voice. "I'm not sure. A staffer called me this morning and brought this to my attention. I figured it would probably be best if you saw this yourself."

She handed over the newspaper. On the front page were two pictures; one of Jackie and Victor escorting the Queen down the aisle of the church and the other was a picture of Mary walking down the aisle at the Christmas Eve Service the day before, with her hands folded and head high in the sky. The article read:

ROYAL BEHAVIOR DOESN'T MATCH ROYAL WORDS

Official statements from the State Palace have quelled questions regarding the Queen's health and stability for the past few months. However, sources have confirmed that HM The Queen had to be escorted out of the Christmas service by her two grandchildren, HRH Prince Victor II and HRH

Princess Jacqueline. After the service, HRH Princess Mary (next in line for the throne) was observed carrying out the Royal Procession, a tradition only performed by the sitting Crown or the acting Regent of the nation. Just weeks ago, Princess Mary herself also issued a statement that implied health concerns for the Queen. All this conflicting behavior from the Palace has begun to paint a strange and confusing image for the people of Iakos of the health and well being of Her Majesty.

Before Victor could read anymore, Margaret suddenly snapped the paper closed and slammed it onto the table with a BANG! "MMMAAARRRYYY!" she bellowed, making the whole room freeze. Mary and the Duke ran into the room from the balcony. Mo Li leaned forward to stand and bow to the entering members of the Royal Family, but was halted by Margaret's arm snapping across her chest like the safety bar of a rollercoaster.

"Yes, Mother. What is it?" Mary frantically asked.

"The Royal Procession? You carried out the Royal Procession?"

"No, I just left the church," Mary replied, with a false confused look on her face. Margaret reached forward, almost falling over and grabbed the newspaper. Victor and Mo Li steadied her as she recoiled her arm and she threw the folded newspaper at Mary. Mary flinched as it smacked her chest and slid down to her outstretched hand. She opened it and looked at the picture of her.

Mo Li stood slowly and began backing out of the room. "Maybe I should go," she softly pleaded as she continued away. She'd never seen the Queen show this much emotion outwardly, especially anger.

"No!" The Queen commanded without even turning around. "No one leaves." Mo Li froze and folded her hands with her head down. "You do NOT deputize for me without my expressed and official orders, is that clear?"

"How'd they get a camera into the sanctuary in the first place?" Rose interjected in an attempt to lighten the blows swinging at Mary in front of her own children and new husband.

"Do NOT interrupt me again," Margaret barked at Rose. Rose retreated to her husband who embraced her in a hug. Margaret returned her focus back to Mary. "Making statements without my orders, carrying out Royal Procession, getting married without Royal Consent... are you sure I'm the one with the brain tumor? Because the way you've been acting this year, I swear one would think you're the one with irrational behavior."

Mary took a huge risk and mumbled, "It's not irrational."

"Then manip-mani-manipulative. One or the other... either way, it's unacceptable. I'd suggest you keep your head down to the public for a long t-t-time if you want that ring to mean anything af-fter I'm gone."

Mary's head sagged like a whipped puppy, while Victor felt like he wanted to crawl under something. Everyone but Margaret seemed to quickly glance at Victor before returning to their stoic gazes toward the ground.

What the hell just happened? Victor thought.

January

<u>Chapter 11</u>

Victor stared out of the window of the kitchen as he looked at the cheering crowd gathered outside the front gate of the Palace. He raised the brown mug to his lips and blew lightly to cool his ginger tea. With the cup inches from his mouth, the prince slowly inhaled the steam allowing it to fill his lungs. He then sighed and carefully sipped the tea, choking slightly at the burn on his throat.

"Woah, careful," Vince softly spoke as he stepped closely behind Victor and rested his chin onto Victor's shoulder. Several moments passed as Victor continued to stare out of the window. His nerves were visibly getting to him, despite his best efforts to mask them. "What's the matter?"

Victor thought for a moment on how to put his feelings into words. "I'm just concerned about the Queen's New Year's Address."

"Why? You can read from a teleprompter, right?"

Victor giggled, "Of course, but that's not what I mean. The Queen can barely finish a sentence without stammering, now."

"Yes, but that's why she has you," Vince whispered as he gently slid his hands under Victor's new military jacket and pulled him tightly into a hug. Victor leaned into the embrace, resting his head back on Vince's.

"And Mother too."

"Well, then what's the problem?" Vince asked.

Victor paused for a moment. "I know my mother. She may use this to try and win support from the people."

Vince stood upright and turned the prince around to face himself. He held him by the arms firmly but affectionately. "Then let her do it. You are not there to win public support. You are there to support the Queen in *her* duties and nothing more. If you focus on that, it will show you as the loving and devoted grandson that you are."

The prince took a sip of his tea to distract his lips from carrying out what they wanted, but Vince wasn't having it. Just when Victor lowered his mug, Vince quickly swooped in and pressed his lips against Victor's. Taken aback, Victor's first reaction was to push him away with a hand to the chest, but Vince caught his hand and held it onto his chest as he gently comforted the prince with his lips.

"Ahem!" The sound of someone clearing their throat sent Victor and Vince into different directions. Vince turned to find Jack standing at the door of the kitchen with a disturbing grin. He was dressed in a blue suit that showed off his broad and toned shoulders and arms. "Now what do we have here?"

Victor bashfully wiped his lips and replied, "What, Jack?"

"Grandmother said they are ready for us."

"Thank you!" Victor said as if to scream *GET OUT!* Jack somehow grinned harder, turned around and left.

Victor looked at the handsome man on the other side of the kitchen counter. He thought about walking up to him and stealing another kiss from him. Luckily, he was still partially in his right mind, so he decided to hold off on that. "I really should go," he said.

"Go ahead. I'm not going anywhere."

Victor smiled, placed his mug onto the counter, and hurried out of the kitchen and down the hall. He made his way to the main staircase and ran up the stairs and around a few corners until he made it to the Throne Room. When he entered, the Queen was seated in a chair in the middle of the room surrounded by her dresser, a videographer, Mary, and Mary's makeup artist. He looked around the room, when suddenly the large camera, the bright lights, and the Royal Crown of Iakos resting on a pillow atop a waist-high table next to the Queen all became daunting. His palms and forehead grew damp with beads of sweat. Behind the chair was a low, raised platform where the rest of the family conversed with one another. The women were in simple, yet elegant dresses and daytime jewels, while the men were dolled up in blue suits and military uniforms. The videographer bowed and gestured Victor over. He complied and stood on the left side of Margaret's chair.

"No, sweetie," Margaret said. "You stand on my right. Mary, you stand on my left." Victor's eyes grew big and he resisted the urge to look at his mother's reaction. Normally, the heir apparent stands on the right of the sitting monarch.

Mary scoffed loudly. "Mother, that's my place."

"Are you sure?" Margaret challenged. Mary stood speechless as she turned and looked at Victor but he refused to make eye contact. He just kept his eyes on the camera as he obeyed and stepped to the right side of the Queen.

The videographer clapped his hands three times, "Your Royal Highnesses, Your Majesty, we have one minute before we're live." Outside of the window, a military band began to play the Iakos National Anthem. Mounted to the top of the camera was a screen that read, STANDBY. Mary reluctantly stood on the left side and turned on her public smile. Behind the three primary members in the front, the rest of the primary Royal Family took their places in a line on the platform. The words on the screen changed to numbers counting down from 20. When the number reached 5, Victor held his breath and smiled.

"Three, two," the videographer mouthed "one" and then pointed to the Queen.

"Every year, the world puts aside our differences to celebrate the beginning of a new year," the Queen began reading slowly. "People from all corners of the world, in every time zone, shed the old to usher in the new."

Mary's name appeared on the teleprompter and she began to read. Victor barely noticed what she was saying. He just wanted to make sure that when it came time for him to speak, it would appear natural. Normally, it would just be the Queen speaking, but this time, Margaret had asked them to join in because her aphasia was becoming more prominent. She never stuttered or had trouble finding her words prior to the cancer but with each week that passed, it grew worse and worse.

Finally, Victor's name appeared and something inside of him turned on. Confidence and authority rushed over him and he began to speak. "As we usher in a new year, we celebrate the lessons and growth of the past as well as hope for the future. We are truly grateful to God in advance for the blessings that are to come in the year we are beginning and are hopeful that all of Iakos will share in those blessings. It is with great pride and joy that we wish all of The Kingdom of Iakos, and every nation across the globe, a prosperous and peaceful New Year!"

The entire family, in one chorus, concluded with a boisterous, "Happy New Year!" The whole broadcast lasted about 3 minutes but was a standing tradition for the Kingdom to hear from the monarch on New Year's Day.

"And we're out," the videographer announced and the room took a breath and the tech staff joined the crowd outside in cheers and applause.

Margaret called Rose over to her. "What time were you two thinking of heading back to Makria?"

"Well, we'd considered this afternoon and then I'd be coming back next week to take care of you."

Margaret sat pondering for a moment, and then looked up at Rose. "I'd like Margie to stay with me until you return next week."

Rose turned and called for Margie to join her. Margaret asked her granddaughter if she wouldn't mind staying with her to help her for the week.

"Sure, I'd love to!" Margie exclaimed. "But what about Victor? He isn't taking care of you?"

"No, I n-n-need him and Mary to do something else for me."

Victor stepped in front of the chair to see her face. "What would that be?" he asked.

"Per doctor's orders, I need to delegate a few responsibilities. I would like the t-t-two of you to attend a few public appearances this month in my name," Margaret said.

Mary's face turned red, even through her makeup. "Victor *and* me?"

"Not together," the Queen replied. "I've split the duties between the two of you." She raised her right hand and waved over

Mo Li who was standing in the corner with two folders in her hands along with her tablet. Mo Li gave one to Mary and one to Victor.

Victor opened the folder and began to read. The first page was an itinerary for January featuring three bullet points:

- Opening night at Parados Theater Company
- State Luncheon at French Embassy in Iakos
- State Dinner at White House *(US)*

Victor studied the details below each one and looked up at his grandmother. "This last one?"

"What about it?" Margaret asked.

"You want me to fly to The United States in your name?"

"Yes," Margaret replied with certainty.

Victor had to play this right as to not offend his mother. "Wouldn't that be better suited for the Heir Apparent to go to a State Dinner in your name?"

Margaret turned and read Mary's face. She attempted to mask a micro-expression of pride, but Margaret was more concerned about the good of her nation and less about placating to her daughter's inflated ego. "No, it's time you get some real diplomatic exposure. Mary has her own itinerary."

Mary looked hers over and then looked up with an all too familiar look. "But mine are all domestic. Medal ceremony, a museum opening, and a dedication of a library in Father's name? These duties are all cosmetic," she almost whined.

"Well, I need you there. Is that a problem?"

Mary returned to her default, fake smile and replied through her teeth, "No, ma'am!"

"Good. Will you be returning to Rousel Palace tonight?"

"No," Mary said. "We're leaving within the hour."

"Ok. If you have any questions, ask Ms. Zhang here. She has all of the details."

Victor smiled at Mo Li, who returned the nonverbal equivalent of "way to go".

* * * * *

Victor struggled with the bow tie around his neck. He stared at himself in the long bathroom mirror above the sink and sighed. He could hear the audience through the closed door. The play he'd just watched was the furthest thing from his mind. The star-studded audience was filled with celebrities from across Europe and The United States to celebrate the new Iakos National Theater. The theater was founded as a first step to promoting the arts in the country, an initiative the Queen began a few years prior and he supported wholeheartedly. His mother, however, wasn't too thrilled but what else was new.

Victor found himself lost in his thoughts about all that his grandmother had done during her reign; everything from a push for modern technology, improved international relations, and so much more. During this time, Iakos was finally a competitive country in the international market, industry, trade, and even military. The reality was sinking in that all of this would be his responsibility, and there was a real chance that it could come sooner than anyone had previously expected.

"Why, hello there," a voice spoke from behind him. Victor hadn't noticed anyone enter the room and nearly jumped out of his skin. He spun around aggressively to find Marcus Frazier standing there with a smile. Victor was frozen as Marcus threw his hands up in surrender. He slowly placed his hands at his own sides and bowed at the neck. "I'm sorry, Your Royal Highness. I didn't mean to startle you."

Victor studied the young performer's face and recognized the same half-smile smolder from two months ago. "You didn't startle me."

Marcus slowly crossed the bathroom and stood close to him. "Good."

"What are you doing here?" Victor whispered.

"I came to see the show, same as you."

Victor gazed into Marcus' enchanting eyes. "I'm sure you have a love for theater," Victor sarcastically but playfully replied.

"I couldn't pass up an opportunity to see you," Marcus spoke softly in his deep voice.

Victor innocently furled his eyebrow. "Why do you want to see me?"

Marcus looked down at Victor's lips, "I think you know why I'm here."

Victor felt himself being pulled into his gaze but somehow found the strength to step back. He needed to put distance between himself and Marcus but the counter stopped his retreat, allowing Marcus to make up the distance with one step. He grabbed Victor by the waist but Victor turned his head. "No! I cannot do this," Victor pushed Marcus' hands off and walked over to the towel dispenser.

"Ok." Marcus surrendered. He leaned up against the sink trying to maintain his suave facade. "I'm confused. You're the one who kissed me."

"That was a lapse in judgment - a lapse in judgment that happened two months ago. I haven't heard from you since."

"So, you wanted to hear from me then," Marcus teased in a sultry voice that didn't seem to work on Victor anymore.

"I'm more surprised that you remembered," Victor teased back.

Marcus furled his eyebrows. "Why wouldn't I remember?"

"Maybe because it was *two months ago*."

"Oh, so two months means you don't want to kiss me again?"

Victor knew that his answer didn't match what he wanted to say. Truth be told, something about Marcus made him want to kiss him again. Was it the sense of danger - the risk of kissing him? Or was it because a part of him needed to step out of the boundaries of the palace? Either way, it couldn't happen today, not at this moment. He had a speech to give in about five minutes and he didn't need any more distractions. "I can't kiss you. My circumstances have changed and I can't go there again."

Marcus stared into Victor's eyes from across the room and asked the forbidden question, "What is going on with the Queen?"

Victor's upbringing kicked in and he began to rattle off the party line. "I cannot comment on the Crown."

"Jeez, do you all have any original thoughts? Come on, it's me. Talk to me like a person, not a thing."

"I am. I just cannot comment — "

" - Comment on the Crown." Marcus finished his sentence. "When you're ready to divert from the script, give me a call." He crossed the room toward Victor extended his hand. Victor flinched and stopped Marcus' hand by the wrist just by his side.

Marcus reached down into Victor's pocket and pulled out his cellphone.

"What are you doing?"

"Just making sure you can," Marcus replied typing rapidly into the phone.

"I can what?"

"Call me!" And with that, he replaced the phone in the pocket, turned, and began toward the door. He stopped just shy. "You have to talk to someone, before it destroys the real *you*. Oh, and put a password on your phone." Marcus left the room.

What the hell does that mean? Victor thought. He took one last look at himself and then left the room. "Way to protect me guys."

"I'm sorry, sir. I thought he was your friend," the guard said.

"Good thing he wasn't an assassin," Victor spat. The four security guards formed a star around him with one guard leading the way, two along his sides, and one trailing behind him. They walked down the hall to the entrance of the conference room and stopped. Victor's nerves exploded throughout his body. His hands began to tremble and his legs grew weak, but Victor caught himself and quickly began to suppress his nerves. He reminded himself that he was there in the name of the Sovereign, so nothing could affect his duty to achieve perfection. He took a deep breath, filling his lungs down to his diaphragm, and blew out every shaky, uncertain, and insecure cell in his body.

Through the large wooden doors in front of him, he heard the PA system blare a deep voice, "All rise for His Royal Highness, Prince Victor II of Spiti." A large rustling of the audience standing thrusted Victor into a state of still to which he was beginning to grow accustomed. The double doors opened and a well-lit ballroom burned his eyes, be he dared not squint or flinch. He slowly entered the room and processed down the pathway between the tables. Everyone stood applauding, bowing or curtsying as he passed. Once on the stage he was instructed to sit at the chair in the center.

As the Artistic Director of the new theater gave his speech praising the Queen for her policies on the arts, Victor scanned the room to study the temperature of the room. Everyone seemed to agree, so Victor breathed a sigh of relief. At least he didn't have to win the crowd over. He listened to the speaker, but didn't hear a word he'd said. Victor's eyes fixed on the dapper young singer sitting at the front table staring back at him. Marcus looked at him with a face that Victor couldn't decipher. *What did he mean by 'You have to talk to someone, before it destroys the real you'?* How was my position destroying me? He wanted to talk to him more but finding private time would be a struggle. *And who does he think he is to ask a question like that?*

"And now, His Royal Highness would like to say a few words. Prince Victor?" The director stepped out of the way allowing for Victor to step up to the podium as the audience applauded.

"Thank you!" Victor spoke, placing his black binder of written remarks on the podium. He looked around the room in surprise as everyone, one by one, rose to their feet. He hadn't spoken three words and yet was receiving a standing ovation. The pressure was on, but he was willing to rise to the challenge. "Thank you," he repeated, in attempt to quiet the room but the applause continued. At this point, he began to blush. *How do I quiet this room?* He spoke, "Thank you!" One last time with authority, emphasized by a raised hand. Just like that, everyone slowly took their seats. *Cool!*

"Thank you for attending the opening night at the Parados National Theater, our nation's first government sponsored theater." The audience politely applauded, forcing Victor to pause briefly. "This theater is the first phase of Her Majesty's initiative to expand the arts in our country. We have excelled in technology, medicine, and finance in recent years and we should continue this trend as we become competitive on the international stage." He realized how scripted and artificial he sounded and suddenly, he realized what Marcus meant. He knew his remarks backwards and forwards, so why not paraphrase and make it his own. "You see, the arts have a way of touching people in a way other fields cannot. Literature, music, theater, and other media can provoke thought, challenge convention, and expand the world in which we live. I think it's time that Iakos joins in the traditions that our Western sister nations have been doing for millennia." The audience clapped and cheered. "This theater is the first step in that direction and as our nation continues this mission, we encourage all of you to support the arts as you have other fields. And as the arts blossom, let our imaginations and minds blossom with them as we move forward in an ever-changing world. Thank you!"

The audience rose to their feet and applauded vigorously. He descended from the stage and took his place at a table designated for the Royal entourage. The rest of the evening was filled with speakers singing praises for the Queen, reinforcing the importance of the arts, and expensive yet small-portioned cuisine. Afterward, Victor made small talk with some of the most prominent actors, directors, playwrights, producers, and other bigwigs of the American and European theater worlds. He made his translator earn his salary as people engaged conversation with the Prince.

After about a half an hour, the motorcade pulled to the front of the theater and Victor gave one last wave to the citizens outside the theater and flashing cameras and climbed into the SUV. As the string of cars pulled off down the street, Victor's pocket started to vibrate. He retrieved his phone and read on the screen, TEXT: Marcus Frazier. He unlocked the phone with his new password and read the teasing text message, "Just making sure you have my phone number so you can call me when you're ready. It's Marcus." Victor rolled his eyes and replied with the face that made sure Marcus knew how we felt.

Chapter 12

Margaret sat with her eyes closed listening to the newscaster drone on about the day's events on the small radio near the window. Just as she felt the small of her back relax, she heard footsteps enter her room and suddenly the tension returned. Her eyes fluttered open to find the Parliament Speaker and Mo Li bowing and curtsying respectively.

"Good morning, Your Majesty. The Parliamentary Speaker is here. You remember that he requested an audience with you this morning, if you feel up to it," Mo Li said.

"Yes, of course that's fine. Thank you," Margaret replied. Mo Li nodded politely and left the office.

Gabriel walked over and sat next to the Queen, "I'm sorry for the urgent request, Your Majesty, but there is something that I wish to discuss with you … and it's a, sort of, sensitive matter."

"Sure," Margaret replied, repositioning herself on the couch. "Go on."

"Well, some of the members of Parliament have brought to my attention some rumors about Prince Victor."

"Really," she said, "what about him?"

Gabriel chose his words very slowly and carefully. "Well, there are rumors speculating about his sexuality, and some of the more Conservative members have grown a bit restless." Margaret's stone face gave no indication on how closely he was treading to the ledge, so he stopped and gave her time to respond.

Margaret paused briefly, swallowed hard, folded her hands in her lap, and began to speak calmly. "Are you asking me my personal opinions about my grandson's *alleged* sexuality or my official policy views? Because the latter are very clear."

"No, ma'am. I know the Crown's stance on discrimination on the basis of sexual orientation for public service, marriage, employment, etc., but being that this isn't a true employment but rather an anointment, I wanted to get your advice on how to address the matter with Parliament. How do I curb a powerful group of people who are content in their bigotry?"

121

Margaret sat for a moment, trying to find the right words to say. Then, a memory brought a nostalgic smile to her face. "My late husband, Prince Victor, used to always tell me something. He would say, 'Margaret, your op-pinion is always valid simply by its nature of being an opinion. H-however, if one wishes to turn that opinion into action, policy, or law, one must consider the opinion of those who must abide by it. Do they have a right to have an opposing opinion? Of course! But what damage could occur to those citizens by following a law that they oppose.' A person's wallet can recover from tax increases. Nations even recover from wars, but a person's psyche ... the kind of damage that comes from being forced to live in secret and hide ones *true* self," Margaret paused, her eyes glazed as she looked inward, "That is not something I'm willing to do to my people, regardless of personal opinion."

The Speaker simply nodded and stared at the Queen, as she came back to the present world. She continued, "Now, according to the Constitution, I do not have say over Parliament so I cannot tell you what you must do. However, between you and I, it sounds like these Members of Parliament should be reminded that they were elected to represent the views of their constituents, not to impose their personal views on the rest of the country or the monarchy in whose government they serve."

"Yes, Ma'am! Thank you," he said rising to his feet.

"Furthermore," she added, "you might remind them that they are not electing a president. They are simply deciding whether or not to accept my amendment."

"Yes, Your Majesty." He began to leave, but stopped and turned back at the Queen. "How are you feeling, Ma'am?"

"What do you mean?"

"Just, are you feeling well today?"

Margaret smiled softly. "I am well, Mr. Speaker. Thank you for asking."

He bowed his head and left the office. Mo Li reentered behind him holding a stack of papers. She placed them on the coffee table next to the Queen and sat beside her. "Can I get you anything?" Mo Li asked.

"Yes, could you get me my grandson on the phone?" Margaret spoke taking the paper off the top of the pile.

"Yes, Ma'am." Mo Li pulled out her phone and began scrolling through her contacts.

* * * * *

Victor peered out the window as the motorcade traveled down the street, fidgeting with the pin on the left side of his jacket. He ran through the brief welcome remarks he was given to welcome the new ambassador of France, but he kept stumbling over his words. He pulled out his phone and searched the man he was to introduce, however, just as the picture of the man loaded on the screen, the phone began to vibrate and the screen read, MO LI ZHANG - PSS. He tapped the screen and put the phone to his ear. "Yes, Mo Li. I am on my way to the embassy as we speak. I should be there in roughly five minutes."

"That's good," Mo Li replied, "But I have the Queen for you, Your Royal Highness."

"Oh. Ok sure."

Victor heard a jostling on the other end that he assumed was Mo Li passing his grandmother the phone. "Victor."

"Good morning, Grandmother."

"I just had a brief audience with the Parliament Speaker," Margaret began.

Victor's nerves lit up. "Oh? What about?"

"You, actually."

"Me? Whatever for?" Victor asked, confused. *Why is he talking to the Queen about me?* He thought to himself.

"Rumors that are circulating throughout Parliament about you."

"Rumors? About me? That's new," Victor chuckled.

"Victor, this isn't funny," Margaret scolded. "What did I tell you about discretion? We are in a rare situation in with Parliament is able to appoint the Sovereign rather than the hereditary succession that has existed for centuries. And hypocritical as it may be, you cannot slip up and give them a reason to resent you."

Victor grew increasingly confused. "I'm sorry, but what is it they are saying I did?"

"I'm not sure, but you are now in the public eye and, therefore, under an enormous amount of scrutiny. As you make

123

decisions going forward, you must understand that in our position, perception in some cases is more important than the truth. Your sexuality is not my concern; however, the stability of this nation is very much my concern and you are the clear stable choice. Do not complicate this matter further with personal gratifications until stability is restored. Do you understand what I'm saying?"

"Yes, Ma'am." Victor replied, shell shocked by the tone of his grandmother as well as her words. "We are arriving. I will see you in a few hours."

"Ok, God bless." The phone disconnected. The motorcade pulled into a stone gate and drove toward the front entrance of the semi-Tudor-style mansion. Victor's stomach growled because he was saving his appetite for this brunch. Just as the cars stopped in front of the door, Victor's phone vibrated from inside his pocket. He quickly retrieved it and, of course, at the most inopportune moment, the screen read "MF: Just thinking of you. Have a good day. -MarcusMarcus". Ever since the theater opening earlier that week, he'd been getting more cute texts like this one, even more than those from Vince. The chauffeur knocked on the window and he noticed the Ambassador standing in front of the entranceway waiting for him. Victor shoved his phone into his pocket without replying and pulled the handle on the door.

He climbed out of the SUV and walked over to the young Ambassador. "Bonjour M. l'Ambassadeur. Comment ça va?"

The ambassador's face lit up. He was about thirty years old and looked just as youthful. He had on a black wool coat over a simple black suit with a coral blue tie and the pin with the French flag on his lapel. "Ah, ça va bien, merci. Et vous?"

"Ça va aussi."

"Mon équipe ne m'a pas dit que tu parle français."

"Oui, j'ai appris à l'école," Victor replied with a sense of pride.

"Ah, shall we go inside?" The two walked into the building and into the banquet hall just across the hall from the door. It was designed with tan carpeting and round tables with tall centerpieces. The ambassador escorted him to his seat next to himself. The first course was brought out and then a few welcoming speeches were made. A young French man walked over to the table, bowed to Victor and then walked to the large black piano. He paused for dramatic effect and then began playing the French national anthem. Everyone stood as the song played and then he modulated to a few keys down and then they all sang the Iakon National Anthem. Victor sang out proudly as if in a competition for which man was more patriotic.

Finally, they all sat and an older French man took to the podium. "Je voudrais souhaiter la bienvenue au premier prince d'Iakos, le prince Victor." The room burst into applause.

Victor stood and took the old man's place at the podium. His nerves were safely smothered deeply away. "Merci beaucoup. Et merci à l'ambassadeur pour ce brunch délicieux. La relation entre nos deux pays a été l'une des plus fortes dans l'histoire de nos pays. Nous avons résisté aux dangers de la guerre et nous avons réussi dans le commerce. Alors que nous allons vers l'avenir, j'espère suivre ce partenariat. C'est donc un honneur de présenter le nouvel ambassadeur, l'ambassadeur George Martin." Every face in the room seemed to be beaming with pride, not just at the prince's french, but also at their new ambassador.

He approached the podium and shook the prince's hand. Ambassador Martin spoke into the microphone, "And we share that hope, my friend."

The rest of the event was filled with sheer diplomacy - sucking up, ego stroking, and most of all flattery, lots and lots of flattery. By the time Victor left, he was ready to crawl in a corner. One would think that he would get used to being in a room with all eyes on him, but he was beginning to realize that that might never change for him. Ambassador Martin escorted him to his car, they shook hands, exchanged pleasantries, and then Victor climbed into the motorcade and left.

Finally, in privacy, Victor's smile melted away as his grandmother's voice came roaring back into his head. He felt like the sky had grown cloudy even though the sky above him was clear. Victor leaned forward and told the driver to head back to the State Palace, then pulled out his phone and dialed. He placed the phone to his ear and waited as the line rang.

"Hey Vic, what's up?" Jack said.

"Hey! You got a minute?"

"Yeah sure. Everything ok?"

Victor paused for a moment and then honestly answered, "No."

"Ok, I'm listening."

Victor sighed. "According to Grandmother, Parliament? asking questions about me."

"About you? What about you?"

"You know," Victor covered his mouth and whispered into the phone, "Marcus."

"WHAT?" Jack yelled making Victor pull the phone away from his ear. "How do they know?"

"I don't know, Jack."

"What did you do?"

"Nothing," Victor pleaded. "She said that there were rumors, but I don't know how that's even possible. I've only seen him once since the party and that was at the theater event."

"The theater opening? He was there? Well, that's kind of creepy." Jack paused, and then his voice calmly asked, "Are you seeing anyone else?"

"First of all, I'm not seeing Marcus. But kind of, Vince."

"Oh, so you two are official now?"

"Kind of. No. I don't know," Victor stammered.

"Well, you better figure it out soon because you cannot afford to lose Parliament's support, especially with Aunt Mary acting the way she's been acting lately. She will hang herself, but you just have to let her."

"So, you're telling me to go back in the closet too?" Victor asked.

"No, I'm not. Well, yea, you might have to until you're crowned. Wait, 'too?' Grandmother told you to go back in the closet?"

"Yes, without saying it. You know how she talks."

Jack chuckled, "In code, yes I know. I'd say, just chill. Focus on this trip coming up and leave the guys alone for a while. Go vegetarian."

"What?"

"You know, don't eat meat!"

"Ewwwww! I hate you! Good-bye." Victor's face grimaced as Jack's hysterical laughter was abruptly silenced by Victor's thumb hitting the end button on the screen. Despite his uncomfortable sense of humor, Jack had a point! He had to try and let go of relationships and put all his energy on this upcoming trip to the US.

Chapter 13

"Would you like anything else, Your Royal Highness?"

"No, thank you," Victor replied with a mouthful of cheeseburger. The flight attendant left and returned to the front of the plane. Victor quickly swallowed his food and then picked up his phone that he'd been hiding under the table. "I'm sorry, the flight attendant was talking to me."

"It's ok," Vince replied with a chuckle. "Are you eating?"

"Yes, a cheeseburger. But it isn't anything like yours." Victor flirted.

Vince chuckled, "Better not be."

Victor sat silent for a moment. He desperately wanted to keep the conversation light and sweet, as it usually was, but he needed to tell him about the Queen's *request*.

"Victor, are you still there?" Vince said.

The prince realized that he'd been sitting silently on the phone longer than he expected. "Yeah, sorry."

"Is everything ok?"

"Yeah, sure. Why?"

Vince cleared his throat. "Come on, talk to me."

"Well, I had a conversation with my grandmother last week and I think we should slow things a bit." As Victor spoke, his voice began to shake, along with the rest of his body as if he'd been standing in Antarctica.

"May I ask what she said?"

"Basically, rumors are circulating so I have to proceed with caution."

Vincent paused. "Are you saying that you don't want to talk to me anymore? Because that's pretty much all we've done."

"Um, my lips beg to differ."

"Hey, that's not my fault," Vince teased.

"Oh really?" Victor said. "You didn't kiss me just the other day?"

"Yes, but you kissed me back."

Victor's brief smile melted away once again. "Well, maybe we shouldn't do that anymore."

"Vic, your public image is what's in question here; not your actual relationships."

"Yes, but I don't want us to continue and then someone find out and splash it all over the news."

Vince sighed deeply and Victor realized what he'd just said. "So, you're saying you don't want to even talk to me anymore."

"No, that's not what I'm saying."

"Then, what are you saying?"

"I'm saying that we have to slow things down."

"We are already making the tortoise look like the hare, the next shift down would be the brakes."

Ignoring the mixed metaphor, Victor immediately changed his mind. He hadn't realized how much he'd developed feelings for Vince and the pain of losing him was greater than he'd ever felt. "You know what? Never mind. I just got a little scared about the rumors and didn't know what to do."

"Well, the first thing you could do is leave that Frazier guy alone."

"I rarely talk to Marcus," Victor lied, hoping it wasn't obvious.

"Vic, he's not a good person. For all you know, he could be the one spreading the rumors." Vince had a point. He added, "And if you want to diminish the rumors, then centralize your focus to the one hidden away."

"Wait," Victor interjected. "You are not hidden away. And I am not interested in Marcus in that way anymore. I told you, that ended months ago, and there wasn't anything really to start in the first place, just one kiss."

"So why have you been texting him constantly for the past few weeks."

Victor looked up and saw the arm of a white shirt peeking from behind the doorway and he moved the phone down to his thigh. "Can I help you?" He called out. A young man emerged from behind the doorway and bashfully put his hand to his chest with a fake surprise look on his face. "Yes, you!" Victor said.

"I'm sorry, sir. I just wanted to let you know that we are about to begin our final descent into Washington DC," the young man said nervously.

"Thank you," Victor replied and the young man left. He put the phone back up to his face. "I'm sorry, I'm not avoiding your question or this conversation but my grandmother's second assistant was listening. I don't know why she thinks I need an assistant on this trip."

Vince began to laugh, "Hey, be nice."

"I'm always nice."

"Uh-huh. Jack isn't the only mean one in your family."

"Shut up."

"See?"

Ding! The seatbelt light chimed on. "Hey, I have to go but I will call you from the hotel tonight and we can talk about this. Promise!"

"It will be early in the morning for me but sure," Vince chuckled. "Talk to you then." Victor tapped the screen with his thumb and fastened his seatbelt to the large, extremely comfortable chair. He rolled up the shade to the window to see the blue horizon give way to a green horizon. The closer it came, the grayer it appeared until it revealed itself to be a large city. The plane made its way over dense foliage, just like the rural areas of Iakos. In the far distance, Victor could see the peak of the Washington monument, followed by a long grey patch of clear land and then a large white building with a dome on the top. All he could think was, *WOW!* The history he'd read about over the years was right there in front of him and he was going to be in it tonight.

The plane made a series of turns until it was on a final path and slowly began its descent. This was always Victor's least favorite part of flying. The rumbling under the jumbo jet began to rattle the plane, which Victor recognized to the landing gear lowering. The dense Earth with the occasional road below gave way to a meticulously maintained field with buildings along the side. The signs, taxiways, and other planes left a reassuring feeling in Victor's head as if to say, "Almost there." Finally, the high-pitched hiss of the engines grew quiet as the plane floated towards America until a loud rumbling and a jostling vibration indicated touchdown. The engines reversed thrust until they slowed to an almost complete stop on the

131

runway. Victor took off his seatbelt and walked over to the bathroom. He switched the light on and checked himself in the mirror one last time before he would de-board to his first trip in America. He knew that he wasn't just there to meet the American president and represent his grandmother, but to win over the international world as well.

"Sir?" the Second Assistant Private Secretary called out to him from the doorway.

Victor sighed. "I'm in here, Mr. Borus."

"Sir, you can call me Nikolai, or Nicky, since we'll be working together for the next five days."

"Ok then," Victor replied walking out of the bathroom. "Nicky, it is."

"I just wanted to go over today's itinerary with you," Nicky said, and then stood staring at the prince.

"Well, go on then," Victor almost barked, making Nikolai flinch.

"First, you de-board the plane and meet the mayor of Washington DC, the governor of Maryland, the American Ambassador to Iakos, and others. Then, we leave by motorcade to the White House where the President and First Lady will greet us. We will have a tour and then you will have a private meeting with the President. Following that, you will have a photo session with the President with American and international press. At 4pm exactly, we will return to the hotel where we will change and prepare for the evening. At 6:30, we will depart back to the White House for the State Dinner." Victor's mind plugged every item on the agenda into his mental calendar. This was going to be a long day, but he was all too excited, more excited about the building itself than meeting the actual president. "Oh, also," Nicky continued, "the Queen's backup secure limousine has been sent here ahead of us to use while we're here."

"And why is that?" Victor asked, as he looked out of the window at the slowly passing buildings and small pocket of people on the tarmac screaming.

"I'm assuming because Americans have guns," Nicky said, very matter of fact.

Victor turned to the young man, "I'm not sure what you mean."

"The Queen said she doesn't want to take any chances in a country that allows guns for pretty much anyone."

"I think that she's exaggerating."

"You've seen the news. All of those mass shootings."

"Those can happen anywhere. Not to mention, riding around in an armored Rolls Royce may give the wrong impression." Victor rebutted. "But I guess there isn't really a choice, is there?" The plane slowed to a stop next to a long, red carpet with a staircase at the end. "What's with all the pomp and circumstance?"

Nicky smiled. "You are the Prince of Iakos."

"Yes, but the second-in-line. I'm not even the Head of State."

"Americans love royalty! I guess it's because they don't have it here, besides the celebrities they love to 'crown'. King of Pop, King of Rock and Roll, Queen of Soul, even Queen B, it's actually kind of comical." Nicky began to laugh, but Victor's unamused facial expression smothered the young assistant's laughter.

Victor turned completely to face Nicky. "And it's those kinds of jokes that cannot happen on a diplomatic trip." Nicky was frozen in place like a puppy that had been whacked on the nose. Victor noticed how this new authoritative energy was affecting Nicky and backed off. "How do I look?"

Nicky quickly looked him up and down and smiled. "You look good, sir. We should get going." Nicky turned and shuffled to the back of the plane where he and the rest of the accompanying staff would de-board. Victor grabbed his coat and made his way to the front of the plane and stood next to the door. The stairs rolled up as the door unlatched and swung open. Cold air rushed in and Victor quickly put on his coat and black gloves, and wrapped a grey scarf around his neck, tucking the ends into his coat. Two guards flanked the doors within the plane and awaited confirmation from security for Victor to exit the plane. As he waited, Victor swallowed his nerves and anxiety. The pressure was now on and he had to represent the nation with more than just the pin on his lapel flying the Iakon flag.

Finally, the guard to his right put his finger to his ear, nodded slightly, and the two guards snapped to attention followed by a bow. Victor painted a smile onto his face and stepped out into the cold. The roar from the small group of people at the end of the carpet was louder than he expected. His political smile slowly morphed into a genuine, flattered smile as he descended the stairs and greeted the US officials along the red carpet. Hand after hand he shook trying to focus on the US officials: a line of white men that seemed longer than usual. Finally, at the end, he turned and waved to the crowd of people behind the barricade. He smiled brightly and gave a gentle wave high in the air as the women in the crowd screamed louder. Victor chuckled silently to himself at the enthusiastic girl in the front held an 8.5x11 picture of him in one hand and frantically waved with the other. Victor felt a hand on his back moving him along down the carpet toward the limousine, which idled at the end. He longed for the warmth of the car but he knew he had to pass the press pit first on his way.

He slowly walked toward it, waved briefly and then started off to walk. The cameras fluttered frantically and reporters screamed out questions at him while extending microphones toward him in the off chance that he would answer. One woman's voice pierced through the rest, yelling, "Your Royal Highness, what do you think of the president's trade policies with Iakos?" Victor smiled and walked off to the car. He wasn't used to the American bluntness but it was strangely refreshing for him. A question that loaded would rarely be thrown at a member of the royal family in Iakos out of traditional respect and deference; maybe a staffer or a member of parliament but not a royal. The security guard opened the thick, heavy door and Victor climbed into the mini-tank where the rest of his close entourage waited for him.

The motorcade made its way through the streets of the capital city, which were lined with what seemed like the entire city. Victor sat amazed by the quantity and the excitement of the people, but what amazed him more was the diversity of the crowds. There were people from every conceivable race, gender, and walk of life. He turned to Nicky, "Do all of these people think the Queen is in this car?"

Nicky's face looked puzzled, "No. Why would they think that?"

"Well, there usually are crowds like this for her, but not a prince. She was originally supposed to be coming on this trip, right?"

"We've spent quite some time promoting this trip for you, sir," Nicky explained. "The Queen asked us to set this up a few months ago."

Victor stopped for a moment until it dawned on him. The Queen just used the doctor's order as an excuse and had planned on testing him for a while. Victor smiled to quickly disguise the increase in pressure. His focus needed to shift from representing the Queen, to showing his grandmother that he could handle the responsibilities of the Crown. He'd been planning on doing that anyway, but the stakes seemed to skyrocket in his mind.

The police-led motorcade made its way down the street until it slowed around a turn and then entered one of the most famous homes in the world. Victor looked up into one of the trees and noticed a man dressed in all black with a large gun. *Wow, even their trees have security*, Victor chuckled to himself. He looked up at the large building and realized it wasn't as big as the State Palace of Iakos, but it was more secure. He could see men on the roof, in the garden, men walking dogs — security everywhere. Finally, Victor's limousine slowed to a stop in front of a wide staircase with only a few stairs. At the top of the stairs stood a man who appeared on the higher end of middle aged and a woman who was visibly younger. Victor had heard horror stories about the current President of the United States from his pre-trip briefings from Mo Li, but he liked to experience people for himself before he judged. So he braced himself but kept an open mind.

"Don't forget you have to let him extend his hand first, as per the agreement," Nicky said.

"Agreement? With whom?"

"The agreement with the White House. You must let him extend his hand first. I guess it's a dominance thing. I don't know."

Victor groaned and sarcastically mumbled, "Oh, great. He's got a sensitive ego. This should be fun."

Victor took a deep breath and then tapped the window. The guard opened the door and suddenly the frantic click of cameras sprang into action once again. He stepped out, put on that handy-dandy smile, and walked up the stairs. The president stood about 5'9" tall with a full head of sandy brown hair all neatly combed back which didn't match the grey in his eyebrows and stubble. He bulged from a dark blue suit, red tie, and a white shirt; and appeared to be about 6-7 months pregnant with beer and hamburgers. Victor began to extend his hand just to be *that guy* but his grandmother's voice in the back of his mind quickly snapped his hand back down. "Hello, Mr. President."

"Hello, Your Highness," the President greeted with a broad diplomatic smile that put Victor's fake smile to shame. He turned to his wife, "His English is good."

"Honey, it's Your *Royal* Highness," the First Lady whispered to her husband.

"Shut up!" the President softly warned through his teeth, never cracking his smile. Victor's eyes slammed open at the utter disrespect he'd just witnessed and his smile melted into a contorted face of disapproval. This was one of those moments where no amount of mask would cover his true feelings.

"It is fine," Victor defended. "The titles tend to confuse people, sometimes even in my own family. And English is our official language." He gave the First Lady a reassuring smile that seemed to settle her. The President placed a hand on Victor's back and extended the other toward the bleachers of photographers and journalists immortalizing every millisecond of their meeting. Victor stepped to the President's side and posed for the cameras, ignoring the break of protocol in touching a Royal.

After a few drawn out moment, the President waved one last time and turned to Victor. "Shall we get out of this cold?" Music to Victor's ears. He gave one last wave himself and then turned to enter next to the First Lady.

They walked down the hallway with the bright red carpet atop a marble floor. He turned around to compliment the president's home but he didn't see the man behind him. The prince looked back through the door that led outside and noticed the President had gone back out to wave. Victor turned to the beautiful woman standing next to him with a puzzled look. "He prefers to be the last person to wave," the First Lady said.

"Does he have a lot of personal protocol rules too?" Victor sarcastically and quietly teased to her; she gave a half smile and nodded. A look behind her eyes told a dangerous story and Victor immediately read through the makeup. A slight discoloration sang a devastating truth. He threw away all protocol in that moment

136

and gave her a comforting handshake and smile before turning to the now entering leader.

The doors closed behind the American leader as he took off his coat and held it out. A few seconds passed but no one took it so he dropped it to the floor and walked over to Victor. "Let's take a walk. I hear you have a fascination with the Kennedys."

"Yes, sir. Well, the whole Kennedy era," Victor replied watching a slender woman wearing an apron retrieve the coat from the ground and brush it off. *This man's ego puts my mother's to shame.*

*   *   *   *   *

"Honestly, I didn't think the room was really an oval. I thought it was just a name until I got here on Inauguration Day," President Taylor said. Victor gave a loud laugh intended to flatter the man, though he really was laughing at his expense. The elder of the two spent the last hour walking from room to room in the presidential mansion making conversation consisting of one topic alone: himself, despite Victor's many attempts to steer the conversation in any other direction. Now, they sat in the Oval Office making small talk. "I have to admit something."

"What would that be?" Victor played along.

"I was a little disappointed when I was informed that Her Majesty wouldn't be coming."

Victor didn't know how to take that statement, so for the sake of diplomacy he chose to ignore the implication and take it at face value. "Well, I can say that she was disappointed in not being able to make the trip."

The President lifted his glass of scotch,' to his mouth and sipped. "So why couldn't Her Highness come?" he said mockingly.

"*Her Majesty?*" Victor politely corrected.

"Oh, I didn't know they weren't interchangeable," his Southern drawl seeped through. Clearly, that drink was getting to him a little earlier than the President had planned.

"No, Mr. President. They aren't," Victor replied with the only bit of a smile he could muster which ended up reading more of constipation.

The heavy man chuckled and then sat as if waiting. Finally, he asked. "So?"

"So?"

"Why didn't *Her Royal Majesty* come?"

At this point, Victor fought every urge, as his little brother would say, to "roast this clown". Instead, he kept reminding himself of the importance of America to Iakos' global trade market. He gritted his teeth and attempted to reply with as little aggression he could. "Well, she was not able to attend for a few reasons, but I cannot comment on the Crown."

The President blurted a throaty laugh that echoed throughout the room. "Thank God for the First Amendment."

That's it. Enough is enough! "Pardon me? What exactly is that supposed to mean?"

"I'm just pointing out the beauty of democracy," the President bragged with an obnoxious smirk as he reached for a refill.

"The beauty fades, I assure you," Victor replied, hoping the President would catch on to the double meaning.

"The beauty of a constitution," he continued, not even listening to the prince.

Victor sat back in his chair and, though his heart blared in his ears, he appeared calm on the outside. "Are you familiar with the term '*constitutional* monarchy,' Mr. President?" The smile melted off the old man's face. "We do have a constitution, and a Parliament democratically elected by the *majority* of the Iakon people. We even have a judicial branch. The only difference is that our Executive branch is run by a monarch rather than a president or a prime minister."

"Wow, you certainly know a lot about our government, Your Royal Highness."

"I read," Victor replied. *Ok, that one was an accident.* The two men sat in their seats having a literal staring contest. Victor didn't know what to expect from President Taylor, but he knew that if he backed down now, this bully would try and railroad Iakos for the rest of his presidential term. President Taylor lifted his glass and gave Victor an impressed smirk, allowing Victor to finally breathe. *That could have ended badly.*

Chapter 14

Victor's mind reeled as the hot shower kneaded the tensions from his shoulders. His conversation with the Queen outside of the French Embassy was stuck on replay. It seemed so out of character for her. She wasn't thrilled when he'd come out years ago, but over the years, he'd assumed that the idea of his sexuality had - normalized? The part that frustrated him was not knowing if the purpose of her demand was her opinion or solely for the appeasement of Parliament. She'd never suggested anything like that to him before. Suddenly, the light in the room seemed to grow brighter as it dawned on him. *It could be the tumor.*

He reached down and turned the metal knob on the wall. As the water stopped, Victor grabbed the towel hanging on the rod just outside of the shower and stepped out onto the cold tile floor. He patted himself dry and jumped into a pair of blue boxer briefs and plaid, flannel pajama pants. Then, he set the towel in the corner of the bathroom floor and walked into the bedroom. He flopped onto the bed right in front of his laptop and opened it. Victor typed, 'Side effects of Glioblastomas' into the search bar and waited. Websites from every end of cyberspace were compiled into a list in front of him. On the right was an excerpt of an article from the Mayo Clinic. He clicked it and began to read the list: Headache, nausea or vomiting, confusion or a decline of brain function, memory loss, *personality changes and irritability...* "Could this have been the reason?" Victor asked to himself aloud.

KNOCK, KNOCK, KNOCK! The rapping at the door made Victor all but jump out of his skin. He reluctantly climbed off the bed and shuffled over to the door. He looked through the peephole to find his security agent. Victor opened the door with a little more aggression than he'd intended. "Yes?"

The guard bowed at the neck. "Your Royal Highness, your private secretary would like a word."

"It's fine. Thank you!"

The agent stepped back, bowed, and disappeared around the corner for a moment. When he returned, he was followed by the

139

90s-boy-band look-alike. "Can I help you, Nicky?" Victor asked forcefully.

"Uummm, I just got a call from Ms. Zhang. She wanted me to show you this," the young man said as if he were afraid of the prince's reaction. He was clearly intimidated by Victor so Victor tried not to make it worse. He stepped back allowing Nicky into the room and closed the door behind them. They walked over to the bed and sat at the foot. Nicky tapped the tablet and handed it to Victor. It was a newsreel with the heading, BREAKING NEWS: PRINCESS INSULTS FRENCH AMBASSADOR. Victor looked at Nicky and burst into nervous laughter.

"This can't be real."

"Unfortunately, sir, it is."

"Which princess? My mother?" Victor asked. All the young boy could do was nod his head and fight back a laugh. "But how? I just met the man a few weeks ago and he was as nice as can be. What did she do?"

Nicky sighed. "Where do I begin? Ms. Zhang said that she was late to arrive to the meeting."

"What kind of meeting was it?"

"It was a meeting to discuss France's contribution to the new art initiative. The Queen has been pushing for their help. They were really interested in it and wanted to see how they could help and maybe create their own."

"Wow," Victor replied. "Well, how late was she?"

"Apparently, she was about an hour and a half late," Nicky said.

"An hour?" Victor exclaimed. "Did she give a reason?"

Nicky shook his head. "She just showed up as if she had been on time. Then, according to some of the staff in the meeting, she seemed unprepared. They said it was as if she hadn't read any of the prep booklets on the initiative and didn't seem all that invested."

"It's no secret that my mother isn't a fan of the new art programs. She would prefer the money and resources go to STEM fields." Victor got up and walked over to the mini fridge and pulled out a chocolate bar that he'd stashed inside after the state dinner.

"Yeah, like they need any more government money with the booming private sector," Nicky said, sarcastically.

"Exactly. What are we doing to fix this problem?" Victor asked.

"Well, that's not all that happened."

"Jeez, what else?"

Nicky paused as if he didn't want to say it. "She kind of insulted the ambassador to his face."

Victor gasped. "Oh, my goodness, how?"

"She insulted his age. According to the bloggers and online newspapers, she insulted him by saying that she could smell the Similac on his breath."

Victor's jaw hit the floor. *What did she hope to gain from that?* He began pacing around the room, trying to figure out what her endgame was.

"If you're thinking about how to fix this, Ms. Zhang and Her Majesty are on it. The palace is in full damage control mode," Nicky tried to reassure him but to no avail.

"I'm sure they are tired of being in that mode on account of the Princess. It's like she's trying deliberately to destroy her chances to be crowned." Victor took a bite of the chocolate and sat on the bed. Suddenly, his phone began to vibrate in the pocket of the suit jacket that hung from the chair in the corner. Nicky got up and retrieved it for Victor. Victor looked at the screen and a smile spread across his face. "Hey there. What are you doing up so late?"

"I wanted to catch you before you went to bed. Please tell me you heard what happened today with your mother," Chef Vincent asked through the phone.

"Yeah, I just heard," Victor replied.

Vince chuckled. "It's been all over the news here."

"I just read an article online and there's a video clip of the new report. What made her to insult him like that?"

"They said that he allegedly called her out for being late so she snapped back at him," Vince replied. "The story was allegedly leaked to the public by a source in *your* family."

Victor froze. "A source? Someone is leaking information? Does Her Majesty know who it is? Is there an investigation?"

"Victor, that's all I've heard. I'm just the cook. But the butler staff was all a buzz today. I'm assuming there will be an inquiry."

Victor realized that he wasn't talking to a member of the family. *Could he become a member one day?* His mind rocketed from point to point until it froze at a realization. He instinctively lowered his voice, "Do you think the mole knows about us?"

"Jeez, I hope not." Vince replied, his chuckling seizing instantly. "At least until you hear from Parliament."

Victor sighed as the lights in the room seemed to dim around him. Suddenly, he remembered the young man was sitting at the foot of his bed. His body stiffened, "Um, I have to go. I should call my grandmother."

"Ok, be good! And text me in the morning."

"Will do. Bye." Victor tapped the screen and put his phone on the bed. He slid closer to the foot of the bed and looked at Nicky as if to say with his eyes, *"You didn't hear that, did you?"*

Nicky sat confused, as he was only a few feet away from him, but then the subtext dawned on him. He smiled innocently and returned to his iPad.

Victor stood up, "Good man!" He walked over to his luggage and pulled out a thin black secure cell phone, or so it appeared on the outside. Once the screen emitted a green light, he scrolled down the short list of contacts until he saw the number that he recognized to be the secure line to the Queen. He pushed the call button and put it to his ear. Instead of the normal tone indicating the phone ringing on the other side, it simply beeped every few seconds until a voice came on the line.

"Palace line. How may I direct your call?"

"Hi. This is Prince Victor for Her Majesty." The line went silent for a few moments. While he waited, he turned to Nicky who was busy typing away on the keyboard engraved into the cover of his tablet. "What are you doing?"

"I'm checking my email," Nicky replied. "We've just received an itinerary change."

"A change? What changed?"

"I'm not sure, that's why I'm checking it," Nicky replied sarcastically, followed by a chuckle. Victor mocked the chuckle silently and walked over to the window on the other side of the room. From that height, the glass revealed the entire Washington Mall. Victor was amazed at how well the trees hid the White House from view.

"Victor?"

"Hi, Grandmother. How are you feeling?"

"Bothered. I'm assuming you called because you've read the latest headlines," the Queen said, sounding preoccupied.

"Yes, ma'am. We just received an itinerary change, also. Nicky is checking it now."

"Nicky? Who's Nicky?"

Victor furrowed his brow. "My private secretary for this trip?"

"Oh, yes! Mr. Borus. Has he been helpful?" the Queen asked.

"Yes, ma'am. He's very good at his job."

"Good, that's good."

A tap on his shoulder made Victor jump. He turned to find Nicky holding a tablet to his face. Victor pushed it away slowly with one finger until he could read it. Days 3, 4, and 5 were marked in red with a line through it. "Um, Grandmother, did you cancel New York?"

"Yes, dear. Unfortunately, we have a lot of damage control to do here and I need you back home."

"Grandma, with all due respect, I don't think that is wise or all that necessary. This is my first royal tour. Is what Mother said to an ambassador of an ally so bad that I need to return home?" Victor went on to explain how this trip was intended to nurture the relationship between Iakos and the US, and how cancelling the New York City part of the trip and leaving for a domestic political problem would do just the opposite.

"So, then what do you propose we do, Victor? The main event of the trip was the State Dinner. Everything else is cosmetic."

He stopped and thought for a moment. "What exactly do you need me to do that requires me to be stateside?"

"I need you to make a statement walking back what happened to the French people on my behalf. Then, I want you to meet with the ambassador and try to mend the bruises he's now publicly suffering," the Queen said. "And then fulfill Mary's remaining duties for a while."

"The Palace Press Secretary can issue a statement. And I can have that conversation with him over the phone."

"Victor, someone can't hang up on you to your face. In person, one can read facial expressions, body language, and so forth. One can get a genuine sense of the intentions."

"One can do that through video chat, as well," Victor pleaded. "That's what technology is for, ma'am."

The line went quiet. Victor could only hear mumbling as if his grandmother had her hand over the receiver. Finally, the ambient noise changed back, "Fine. You can video call him in the morning, your time, but I still would like you to come home tomorrow morning. No New York leg. I wasn't too fond of that idea anyway; too many people, too many possibilities of something happening to you. Not to mention, our country needs leadership right now."

Victor smirked. "Grandma, America is not as bad as Iakon news makes it out to be."

"Victor, l-l-let me be as c-cl-clear as possible. Here in Iakos, you are an exotic-looking young prince, and next - I mean second-in-line for the throne." Victor cringed at the word, *exotic*. The Queen continued, "But our American brothers and sisters have a history of seeing darker skin as something lesser. Some parts of the world see that you are of mixed race and label you, using nomenclature designated to treat people less than they deserve. Your father's race has caused some discomfort in certain parts of the country. They weren't happy that your mother married a gentleman of African descent, but Mary insisted that she loved him. So, we welcomed him into the family."

Victor listened to his grandmother's every word as images of videos from his American Society class flashed in his mind. "Respectfully, Grandmother, one could then argue that that makes this trip even more important. It's not everyone here. The response to my arrival has been better than any of us expected. The world needs to see how the idea of race is changing around the world. Besides, sooner or later, the Kingdom of Iakos will have a 'Black' king whether certain people want it or not."

The Queen didn't respond at first. Victor immediately grew afraid of what her response would be, so he continued. "If you'll allow me, I'd like to keep at least one of tomorrow's engagements here in Washington if you feel *that* strongly about New

York - the elementary school and the press conference thereafter. Those kids have been looking forward to it and I'd like to see them."

Seconds felt like years until she finally replied, "Ok. You'll have the press conference at the airport," the Queen said with what sounded like a smile. "You know, you make me so proud, Victor. You are becoming an incredible young man. I had a conversation with President Taylor before all this nonsense broke in the news and he was very impressed with you. I am most proud of the way you represented the Crown, yourself, and your country."

Victor's eye began to tear slightly at her choice of words: *your country.* "Thank you, Grandmother. That means the world to me."

"Now, come home."

Victor sighed in relief. "Thank you! Get some sleep. I'm off to bed, as well."

"Now I have to call your mother. Good night." The phone went dead. Victor's face had a clear expression that every kid who witnessed his or her classmate get in trouble would recognize. *Ooooooooooo. She's in trouble!*

*   *   *   *   *

"Ok, kids. I'd like you to give a warm welcome to the Prince of Iakos, His Royal Highness, Prince Victor!" the principal announced into the podium. She extended her left hand to the prince with a smile as the kids erupted into claps and high-pitched squeals. Victor was completely caught off guard and winced as the screams sounded like a jet engine. He knew the school was excited to have him come, but he didn't expect them to have such an adoring and hysterical reaction. It was as if he was a pop star that had come to give back to the community.

He walked across the stage and embraced the principal in a handshake, then took her place at the podium. He stood waiting for the children to calm down, but seconds turned into minutes as the screaming continued. The teachers and chaperones tried to calm them but to no avail. Victor had an idea, "Hello children." The screams got even louder. "Hello. All right, let's settle down a bit." The room began to quiet noticeably, but he figured he'd have to say it again. "Settle down, please. Thank you!" Finally, the room got to a

145

manageable level, so he began. *Cool.* "I want to thank Principal White for inviting me to your school today. I'm so honored to be here. First, let me start by saying that I'm not the kind of person to tell tales to children, so I'm going to be honest with you." He pulled the microphone off the clip that was attached to the podium and walked to center stage as he spoke. "I'm not going to give you rose colored glasses and make things pretty because that's not what you need. I'm going to be honest and then you're going to be honest and then we'll have a great time. Deal?"

"Deal," the kids called out.

"Deal?" Victor yelled louder.

"Deal!" the kids screamed back.

"Great. So, my grandfather, His Royal Highness, Prince Victor the First, may he rest in peace, was known for his sayings. He'd have these phrases that seemed to make no sense at the surface, but once you started to think them over, you would begin to understand the weight of them. They would be things like 'There's nothing common about sense' or 'Victor, that's a head up there, not a foot.'" The children burst into laughter while the others groaned "ewwww," clearly imagining a foot on someone's head. Then he continued, "But one of them really stuck out to me as a child. 'Good, better, best. Never let it rest, 'til your good is better, and your better best.' Can you guys say it after me?"

"Yeeeeees," sang the children.

"Good, better, best —" Victor started.

"Good, better, best —" the children replied.

"Never let it rest —"

"Never let it rest —"

"Until your good is better —"

"Until your good is better —"

"And your better, best."

"And your better, best."

"Now what does that mean?" Victor asked. Of course, he knew that the saying was a bit dense for the children so he just continued. "This saying means you must always be working hard to improve yourself to be your very best and reach the impossible. At your age though, I never could really figure that out. It seemed to praise being perfect, right? And it conflicted with some of his other sayings like 'Always shoot for the stars, so if you fail, you'll land on the moon.' The first saying is intended to mean to never give up and strive for excellence always, while the other means you should dream the impossible but prepare an alternative - a fall back. As I got older and went to university, I had the worst time battling between these two sayings that I'd heard over and over and over again all of those years." Victor's emphasis on "and over and over" made the children chuckle. "I'd ask myself, *Should I give all of my energy to plan A or take some energy away from plan A to create a plan B?* Raise your hand if you think you should stick to plan A?" Most of the younger children raised their hands along with a mere handful of the older students. "Ok, lower your hands and now raise your hands if you think having a backup plan is a good idea?" The rest of the kids' hands shot up. "May I ask why you think that?"

A long silence lingered before one of the more cynical 8th graders called out, "It's safer."

"Yes," Victor agreed and began pacing around the stage as he continued. "You are absolutely right. It *is* the safer plan. You wouldn't really have to worry and you'd always have a sense of security, which sounds favorable. But one could argue that the same security would mean that you might not work as hard or with the same passion if you always have a safety net? Think of it like gymnastics. Gymnasts train day in and day out on vault, bars, pommel horse, and other apparatuses using those large padded cushions and nets under them in case they fall. Now when they compete and it's time to achieve the seemingly impossible in front of judges and cheering crowds, they take away the cushion that takes away any option of 'safe' failure. Now some thrive under this pressure and see it as a cool challenge, and they do everything they can to win gold, right? But what about those gymnasts who can't do their hardest tricks without the safety net? What does that say about them?"

"They didn't really want to achieve the impossible; they simply wanted the praise of the impossible," an older teacher rebutted loudly.

Victor paused and studied the teacher. "That is one conclusion, yes. Intentions are very important to achieving the impossible. But this brings me to my point: no matter what your intentions are, don't be afraid to try it. Sticking to plan A works for some of you, while others need a backup plan. Only *you* will know

147

which works for you and neither is wrong — just different. Always strive for your wildest dreams, in the way that works for you. Ok? Does everyone understand what I'm saying?"

"Yeeees," the children replied.

"Great. That's all. I told you I'd be short and sweet."

The children all jumped to their feet clapping and cheering the prince. Victor replaced the microphone and proceeded to the side of the stage where the principal stood with a smile on her face.

The next hour was filled with thousands of photographs taken with students, staff and their families. He left the building and just before climbing into the limo, he turned and gave one last wave to the children who were spilling out the door and windows of the school, trying to capture the last moments of his visit with their phones. Victor could finally allow his face to rest from the smiling. Inside the limousine waited Nicky who typed away on his tablet. "Are the suitcases on the way to the airport?"

"They are already aboard the plane along with the rest of the staff," Nicky replied. "It's just you and me."

"Great. Have you been in touch with Ms. Zhang about my remarks when I land?"

Nicky nodded. "Yes, sir. They are in my bag. We can go over them on the plane."

Victor sat back and looked out of the window watching Americans wave along the barricaded streets. "Did they leave these streets barricaded overnight?"

"No," Nicky replied with a chuckle. "Our security and the Secret Service had them put back up early this morning when we got word that you were being called home."

"How'd the people in New York respond?"

"Disappointed," Nicky replied, paying more attention to his phone.

* * * * *

Victor threw his phone into the seat across from him and sat back in his chair looking out the window. "I'm not going to reply. I'm not going to reply," Victor chanted softly to himself as he tried to ignore his phone. The text messages from Marcus had a firm grasp on his heartstrings, or so it seemed. They never talked about a relationship or anything like that. Marcus simply would let Victor talk or vent or just release a sporadic stream of consciousness. Marcus was a much-needed ear for Victor, to which Victor had become borderline addicted and with the new non-disclosure agreement between them, the dam had burst.

DING! The cell phone chimed in the chair in unison with the seatbelt light above Victor. He adjusted his head to be able to see ahead of the plane. They broke through the clouds to show the approaching coast as the city became more visible. The jet floated toward Earth for a few minutes until they landed at Parados International Airport. Before they had come to a stop, Victor had unhooked his seatbelt and was on his feet. They taxied to the royal hanger where the Royal Jet resides. A large ground of reporters and citizens had gathered and waited in the chilly morning air.

Nicky entered the "living room" of the plane with Victor's coat draped over his arm. After helping him into it, he fixed his tie and made final adjustments to his suit. A nervous and annoyed Victor swatted Nicky's hand away. "Are you ready, Your Royal Highness?"

Victor took a moment to take a mental inventory of everything he wanted to go in the car with him to the palace. Almost gasping at his absentmindedness, he stepped over to the chair and retrieved his phone, slid it into his coat pocket, and then he nodded. Nicky shot him a quick smile and bowed, "It was great working with you, sir."

"It was great working with you, as well, Nicky," Victor replied. The younger of the two walked toward the tail door and Victor made his way to the main door.

Once there, he took a deep breath and centered himself. He was kind of disappointed that he only got to spend one night in the United States, but he figured that he'd be back one day soon to carry out the cancelled engagements or maybe a longer tour. Victor turned on his public charm and stepped into the brisk air as the crowd roared about 30 feet away from the plane. He slowly made his way down the stairs, to make sure he didn't fall in front of the live cameras. Finally, he walked up to the swarm of reporters all shoving their microphones into his face.

"Hello, my fellow Iakons," he read. "As always, it is great to be home no matter what the circumstances. I enjoyed the State Dinner with President Taylor of the United States, and enjoyed spending this morning at a Washington DC grade school. Unfortunately, duty called me home prematurely. I'd like it to be known that the entire Royal Family and myself have great respect for French Ambassador whom I've had the pleasure of welcoming to the new French Embassy here in Parados, just a few months ago. Our relationship with France is a centuries-old relationship; one that is strong, important, and one we cherish. This morning, I spoke with the Ambassador myself to convey our deepest regret at the recent behavior from members of the Royal Family and to reinforce that this, in no way, reflects the views of Her Majesty, the Royal Family, or the Iakon people. That is all I will say on this matter. Any more questions should be directed to the Palace Press Secretary. Thank you." The large security men parted the chaotic sea and Victor calmly walked through to the idling row of SUVs and police cars.

February

<u>Chapter 15</u>

"No! Stop," Victor pleaded to his lover as he squirmed away from the lips chasing his neck.

Vince stepped away, submitting reluctantly to Victor's request. Instead, he turned Victor by the waist and pulled him close. "But you taste so scrumptious, I need to taste some more." He leaned forward and kissed the prince's forehead.

"Well, sugar is only good in moderation," Victor half-heartedly struggled to push Vince away.

"Yes, but that implies that I'd get more than a taste. When do I get to have more than the sampler?" Victor snickered nervously and turned away from him. Victor slowly stepped onto to his bed and sat on the edge with his eyes fixed on the floor. Vince watched him from the window, waiting for an answer that he soon realized wouldn't come. He slowly made his way over and sat next to Victor. "Hey," he almost whispered as he bumped him on the shoulder. "Are you ok?"

Victor turned to Vince with a storm brewing in his eyes. "I'm just not ready."

"You're not ready?"

"You know, to take things to that level," Victor whispered.

151

Vince read his lover's eyes and recognized that there was something deeper there. He desperately wanted to know what was the cause of the pain that he was witnessing in Victor, but he decided not to press the matter. "It's ok." Vince brushed Victor's cheek with the back of his hand and smiled reassuringly. "I will wait as long as you need. There is no rush; I'm not going anywhere. Hey, I have an idea. A friend of mine from culinary school is opening a new restaurant downtown tonight for Valentine's Day. I figure it would be great for business for a member of the Royal Family to enjoy a meal there and good for a particular member of the Royal Family to take a break from official duties."

"I can't," Victor began to complain. "I have two meetings tomorrow morning, and I have to prepare for the ruling of Parliament-"

"Baby, you have been going nonstop since you've gotten back from your trip to the States. You've been balancing ambassadors, press conferences, events..."

"It's my responsibility; my duty. Grandmother pulled Mother's duties until the ruling, so I must pick up the slack. The Queen can't handle any of Mother's responsibilities right now, it's all on me."

Vince chuckled. "You've proven my point, you need a break and I need a favor. Why not merge the two?"

Victor stopped and allowed himself to lower his guard enough to consider the invitation. "Ok, I have to request permission from the Queen but it shouldn't be a problem."

"Great! I'll see you tonight." Vince replied with a huge grin on his face. He grabbed Victor's face and kissed his lips deeply with a soft nip to the prince's bottom lip. Then, he got up and danced over to the wall. Victor followed over and placed his thumb on the almost invisible circle on the wall. The secret passageway door clicked open and he pushed it open for Vince who disappeared down the dark hall. The prince quietly closed the door and practically ran to the Crown suite.

Just outside the door, the sound of a particular voice made his hair stand up all over his body. He stopped and steadied himself for a moment, then entered the bedroom. "Good morning," Victor announced with a small bow, then walked over to his grandmother and planted a kiss on her forehead.

"Good morning, dear," she replied.

"Hello Victor," Mary said without turning toward him.

Victor ignored the disrespect and turned his body to only face his grandmother. "Do you think you will feel up to going down to the office today?"

"Yes, she is," Mary interjected. "I will be going down with her and helping her today."

Victor snickered. "Oh, boy."

Margaret reprimanded Victor with a light pat to the back of his hand, although her smirk seemed to lighten the impact.

"I'm glad you are feeling better," Victor spoke to his grandmother.

"Yes, I think it was just a little bug or something," Margaret replied. "No need to be worried."

"That doesn't mean I won't," he replied. "You don't really have the strongest immune system at the moment. You should definitely stay out of the cold."

Mary walked around to the side of the bed where Victor was seated and stepped in front of him. She reached down and pulled back the blanket from Margaret's lap. The Queen slowly swung her legs over the side of the bed.

"Grandmother, may I ask you something?"

"Sure," Margaret replied with labored breath as she pulled herself to her feet using Mary's hands to hold herself up.

"I've been invited to a restaurant opening this evening and I thought I might go. I just wanted to get your permission before I confirmed."

Margaret sat on the chair in the middle of the room as the Royal Dresser entered the room and began to undress her. "No."

Victor turned to the side and faced away from her. "No?"

"I-I-It's t-t-too pop culture. Do you remmmmember what we spoke about?" Margaret used her eyes to indicate to Victor that she didn't want to elaborate further in front of the princess.

Victor had to figure out a way to go. He wanted to have this chance to have a normal night with Vince. "What if I brought Jackie?"

"Victor, it still associates you with the frivolous. Now enough!"

"Yes, ma'am!" Victor stood, disappointed. He bowed and left. As he walked down the hall, he reached for his phone and scrolled his contacts. He jogged down the stairs of the Residential Lobby and then pressed call, slamming the phone to his cheek. As the phone began to ring, he stormed down the hallway toward the kitchen.

"Hey, you. Is everything ok?" the voice said.

"Hey. Are you busy tonight?" Victor asked.

"Um, no? Why?"

Victor stopped walking. The wheels turned in his mind and then before he could stop himself, the words came out, "I need your help."

"Anything! What do you need?"

* * * * *

"Will you stop fidgeting with it?" Vince whispered over the table.

Victor wiped the beads of sweat off his forehead with the back of his hand and then wiped his hand on the napkin resting in his lap. "My goodness, this is so hot. I shouldn't have done this. This was so irrational of me."

Vince reached across the table and placed his hand on Victor's. "You look great. Different, but great. Jackie did an amazing job and no one has said anything so far. Now take a deep breath and figure out what you want to order."

Vince is right, Victor thought to himself. He looked around and nobody was paying attention to him, so he began to study the menu. The picture of the coconut shrimp on the top right corner caught Victor's eye. Immediately he placed the menu on the table next to him and smiled broadly. "I know what I want," he said gleefully. He reached forward, retrieving his tall glass of water.

"Wow, you know what you want to order already? You only looked for a second."

"Yup," Victor bounced.

Vince chuckled at how cute the prince looked, even with the prosthetic nose, sandy blond wig, fake eyebrows, and dark brown contacts.

"I'm torn between the coconut shrimp and the Mediterranean chicken," Vince replied, without even looking up.

"Get the chicken, because I'm getting the shrimp."

"What?" Vince said with big eyes. "*You* are gonna share your food?"

"Hey, it's a special occasion."

Vince smiled at the excitement oozing from the bouncing man in front of him, "That it is."

A young woman walked up to the table wearing a black polo shirt and black trousers with an apron around her waist. "Alright, gentleman. Are you ready to order?"

"Yes, ma-"

"Yes, we are," Vince jumped in. "I would like the Mediterranean chicken."

The waitress began vigorously scribbling in her notepad and then looked up at Victor. "And for you?"

"And he will have the coconut shrimp," Vince replied.

A look of complete and utter confusion was plastered all over her face. She slowly looked back and forth between the two and then looked directly at Victor. "Is that what you would like dear?" Victor simply nodded and then she wrote it on her pad, took the menus, and walked off after shooting Vince a look.

"Ok, what was that?" Victor whispered.

"Everyone knows what your voice sounds like. I was just protecting you."

"Well, stop," Victor asserted, off-voice. "You're making things suspicious."

"I'm sorry. I'm just new to all of this clandestine stuff. This isn't my world," Vince whispered.

Victor stopped and sat back. Vince's words hit the prince like a ton of bricks and he could see it all over the prince's face. Vince immediately wanted to suck the words back into his mouth. "Well this is my life, at least for now, and if you don't want to be a part of it-"

"I do. I just need you to give me some time to get used to the attention."

"Get used to the attention? How long have you been working for my family? You're not used to it yet?"

155

"No. Of course not! I'm used to being behind the scenes. Not at the table." As his lover paused, Victor tried to digest Vince's point of view. He played with his watch as Vince continued, "I'm also not used to hiding who I am from the world. That's not me and I know that's not you."

Victor swallowed hard and leaned forward. "You know that this is only until Parliament makes a decision. Then, either way, we will be free to be who we are."

"Can we survive that long? They haven't even begun arguing the case."

"What do you think?"

Vince nervously looked around the room and then back at Victor. "I hope so, because I'm in love with you."

Victor froze, not breathing, not moving. He couldn't believe what he'd just heard. That was the first and only time anyone had ever said that to him and he didn't even know how to react. He grew dizzy, realized he'd he needed to take a breath. He slowly inhaled, "Really? How do you know?"

"Because every day, you're the first and the last person I think about. Every part of me wants to protect you from everything you go through on a daily basis and I don't ever want to spend a day in this world that you are not a part of my life."

Victor noticed his hand trembling under the table, but before he could respond, a plate of large, golden brown shrimp surrounding a small glass bowl filled with cocktail sauce stole his attention, along with piping hot potato wedges. His mouth began to water and his stomach began to growl. Vince couldn't figure out which was more amazing, how quickly the food came or how quickly Victor had become distracted by it. Within seconds, Victor had a mouthful of food and was reaching for the next shrimp when suddenly a scream came from the other side of the restaurant. Victor gasped and began coughing violently, sending bits of partially masticated shrimp across the table. As he caught his breath, he turned around to find his sister and all her sparkling splendor entering the restaurant with security.

"What is she doing here?"

"Well, the whole point of me coming here was originally supposed to be publicity," the prince whispered. "This way, the restaurant gets its publicity and everyone is focused on Jackie and nowhere else." Vince raised his eyebrows in surprise. Thoroughly impressed, he raised his glass and Victor connected his with a clink.

The rest of the evening went on without excitement. Victor enjoyed watching people fawn over someone else, though he had to admit that it felt weird. The two left the restaurant around 11 p.m. and began walking back toward the unmarked SUVs that were waiting about 3 blocks away. They slowly sauntered down the street trying to enjoy every minute of the evening. Their hands and fingers were tightly intertwined and their steps in sync in the uncharacteristically warm February evening.

"So."

"So?" Victor replied.

"So, do you think you'd be willing to tell me what happened to you?"

"What happened to me?" Victor asked, trying to avoid the probing conversation.

Vince paused for a moment. "I mean, why you decided to take a celibacy vow?" Victor's whole body visibly tensed up as if he were on the edge of a roller coaster. He really didn't want to put a damper on such an amazing night. Vince squeezed Victor's hand. "Hey, you can talk to me about anything."

"I know that."

"So, then, talk to me."

Victor took a deep breath and then began to scan his memories to find where to begin. He wanted to be truthful without giving away too much information. "Back in college, I kind of got a bit crazy. I took some risks with someone I shouldn't have and it put a strain on my family. Grandmother made some decisions that I'm not at liberty to discuss but what I can say is it split the family up. That's the reason my father left. He said that he couldn't be a part of a family whose actions contradicted with his morals."

Vince stopped walking and stared at the disguised prince. "I don't even know how to begin to take that. You're speaking in code."

Victor couldn't look up at Vince. He simply watched his legs as they continued down the pavement. He tried to find the right words, "I was blackmailed my first year of university. My grandmother dealt with the situation in a way that my father hated. So, he renounced all his titles, divorced my mother, and left."

Vince stopped walking again, standing in shock. "What did she do?"

"I'm not at liberty to say," Victor recited slowly, realizing that the implication was enough to send chills down Vince's spine. Victor stared at him, trying to read his face, however, the only expression he could make out was shock and maybe fear. Vince barely blinked as his eyes bore into Victor's soul. "Please say something."

"I-I don't know what to say," Vince stammered.

Victor reached down to take Vince's hand to comfort him but Vince flinched his hand away. "Are you mad?" Victor asked fearfully.

"Mad — no. Afraid — a bit."

"Let me just say this: 'worst case scenarios tend to fill the void of ignorance'. Another philosophical gem by my grandfather. We cannot talk about the Queen or any official, private, or secret information. So members of the Family are to be cautious about refusing to comment on certain matters because people tend to fill in the blanks with the worst possible things. Don't let that happen with us. Unfortunately, this is just part of life as a Royal. I hope you understand that."

Vince swallowed hard and began to weigh his feelings for Victor against the life of which he was getting a glimpse. He didn't like where this was going but the thought of pulling away from Victor felt like ripping his own heart from his chest. "I do understand. Just please be patient with me."

"Of course! Nothing about life with me is easy," Victor warned as they began to walk again.

"You never said it was going to be and I'm still here," Vince tried to reassure him.

They made their way down the last few blocks until they reached a small road. They turned and began walking to the black SUV idling halfway down the street. The front passenger door opened and the chauffeur stepped out opening the door for Victor.

Vince stopped short of the car and pulled Victor by the arm into a long embrace. Their embrace lingered for almost a minute until Vince planted a kiss onto Victor's forehead. "I love you," he whispered into Victor's ear, then turned and walked back toward the main road. Victor watched him leave with a smile and then climbed into the SUV. *I love you too?*

Chapter 16

The next morning greeted Victor gently as he slept until his body naturally awakened. He stayed in bed for another twenty minutes remembering the night before. Full of a joy that he wasn't familiar with, Victor finally climbed out of bed and shuffled into his bathroom. He took his time washing off the night and getting dressed. After sealing the day's look with a spritz of cologne, he made his way to the Queen's bedroom.

He walked into the room to find her dressing with the help of the Royal Dresser. "Oh good, you're up! Good morning," Victor greeted with a bow. Margaret sat in her chair with coldness on her face as she held the row of pearls to her neck while the woman closed the clasp behind her neck. "How are you feeling?"

"Fine."

"Good." Victor replied, taking note of her tone. "I have a meeting a little later with Ms. Zhang about your birthday gala this weekend." Margaret maintained her gaze on the floor in front of her. "Is there anything you want to add last minute?"

"No."

Victor paused and studied his grandmother. She was in full Queen-mode and suddenly his heart began to race. "Is everything ok?"

Margaret turned to the middle-aged woman behind her. "Leave us please."

"Yes, ma'am!" She replied as she curtsied and then quickly left the room.

"What's wrong, Grandmother?"

Queen Margaret pulled a newspaper from between her thigh and the side of the chair and threw it at Victor. He caught it with one hand and looked at the front cover. He studied the picture of his sister at the new restaurant but didn't see the problem. "I don't understand."

"The bottom right corner, behind the text."

Victor looked closely and recognized his disguise in the background. *How did she know that was me? You can't even see*

Vince across the table. He continued to study the image but to no avail. "I'm lost."

"That watch I gave you for Christmas years ago is a one-of-a-kind. It also has a tracker inside. Security has confirmed that you *were* there last night," Margaret scolded.

"You lo-jacked me?"

"You disobeyed me." Margaret's voice began to elevate with every word. "I gave you a direct refusal."

Victor was partially shocked at the violation of privacy, but also impressed at her knowledge of technology. "I wasn't there in any official capacity. It was a simple date." *Oops*.

"Date?"

"Grandmother, I can explain."

"STOP TALKING," she bellowed, catching Victor completely off guard. "I tried to be tactful out of respect for your feelings, but clearly that isn't working."

Victor tried to interrupt. "I'm not…"

She raised her hand authoritatively to silence him. "Let me be *very* clear here. You are not allowed to date."

"I'm what?"

"I want — no —please I need you to be king and, damn it, you won't help me. Instead of making life easy for yourself, and me, you go off and display the greatest lack of judgment I've ever seen from you. What if a reporter made that connection? You wear that watch everywhere." Victor stood silently, trying to wrap his mind around the fact that his grandmother was yelling at him for the first time in his life. "Is sheer stupidity a recessive gene I didn't know about? I thought you would succeed me, but now…"

"Now?"

"…I have a lot to think about."

Victor began to plead. "All because I wanted to feel romantic love for the first time in my life?"

"YOUR DUTY TO THIS COUNTRY COMES FIRST! What part of that don't you get? Love is a feeling that comes and goes. It is temporary. Your primary job as King will be to make sure this country doesn't become a temporary kingdom. It will quite literally be an existential threat to you at all times. You need to learn this *now* if this is what you want."

"It is!"

Margaret sat up in her chair. "Then until we have an answer from Parliament, you need to wait. End it."

Her words felt like a one-two punch to the gut. Victor's mind was completely baffled at the suggestion. "You want me to break up with him?"

"Yes!"

Everything in him wanted to refuse, but he dared not. "Please, don't make me do this," he pleaded with tears threatening his resolve.

"It is just until we get a court date. I should arrange for you a public relationship with a woman, just in case. But, I would never do that to *you*. Short of that, you must not date."

Tears began to well up in his eyes. He'd finally found love and now it's being snatched away from him.
"When does it go to court?" Victor asked with a broken voice and a face now damp with tears.

"I don't know yet," she replied coldly. "But you have to decide what you want. Love or country? Your mother chose for herself, which put us in this predicament. Now you must choose."

* * * * *

Vince's mouth watered at the two filets in the skillet. Next to him were two bowls of white rice, topped with some grilled bells peppers and peanuts. All that was left was the salmon filet and soy sauce. He danced to the music that quietly played from the small speaker behind him as he cooked. Finally, he turned off the fire, picked up the spatula, and placed the fish in each bowl. Drizzling some soy sauce on each bowl, he stepped back and smiled. An almost inaudible sound caught his ear and he turned to find his love standing in the doorway planted squarely on both feet. His facial expression was one he'd never seen before, but he knew it wasn't good. Victor, now since he was caught, slowly entered the room. He looked at the bowls and gave what little smile he could muster.

"Hey there," Vince said with a reassuring smile. He walked around the island and went in for a kiss. Victor flinched and turned his head, making the kiss land on his cheek. Vince stepped back and studied his face. "Is everything ok?"

Victor shook his head reluctantly as he avoided eye contact. "Vincent, I need to talk to you about something."

"Not until you eat." Vince stepped away and picked up the bowl. With the other hand, he grabbed a spoon and turned to Victor.

"Vince, please. This is impo-" the prince was interrupted by a spoon full of food. The extraordinary taste tried to steal his mind's attention, but he fought valiantly to stay on topic. He finished chewing and opened his mouth to speak again. Vince had scooped another spoonful but Victor was prepared. He covered his mouth with his hand making Vince chuckle. He took a step back. "We have to stop."

Vince's smile fell off his face and he set the bowl down. "What? Stop what?"

"Stop seeing each other," Victor replied coldly. His protective shield was in full effect.

After a long pause, a frozen Vince could only manage one word. "Why?"

"Because it's my duty to put my country first."

"And how is ending us protecting Iakos?" Vince asked, now visibly confused. "This isn't *you* talking, it's Her Majesty. Isn't it? What is going on?"

"I cannot discuss the details."

"Victor!" He grabbed Victor's hand and held it to his own chest. "Stop this. Talk to me like a human — like the person I know — like the person I love!" Vince's words put a huge crack in Victor's shield, allowing him to feel more than he intended. He tried to pull away but Vince had a strong grip on his hand. "Please talk to me. I don't want to lose you."

The prince's eyes began to fill and leak down his cheek once again. "I don't want to lose you either. Maybe we can be friends or something. But we cannot date, at least not right now."

A glimmer of hope sparked in Vince eye.

He pleaded, "If not now, then when?"

"I cannot —"

"Discuss it?"

Victor shook his head and slid his hand out of Vince's grasp. "I'm sorry." He turned around and began to walk out of the door.

164

"I'm not letting you go," Vince said in a slightly raised voice.

Victor stopped just before the door and replied without turning around, "You promise?" With that, he walked out leaving Vince without his heart or appetite.

Victor made his way to the private entrance but only made it halfway across the palace until he stopped and pulled out his phone. He scrolled down his contacts and then hit a private number.

"Hello?"

"Yes, Prince Victor for Her Majesty, please."

After a short pause, the Queen's voice filled his ear. "Yes, dear?"

"Country!" He whispered, followed by waterfalls.

* * * * *

Victor studied his family as rowdy conversation filled the tall corridor just outside of the banquet hall. The women of the family were in gowns and jewels while the men all wore black tuxedos. In addition, each member had a large golden pin on the breast of his or her gowns/suit jacket. At the front of the line stood Queen Margaret in a sparkling white gown with a large diamond tiara atop her head. Behind her, the family members were organized in single file except for married couples based on seniority in the line of succession:

The Duke and Duchess of Spiti
Prince Victor II of Spiti
Prince Seth of Spiti
Princess Jackie of Spiti
The Duke and Duchess of Makria
Prince John of Makria
Princess Margaret of Makria

For the last few days, Victor had buried himself in preparing this birthday gala. He wanted it to be special for his grandmother considering this was going to be her last birthday celebration. However, everything seemed to pull his mind back to

Vince. Things that had nothing to do with him would remind Victor of his absence.

Two hands rested on his shoulders and squeezed hard. He flinched under the pressure and turned to see to whom they belonged. Jackie's long white gloves slid off his jacket as he caught her mocking facial expression. She and Jack were the only members of the family who knew about the break up, other than the Queen. Victor had to sit through hours of them orally beating him up about capitulating to such an "unfair demand," but after a while, they finally understood that it was supposed to be temporary.

Through the almost two story doors, a booming voice announced, "All rise for Her Majesty, Queen Margaret I, and the Royal Family." The family began to take a few steps closer to the door so the doors would open with the Queen already in front of them. Once the rustling of the rising people quieted large doors finally rumbled and whined opened and an orchestral recording of the national anthem began to play. The Queen began to walk and the family followed, but after a few steps, they all stopped. Victor could hear gasps so he looked around his mother and stepfather. He noticed that the Queen not only had stopped, was beginning to wobble. Without thinking, he jumped around his mother and grabbed hold of her arm. She took a moment to stabilize herself and then stood upright. Victor knew what the people attending the party would imply and so did his mother. Victor looked to his right to find the eldest princess had come up and grabbed her right arm, but the Queen had pulled away from her and began walking.

Victor knew exactly what was going through his grandmother's head. *Oh, now you want to come help me to save your place in line? Please. One person holding my hand says elderly, but two people reads as weak.* As they started walking, Mary stepped in stride right next to her. Margaret continued to walk, but turned and shot her a look that Victor could read even from behind her head. She was totally out of royal protocol. If you are not holding onto the monarch, you should walk at least two steps behind him/her. Mary slowed her pace and fell behind as they continued down the aisle, up the stairs to the platform where a long table was set for the entire family. Victor walked the Queen to her seat and then took his place a few seats away from her. Once Margaret sat in her seat, then everyone in the room except the staff took their seats as well.

166

Speeches, songs, and even dancing filled the night's agenda with ease as Victor quietly surveyed the attendees and staff, hoping that the chef would be there. Unfortunately, his hopes were not fulfilled but something else took hold of his focus. The Parliamentary Speaker was seated at the table at the very front of the banquet hall. Victor waited for a chance to speak with him but an opportunity wouldn't come until nearly the end of the evening. As people began to dance, the alcohol took its effect on the various members of Parliament, celebrities, government staffers, and a few lucky citizens.

Victor made his way to the table with his second glass of champagne. "Good evening, Mr. Speaker," he greeted.

The Speaker looked up and immediately shot to his feet, offering a slight bow. "Your Royal Highness!"

"Are you enjoying yourself?"

"Yes, sir," the Speaker said. "Please allow me to introduce to you my wife, Alise."

Victor smiled and offered his hand to the middle-aged woman with no extraordinary features except beautiful, long red hair and matching red lipstick on her teeth. "Good evening, ma'am."

"Good evening, Your Royal Highness," she muttered, clearly star-struck at the Royal.

Victor turned to the Speaker. "May I have a word with you briefly?"

"Sure," he replied. Then he turned to his wife, "I will be right back."

The two men made their way to the hallway, a good distance from any unwelcome ears. The Speaker then got right to business. "So, what can I do for you?"

"I'm sorry for talking shop at a party but I do have a question about the Queen's amendment request."

The Speaker sighed reluctantly, "Your Royal Highness, you know I cannot divulge anything…"

Victor interjected, "Oh, no! I'm not asking you anyone's opinion or case information. I simply want to know if a date has been set to hear the case in court."

"Well, this is a closed hearing so the date will not and cannot be divulged outside of the Chamber. You understand what I'm saying?"

"Of course," Victor said. He then silently pressed with a frozen but friendly smile and gaze that patiently awaited capitulation.

The Speaker paused for a moment and then spoke, "You should have an answer by early next month."

Victor's eyes shot open. "Next month?"

"Yes, sir."

"Wow, that's fast. That must mean you are already reviewing the case."

The Speaker smiled, "Sir, that's *your* inference."

"I understand, thank you!" Victor replied, and then began to return to the gala.

"Sir, if I may have a question in return," the Speaker quietly called out. Victor turned slowly. "Is the Queen well?"

"You know I cannot speak on the Queen," Victor replied.

"And I cannot divulge case information on closed Parliamentary hearings."

Victor paused and thought for a moment. He figured, *if he could put himself on the line for me, so could I*. He shook his head suggestively and said, "I cannot speak on the Queen."

"Oh," Speaker said, understanding the code in disappointment. "I'm so sorry."

"Sorry for what? I didn't say anything," the prince replied with a half smile. The Speaker bowed deeply, turned and proceeded to the party.

As jovial as the party had become and despite the good news he'd just received, all Victor's downtrodden heart wanted to do was retreat to the palace and sleep. He turned to sneak out of the building but when he began down the hall he noticed a dark figure of a man in front of the backlit doorway. Victor's heart began working overtime as his feet stopped. The figure then began to walk toward him. He prepared to turn and run away but just as he went to retreat, the light from a room along the corridor flashed on the man as he passed it, revealing a familiar face.

Victor immediately calmed down and began toward the door once again. As he passed the man, a hand grabbed his arm and spun him around. "You're not going to even say 'hello'?" Marcus said.

"What are you doing here?" Victor asked, ripping his hand away from Marcus.

"I was invited. You know Iakos is small. There aren't that many famous people." Victor scoffed and turned to walk away. "What is wrong with the Queen?"

Victor froze and pivoted on his heel. "Excuse me?"

Marcus closed the gap between them and repeated himself in a quieter voice. "What is wrong with the Queen?"

"I cannot comment -"

"Oh, come off it, Victor. Everyone in that room saw what happened at the entrance. Just because no one commented on it doesn't mean they didn't see it." Marcus paused and read Victor's eyes, searching for an answer. "She's sick, isn't she?"

"Mr. Frazier, I'd advise you not to speculate about the Queen's health."

"I didn't ask you for your advice," Marcus spat. It seemed like he was prepared for all of Victor's dodges. "And Mr. Frazier? Really? Don't act like we're not, at the very least, friends. Text messages at three in the morning about your loneliness warrants more than a 'Mr. Frazier.'"

"I cannot be seen with you."

"Perfect! There's no one around."

"You know as well as I that there's always someone around."

"I don't know about you, but I know how to be discreet."

Victor chuckled wryly. "You wouldn't know discretion if it slapped you in the face."

"No one knows that we've kissed."

"And they never will." Victor's tone was laced with threat. If he had to give up Vince for this, he was willing to do anything he could to protect it.

"Come on, Victor. Don't act like you don't want to come visit me later. I'm hosting a few friends over."

Before he could stop himself, he practically vomited the words, "I love someone else."

Checkmate! Or at least Victor thought until Marcus replied, "Well, where is he?"

"I-it's a long story."

"Ah, you're not allowed to date him, huh?" Marcus teased. "A real-life Romeo and Julian."

"Shut up. I don't plan on killing myself for anyone," Victor asserted.

Marcus reached down and grabbed Victor's hand, "Good!" Victor pulled his hand away and began to leave. "You know you can talk to me."

Victor could hear Marcus' footsteps close behind him. "I don't want to talk about it."

"I didn't say about that. I meant in general."

"No, I can't. Not now." Victor stepped out into the cold night and climbed into the SUV waiting for him. The chauffeur closed the door and climbed into the front seat.

Marcus stood right outside of Victor's window. "Talk to someone. You're changing," he called out through the thick glass. Victor knew he couldn't see him, but his words pierced him like daggers.

Victor leaned forward, "Go. Please."

Chapter 17

"Get up!" Jack hollered as he dive-bombed into a sea of white hoping to land on Victor, which he did. Victor groaned in pain and irritation at the 145-pound alarm clock now jumping on the bed. He waited until his body recovered and Jack was in midair before he struck back. With one swoop, he knocked Jack's legs from under him and he crashed onto the mattress.

"What?" Victor groaned.

"Grandmother and Ms. Zhang want to see you."

Victor turned over to face Jack. "What about?"

"All I know is the newspaper wrote something about last night. I'm just following orders. It's not like anyone tells me anything around here."

Victor's mind tried to churn but he was way too groggy. "I guess that means I have to get up then."

"I guess so."

Victor peeled the covers back and swung his feet over the edge, then shuffled off into the bathroom with his eyes half-opened. Just missing the doorframe to the bathroom, he walked to the sink. After running the water to let it warm, he splashed water on his face and filled his mouth with mouthwash.

"Hey," Jack appeared in the doorway. "I noticed Marcus Frazier was there last night. Did you see him?"

Victor spat into the sink and then looked up in the mirror. "Yes, unfortunately. Why?"

"You're *not* dating him now, are you?"

Victor's eyes shifted to Jack's reflection. "What? No."

"Jackie said she covered for your date on Valentine's Day last week and you both got into trouble for it."

"So, people *do* tell you things," Victor teased.

Jack smirked but didn't take the redirection. "So? Was it Marcus? Or the chef?"

Victor paused. "It was Vince. You know who it was." He hadn't said his name since the breakup, so it all but knocked the wind out of him.

Jack's smile slowly faded. "Are you ok?" Victor couldn't even muster a head nod but they both knew the answer. "It won't be forever. You know that?"

"Oh yeah? Say I am crowned? How can I marry someone with whom I cannot produce an heir?" Victor spoke softly, his words lined with worry. Jack sat quietly, unable to find any ounce of humor to give Vince some hope. "What if my mother is crowned and she banishes him just to spite me?"

"Stop it! I doubt that that will happen. You will be King and *then*, you'll have the power to change all that."

"Change, what? Royal protocol? Either way, Parliament can stop that from happening."

Jack stood, growing increasingly confused. "How? They have no say over the succession of the Sovereign, especially on basis of sexuality."

"Yes, they do in this case. And they don't have to cite sexuality as a reason, just pick a legal reason."

Jack stood with a puzzled look on his face as Victor walked to his closet and began to get dressed. "I'm genuinely confused," Jack said.

"Clearly," Victor teased. As he finished dressing, he explained the intricacies of the politics that threatened his chances of succeeding his grandmother. Afterward, they made their way down the hall to the Crown Suite chatting along the way.

As they entered, Victor immediately fell silent when he saw his mother and Mo Li standing at the foot of the bed. His head quickly snapped to the bed where Margaret lay talking to them. The two princes bowed and walked over to the bed.

Mo Li curtsied to the princes and smiled, "Good morning, Your Royal Highnesses."

"Good morning," Victor replied to Mo Li. He then turned to the Queen, "How are you feeling this morning?"

"I'm ok. But we have a dilemma."

"What's going on?" Jack replied.

Mo Li opened her tablet and read from a news article. "'Last night's birthday gala for Her Majesty was a tasteful yet eventful celebration. Insiders described the Queen as appearing vibrant and beautiful, however, it was the first time one could see her age in her actions.' The article goes on to describe Her Majesty as 'feeble' and needed support to move around. The public is no longer buying that nothing is wrong, Ma'am."

The room sat quietly for what seemed like an hour. Then, finally, Victor spoke up. "Grandma, before further conspiracy theories begin to swirl, I think we need to put out a statement. Get ahead of the story."

"No," Mary protested. "If we do that, then we risk panic."

Victor immediately snapped back. "This coming from the woman who stood on the tarmac and fanned the flames of this nightmare, forcing all of us into a cover up?"

"You're the one who panicked and practically carried her down the aisle."

"Would you rather her fall? We need to be a little more transparent with the people. We're already secretive enough. Uncertainty is what causes instability, not bad news."

Mo Li saw the conversation spiraling and jumped in, "Your Majesty, I have to agree with the Prince on this one. We need to issue a statement. Further denial will lead to questions of a cover up."

Margaret lay quietly for moments, internally weighing the pros and cons of either decision. Then, she sat up in the bed with the help of Victor and Mo Li. They helped her to the chair near the window. She breathed a deep sigh and spoke carefully. "Mo Li, draft a statement that says the following ..." Mo Li reached over to the foot of the bed and grabbed the tablet that she'd set down to help the Queen, and began to type. "Her Majesty, Queen Margaret I, has been undergoing treatment for a minor health matter."

"A 'minor' health matter?" Victor protested. "There's nothing 'minor' about brain cancer. There aren't minor health issues that cause the kind of symptoms you've been publicly displaying."

Margaret silenced him with a raised hand, and continued, "'Her Majesty's condition is stable and she in good spirits. In advance, the Royal Family thanks you for your prayers and respect of privacy at this time.' That's it. Nothing more, nothing less. Then instruct the Press Secretary to answer any further questioning with he's 'unaware and cannot speculate on the health and private matters of the Sovereign'; after all, he *is* unaware." She let out a nervous chuckle, but all of those around her remained unamused.

173

The room grew quiet as one of her ladies maids entered the room with a tray filled with bottles of medication. She curtsied and stood in the back of the room. Margaret smiled and gestured for her to come over. The young woman placed the tray on the small table next to the Queen and began opening the bottles. Margaret looked up to her family around her, "Now p-p-please give me some p-privacy so I may dress."

They all bowed and left in a single file. Jack flung his hand across Victor's back to comfort him. Victor gasped for air as he tried to calm his anxiety. "What is the matter with you?" Mary barked.

"What?" Victor replied with little air.

Mary marched in front of Victor, stopping him from walking any further. "Why are you hell bent on making the Crown look weak?"

"The Crown isn't weak. But at the moment, the monarch is. The country should prepare for the inevitable and we should prepare the economy, military, and the government for the fluctuations that come with a transference of power. Not hiding the truth and shocking the world," Victor replied.

"Well, hasn't someone been taking private lessons?" Mary replied sarcastically

"As a matter of fact…"

"Well, clearly it was premature. There must be no vulnerability, no weakness. If you don't know that yet, then you are not even close to being ready."

"And yet, I'm more prepared than you. Funny how that works," Victor spat back. Jack grabbed Victor's hand, which was shaking with adrenaline. Jack pulled him past the princess who followed Victor with daggers until he disappeared around the corner.

Mary then reached into her pocket and pulled out her cell phone. She dialed some numbers and put the phone to her ear.

"Hello?" Princess Rose answered.

"It's done."

"You planted the seeds?"

Mary smiled. "Yes, do you think this may be going too far? Should I be doing this to my son?"

"You should be asking yourself, 'Should your son be trying to overthrow his mother?'"

Mary's voice lowered, "I'm not on the throne yet."

"Well, if you want to get there, then do what needs to be done. 'We do what we have to now...'"

"'...So, we do what we want to later.' I know, I know."

"Then we move on to the next phase."

*　*　*　*　*

Jack, Victor, and Jackie laid in the grass all resting on each other on a wool blanket. Seth sat up in the tree that towered above them, but low enough to join in on the conversation.

"Are you ok?" Jackie asked, tapping Victor's leg.

Victor took a deep breath and rolled his head to the side toward her. "Can you guys stop asking me if I'm ok? I'm ok. Worried but ok. "

"Why are you worried? The statement worked." Seth asked, looking down on him.

"That's precisely why I'm worried. The country believed a lie. Now, whoever assumes the throne won't just be inheriting a grieving nation, but a shocked nation."

Jackie turned to meet him. "Well, that's months away."

"I don't think so. The wig might cover the hair loss from the treatment, but it doesn't cover the change in personality. Lately, she's been on a hair trigger, no pun intended..." Victor said. Jack chuckled as Victor continued, "...and it's getting worse."

Jack sat up making his cousins shift involuntarily. "I think you're just in a foul mood because you miss your chef boyfriend."

"Shut up," Victor almost whispered.

"You haven't talked to him?" Jackie asked.

Victor shook his head as he sat up and rested his chin on his knees. "I'm not allowed to."

"Why not?"

"I don't want to 'give Parliament fuel to use against me' in the words of Grandmother."

Seth readjusted on the branch. "At least she's not making you date a woman."

"I wouldn't put it past her at this point."

"How would she know if you just go into the kitchen and say, 'Hi?'" Jackie asked.

"She knows everything," Victor replied, half sarcastic. "Honestly, I don't think Chef Vince would want me to come."

Jackie rolled her eyes at her brother's stubbornness. "And why wouldn't he?"

"He left me a message the night we broke up, saying that he can't just be my friend. That he loves me too much for that."

Victor's phone rang and he retrieved it.

"Who is it?" Jackie asked.

Victor put the phone to his ear. "Hi, Mo Li. Is everything all right?"

"Well, that answers that," Jack said as he rose to his feet.

Victor flinched and pulled the phone from his ear at the loud voice bellowing in the background. "Your Royal Highness, Her Majesty has requested an immediate audience with you and Prince Jack."

"Okay. I'll be there in a few minutes."

He heard the phone disconnect, so Victor allowed his hand to fall.

"What was that about?" Jackie asked.

"Jack and I have been summoned immediately to Grandmother's room."

"What did you do?" Seth called down.

"I have no idea. Jack?"

"Ya got me. I didn't do anything," he shrugged. "But we better get going."

Victor climbed to his feet. Jack took off running, playfully smacking Victor on the back of the head as he passed.

"HEY!" Victor barked and sprinted after him.

They ran across the grounds and into the Palace, through the halls from corridor to corridor, and into the Residential Suite. Victor caught up to him at the grand marble staircase and pummeled him to the ground. They playfully but viciously wrestled for several seconds until a loud voice boomed from the top of the stairs leaving echoes throughout the foyer. "Get up here!"

Victor's head snapped up to find Princess Rose standing at the top of the other staircase with a harsh scowl pinching her face.

"Mother? What are you doing here?" Jack asked. Victor climbed off his cousin and they ran up the stairs. Rose walked off into the Crown suite. Victor and Jack followed.

Once they entered, Victor looked around. Princess Rose joined the Queen who was perched in the armchair next to the window like a throne. On the other side of her stood Princess Mary with a slight smirk on her face but hidden well so that only those who knew her well could find it. Near the tall, antique dresser stood Mo Li who had buried her face behind the tablet in her hands. Victor felt like he was standing in a sauna of tension.

After a few moments, the Queen turned to Mo Li, "Would you excuse us, please?"

"Yes, Ma'am," she replied. She curtsied and all but ran out of the room.

"What is going on?" Victor asked as Jack stepped beside him.

Mary shook her head. "You couldn't leave well enough alone, could you?"

"What are you talking about?" Victor replied, his words lacking any trace of respect.

Mary went to open her mouth, but Margaret's hand shot up and Mary stopped instantly. "The one o'clock news just had a 'breaking news' bulletin," the Queen spoke, as her hands squeezed the armrests so tightly that her knuckles had turned white. "An unnamed source from inside the Palace confirmed that Her Majesty is suffering from brain cancer."

Victor's jaw fell open and Jack gasped in disbelief. "What? How? Who?"

"Do you know anything about that?" Rose asked in a menacing voice.

"What?" Victor barked. "What are you talking about?"

"*You* were the one pushing for transparency," Mary spoke softly, yet articulately.

"I was pushing for honesty," Victor protested. "Not a breach of confidentiality, and definitely not a leak of the Queen's medical records."

"Victor, I have to ask you. I need to know … did you leak this?" the Queen spoke.

Victor felt like yet another house had fallen on him. He turned and pointed at his mother so that it was clear to whom he spoke, "You did this, manipulative bi-" Before Victor could finish the word, Jack threw his hand over Victor's mouth. Rose clutched her literal pearls.

"How dare you use that language in front of Her Majesty?" Mary barked.

"You are in no position to scold anyone," Victor mumbled under Jack's hand. He grabbed onto Jack's hand and wrenched it down a little more forcefully than intended. Now speaking clearly, he added, "I have not and would never leak anything from here, especially something so personal — so sensitive. I'm not you, Mary!"

"Mary? I'm your mother."

"No, you're not. A mother would never accuse her son of something like this," Victor spat.

"Why should we believe you?" Rose asked, calmly.

Mary added, "How do we know it wasn't you?"

"Because *we* didn't want to make a statement in the first place," Rose replied.

"What would I gain from leaking that you have cancer, Grandma?" Victor pleaded.

The Queen leaned forward in her chair. "I am ordering the NIB to launch an investigation into this matter, on the grounds of an 'illegal breach of medical records' and 'mishandling of classified information'. I am also ordering the immediate investigation into the Royal Physician's office. When they find who did this, he or she will be brought to justice. If that person is in this room, then he or she will be removed from the Line of Succession and restricted from a Royal Pardon, which means that the said party may be subject to legal prosecution. Am I clear?"

Victor began to shake. He couldn't even bring himself to speak, so he just slowly nodded his head. He was sure that his mother had framed him in order to have him removed from the Line. He looked up at his grandmother and the strangest thing happened. The Queen's stern face remained; however, she shot him a quick yet definitive wink. Jack squeezed Victor's shoulder, but the princes were smart enough not to react.

Finally, the Queen broke the silence, "You may go!" Victor and Jack gave a deep bow at the neck, turned and left. She then turned to her side, "Mary?"

"Yes, Mother!" She said with a little joy in her tone, but not enough to seem pleased.

Margaret turned to the other side, "Rose..."

"Yes, Ma'am?"

"That goes for you two, too!"

Chapter 18

The kitchen sat still and quiet, except for the sound of water boiling in a pot on the stove. Victor peaked around the corner, studying the room in search for any sign of the person he longed to see. A sound of metal rustling came from the walk-in pantry closet. Victor instinctively jumped back, afraid of being seen. He waited for a few moments and, then, stepped closer to the edge of the doorway. There he was. Vince had brought what looked to Victor like ingredients for dumpling soup. He stood watching Vince cook as time slowed. One after another, the chef threw ingredients into the pot: some salt, celery, cooked steak meat, among others he couldn't make out.

The world seemed to melt away as Victor homed in on the handsome figure as he filled a bowl with flour, spooned in cold water, and began kneading the mixture in the bowl. Suddenly, Victor jumped out of his skin as his pocket began to vibrate and the loud bells began to chime. Seeming louder than usual, his hands scrambled into his pocket and began jabbing the screen with his finger trying to shut it off.

He looked at the text message, which read, "The Queen would like to see you in her office ASAP. —Mo Li." After the last time he'd been summoned, Victor was not looking forward to going to see his grandmother this time. *Just a few more minutes*, Victor procrastinated to himself with a sigh. He then slowly stepped to the edge of the doorway one last time. Forgetting about the loud message tone, he leaned in to peek around the corner. His eyes met Vince's just two feet away and the prince's body froze. Stuck, Victor wanted to retreat and run to him at the same time.

Vince's face seemed puzzled as he stared at the prince. "Is there something I can do for you, Your Royal Highness?"

Victor gasped slightly. "Y-Y-Your Royal Highness?"

"Yes, Prince. H-R-H. You are the Prince, right?" Vince interrogated coldly.

"Yes, but since when-"

"What can I do for you?" Vince interrupted, as he turned and began walking back to the counter.

Victor didn't know what to say. He didn't want anything from Vince but he knew he couldn't just stand there looking stupid. "I just missed you." *Really? You could have made up an excuse or something. That's what you say.*

Vince stopped and turned, burning holes in the prince's eyes. "You miss me?" He asked as if he'd been insulted. "It was *your* decision to break up with me."

"It was. But that doesn't mean I wanted to."

"What does that even mean, Victor?"

"There are politics involved and what not," Victor said with his eyes staring at the floor to avoid the coldness of Vince.

Vince stopped cooking. "Politics, how? Either you want to be with me or not."

"It's not that simple," Victor almost whispered.

"Yes, it is."

"*You* won't be accountable to millions in a few months."

"What?"

Victor froze realizing what he'd just said.

"What does that mean?" Vince repeated.

Victor turned and began to retreat. "Nothing."

"Ohhhh, no you don't," Vince said as he darted after Victor. He reached him just before they met the doorway and he forcefully spun him around. "Talk to me. What is going on?"

The prince shook his head and whispered, "I can't. It is Top Secret. I'm not allowed to speak about the Queen."

"Victor, take off the title for a moment and talk to me," he whispered, his face close enough for Victor to feel his breath on this cheek. "This illness that the Queen has … the reports about Her Majesty are true, aren't they?"

Victor kept his face turned away because he knew that looking him in the eye would make it harder to not kiss him, let alone not say anything. Vince's warm hands held onto his arms tightly so he physically couldn't retreat, so Vince just waited in silence. The prince slowly looked at Vince and nodded his head as slightly as he could.

"Oh, my goodness. Why didn't you say anything?" Vince squeezed him into a hug and pressed his face to his chest. Once again, Victor's eyes began to well up. He didn't want to cry again but the comfort that held him made him feel safe enough to show his underbelly. Vince continued, "You've been keeping this all inside for God knows how long. I'm so sorry."

Victor consciously threw his protective shield up and pushed himself out of his lover's arms. He looked up into his eyes and whispered, "I have to go. I've been summoned to an audience with the Queen."

"Will you come back for dinner?"

"I don't know if that's such a good idea."

Vince recognized that Victor wasn't ready to deal with the truth yet and he didn't want to hurt him by pushing the prince too far. He finally understood the pressure the prince was under, or so he thought. "I know we're not - us - right now, but you know that I'm here for you, right?"

Victor nodded and turned. He began down the hall wiping his face with his hand. He turned back around after a few steps and the chef was watching him walk away. The hall seemed longer than normal as he made his way through the catacombs of lavish corridors to the Crown Office.

When he reached the office door, he noticed that Mo Li wasn't at her desk. *She must be in there with her.* Victor took a deep breath and knocked on the door. After a lifetime, Mo Li opened the door. Parting from the norm, she had a serious look on her face. He stepped into the room and panned for his grandmother who sat at her desk with her reading glasses resting on the tip of her nose. Victor bowed at the neck and then walked over to her.

"Victor, dear. Come sit," she said coldly gesturing to a chair across from her. Victor obeyed, confused by her tone. Mo Li sat next to him. The Queen took off her glasses and placed them on the table. "We have a problem."

"Ok?" Victor replied nervously.

"The National Investigation Bureau has completed their investigation."

"Already?" Victor's blood pressure shot up, as he feared being framed. "I promise it wasn't me."

The Queen threw up her hand to silence him and he obeyed. "I know it wasn't you, my dear. And I'm sorry for not believing you."

"Who was it? The doctor?"

"It was Princess Mary."

"My mother leaked that you have cancer?" Victor knew she had something to do with it, but he didn't think she carried it out herself. "Why would she do that?"

Margaret sighed, "My guess is to frame you."

"That b-" Victor caught himself and covered his own mouth with his own hand, making Mo Li chuckle. "What's going to happen to her?"

"Well, I've decided not to have her convicted and stripped of her title. It's too easy."

Victor looked at Mo Li and then back at this grandmother, "I'm confused. What's wrong with that? She did it to herself."

The Queen looked at Mo Li with a smirk Victor rarely saw on her face. "Yes, but I have another idea."

"Ok, let's hear it."

Mo Li sat up in her chair, "We leak that she's the leaker."

Victor's face twisted in confusion. "What? Why would you do that?"

"Then Parliament will decide that she cannot be trusted. It will make her look bad to the whole country."

"But, Grandmother, that would confirm that you do have it."

"Well, then you get your transparency," she said with a wink.

Victor smirked back at Margaret. "I've never seen this side of you, Grandma."

"Honey, that's a good thing. Now go on."

March

<u>Chapter 19</u>

"Ouch! I'm going to hurt you," Seth barked while rubbing his forehead.

Jackie cackled at the top of her lungs. "That's what you get for cracking my screen."

"Well, you cracked *my* phone."

"No, you threw it at me."

Seth growled, "Because you laughed at me."

"It's not my fault that I graduated university with a 4.0 and you barely are passing with a 2.4."

"Shut up!" He barked again, throwing his pencil at her. "Math sucks. Now give it back."

Jackie just laughed and continued to fix her hair into a ponytail in the mirror.

"I said, 'give it back' fatso."

Jackie's head snapped to him. "Hey, I'm not fat, dummy."

Victor entered the drawing room just as Jackie charged Seth and tackled him out of the chair. They landed with a thud and she began pummeling him with punches and kicks. He returned fire with martial arts holds trying to subdue her.

"Um, Seth," Victor laughed. "You do realize that she knows all those moves too."

"Plus, I'm stronger," Jackie said, struggling to pin him to the floor.

"Never!" Seth's muffled war cry had Victor laughing hysterically on the floor.

"Why are you two fighting anyway?"

"Because he's failing math."

"Shut up, I'm not failing."

Finally, Jackie had him pinned to the floor with his arms crossed behind his head. "See? Stronger."

Victor just laughed and began slowly backing out of the room. "Where are you going?" Jackie called out to him.

"Just going to get something to eat."

"Great, I'll come with." Jackie released Seth from her hold and climbed to her feet. She fixed herself and then began marching off behind Victor in a spandex workout outfit.

Seth lay on the floor rubbing his shoulders, trying to catch his breath. He held up his pencil, triumphantly, "I still got it back."

She turned to take it from him, but Victor grabbed her by the waist and spun her around. "Let go, crazy." As he left the room, he turned and called out to Seth, "When I get back, I'll check your work. Deal?"

"Thanks," he said through labored breathing.

Victor and Jackie made their way throughout the palace. The closer Victor got to the kitchen, the more his heart began to race. Jackie turned around and studied his face while she power walked backwards.

"Jacqueline, what are you doing?" Victor asked teasingly.

"I wanted to go for a run, but since I'm walking with you, I might as well burn some calories now. What?"

"You look like a '70s soccer mom. All you need is a pair of pink leggings."

Jackie snarled at him and turned her head away from him and kept her stride consistent. Victor began copying her while humming Eye of the Tiger. One quick attempted elbow shot to the rib and Victor stopped his mocking, but he continued to laugh. She continued ahead of him down the corridor while he took his time to prepare to see Chef Vincent. He looked at himself as he passed a mirror hanging on the wall just to make sure everything was in its place. Precious seconds passed, as this walk seemed longer than normal. By the time he made it to the kitchen, Jackie was leaning over the counter with a flirtatious smile on her face and Vince was laughing. *Uh oh! What did she say?* Another cook was in the room so he figured it couldn't have been so bad.

He took a deep breath and walked up to the counter. "Hi."

"Good morning, Your Royal Highness," Vince replied, side eyeing the other cook in the room as if to explain why the formal address. "What can I get you?"

"I just wanted to get some breakfast."

"You know, sir, we usually bring it up to the breakfast room in the morning. You don't need to come all the way down here for it," the other young chef said.

Victor stammered to reply. Just then, Jackie jumped in, "Yes, but I needed to burn off some calories so I figured I'd come down."

"Yes, and I came with her," Victor added.

Vince chuckled. "If you burn any more off, you will have nothing left."

"Hey, it's hard work to look this good and *keep* it," Jackie replied.

"Fair enough." Vince turned to the other gentleman. "Can you go and get me some bacon out of the freezer?"

"Sure," he replied and disappeared into the freezer.

"Okay, quick! Kiss him," Jackie whispered with excitement. Victor's face turned red, as he fought the urge to comply.

"Stop it," Vince said softly. He quickly changed the subject to ease Victor's instant tension. "So, I hear your birthday is coming up at the end of the month." Victor nodded looking down at his shoes. "Would it be totally inappropriate if I got you a present?"

"No, you don't have to get me anything. I'd understand," Victor bashfully replied.

Vince reached over the counter and lifted Victor's chin with his finger so their eyes would meet. "But I want to…"

Victor's phone chirped pulling him out of the gaze. He didn't want to look away, but since his mother's identity as the leaker was made public, the Queen had been running him ragged with political meetings, events, and damage control. He retrieved his phone and looked at the screen. It was a text message from the Parliamentary Speaker. He unlocked the phone with his fingerprint and read the message. *Meet me at Front Street pier in 15.*

He looked up at Vince. "Looks like I'll have to eat your breakfast when I get back."

"I bet you *will* eat his breakfast," Jackie teased.

"Ok, you've been spending way too much time with Jack," Victor threatened to Jackie with a smile. "Behave!"

"Never," she replied plainly.

Victor looked Chef Vincent in the eye, "I'll be back."

"Hurry."

Victor turned and took off out of the room. He jogged down the corridor to the private entrance of the palace. Once there, he climbed in the back seat of the black armored SUV. "Front Street pier please," Victor said to the driver.

"I know, Your Royal Highness. I've been waiting for you," the driver replied as he accelerated more forcefully than normal.

"You've been waiting for me? What do you mean by that?" Victor asked as he scrambled for his seatbelt.

"I got a call from Her Majesty's Private Secretary. She told me to pick you up and bring you to a secure meeting at Front Street pier."

Victor sat piecing together the puzzle. He pulled out his phone and dialed Mo Li. After a few rings, her voice chimed from the phone. "Hello, sir. Are you in the car?"

"Yes."

"Good. Her Majesty couldn't attend the meeting so she sent for you to go."

"Why can't the meeting happen at the palace?"

"After the leaks, the Speaker felt that it would be too suspicious to go to the palace. He felt that it would 'raise too many brows'. So, we must operate with a little cloak and dagger, if that's all right with you."

Victor sighed wryly. "It doesn't sound like I have a choice."

"Good. Once you meet, come directly back to the Crown Office for a debriefing."

Victor snickered to himself at the inappropriate joke that Jack would have made at that statement. *Maybe I've spent too much time with him, as well.* "Will do. Talk to you soon." Victor hung up the phone and flopped his head back on the headrest. He watched the hustle and bustle of city life pass by the window, block after block. Real people, living real lives. Victor's fascination with his future people grew with every event he attended. Finally, it hit him. This meeting would determine his immediate fate, his relationship with his mother, his relationship with Vincent, and the nation's history for decades to come. A large knot in his throat built up with every street they passed. They stopped at red lights and stop signs to avoid drawing attention to themselves. After about 12 minutes, Victor could smell the sea and felt the chill of the coast on his face through the slightly cracked window.

The black SUV turned down the main coastal road, drove for about another minute, then turned right down a service road that went under Parados' Main Port. The cruise ship in the distance had an endless line of tourists, workers, and returning vacationers. They turned slowly into a small tunnel under the dock. After quietly coasting for a few meters, Victor could see a small black limousine idling up ahead. They pulled up alongside the car and stopped. For a few seconds, nothing happened. Victor looked around, but his confusion ended with the click of the door to the small car. Speaker Michaels climbed out of the town car and knocked on the window. Victor leaned over the back seat and unlatched the door.

"Good morning, Your Royal Highness," he said, climbing into the SUV. He closed the door before continuing. "Sorry for all of this inconvenience. I know that you are very busy these days."

"Yes, sir. Is this about the Reque-"

The Speaker shushed him quickly and leaned up to the driver and bodyguard in the front seats. "Hey Gentlemen, do you need a smoke break?"

The men turned to him and read his request on his face. They shifted their eyes to the prince for permission and Victor nodded affirmatively. They exited the vehicle in unison and walked a few paces ahead of the truck. The men never turned their backs to the SUV so they could maintain a line of sight to the prince.

"Okay," the Speaker began. "There were vigorous debates on this dilemma. Considering the importance of the law and the recent circumstances we find ourselves facing regarding Her Royal Highness the Duchess of Spiti, Parliament has decided to *not* change the law." Victor gasped, as his mind kicked into overdrive. He tried dissecting and digesting this information but the words

189

weren't connecting and the Speaker could tell. "This means that Parliament has formally decided that the Queen has legal grounds to pass over Mary as monarch because she broke the law in her elopement, knowingly or not. The only way she can justifiably give her the throne is annulment or to grant her a pardon."

Victor sat back in his seat. His physical eyes were fixed on the Speaker, but his mind's eye witnessed the thoughts racing at lightning speed. "So, the choices for the Queen are 'throne or banishment'?"

"Two extremes … I know."

"I don't necessarily like my mother these days, but I don't want her banished."

"But you don't want her on the throne…"

Victor scoffed, "I don't think anyone wants her on the throne."

Speaker Michaels chuckled. "The only way she could stay in the country is if the Queen passes her over and then *you* grant her the pardon."

* * * * *

"Grandmother, please say something."

The Queen sat in silence, trying to wrap her mind around the news that Victor just shared with her. After a few minutes, she finally spoke, "D-d-did he say a-anything else?"

"That the only way she could be denounced and remain a citizen is for me to grant her a pardon once I'm crowned."

"Interesting," she replied quietly. Her face gave away nothing, a characteristic that one would think Victor would be used to by now, but wasn't.

"So, what are you going to do?"

Margaret sat back in her chair behind the desk and took a deep breath, "I can honestly say that I don't know. I must give this some more thought."

"Okay," Victor replied, capitulating. He stood up and backed toward the door, making sure not to turn his back to the Sovereign. After he reached the door, he turned to Mo Li. "I have one request for my birthday dinner."

190

"Come," she said, advancing towards the door. "I wanted to talk to you about the arrangements anyway."

The two bowed and curtsied respectively and stepped out. They made their way along the corridor. Victor knew he was going to the kitchen, but he didn't want Ms. Zhang to know. So he detoured every once in a while, as they chatted about the menu, the decor, and finally the guest list. "There's one person who I'd rather didn't come."

"Who? Your mother?"

Victor chuckled and replied, "No, that would be petty. I was thinking Marcus Frazier."

"Really? Why? I thought you two were friends."

"It's more like he wants to be more than friends."

"Oh?"

"That stays between us," Victor said quietly but with more authority than he'd intended.

"Okay! I understand. Calm down."

"Sorry, I just don't want Grandmother to have any reason to doubt me right now."

Mo Li pulled him into a hug. "No need to apologize. You are under an unbelievable and unhealthy amount of stress."

"Don't I know it."

Mo Li chuckled. "He will be turned away if he tries to come."

"Do you think that she would grant Mother the pardon?"

Mo Li shook her head and her hands followed. "No, no. That's not my place to speculate."

"I'm asking you as one of the few people who really knows Her Majesty. What do you think?"

Mo Li stopped and slipped into deep thought for several moments. Once she gathered her thoughts, she replied the best way she could. "I think that this will be one of the most difficult decisions of her life and one of her last. I think us focusing on preparing you in the meantime and making her life easier right now is the more important point of focus. She can spot bullshit a mile away so don't stress her about it. Let her figure things out."

Victor sighed, frustrated. *What am I supposed to do with that?* He thought to himself. "How long do you think she'll take?"

"Like I said, she will make the decision when she's ready. You focus on deputizing for her," Mo Li advised, but to Victor, it almost sounded like a warning. She continued nudging his shoulder, "And helping me plan your birthday dinner. We have 3 weeks left."

Victor tried to focus on his birthday dinner but all he could think about was how much his grandmother must be going through.

"Get out of your head, sir," Mo Li teased, attempting to lighten Victor's mood. "Guest list."

Chapter 20

"Are you guys ready?" Margie walked into Victor's room to find Jack jumping on Victor's bed with a groaning birthday boy under the covers. "Jack, what are you doing? You're going to be late."

Jack stopped jumping just long enough to respond. "Late? The party is literally downstairs in the main dining room."

"It's — not — a — party," Victor exclaimed from under the covers. A gray cloud seemed to increasingly hover over his head with every day that passed without hearing what the Queen's decision will be.

Jack turned around to see his sister dressed in a simple royal blue gown and silver jewelry. "Wow, you actually look like a girl."

"Wow, you actually look human."

"I look hot," Jack replied, resuming his jumping as he adjusting his tux jacket pridefully.

"That's not what your girlfriend said."

"I believe 'big' was the adjective you were looking for?" Jack replied.

Victor grimaced and climbed out from under the covers. "Ok, eww!"

"Victor!" Someone yelled from the entranceway startling everyone in the room.

"Damn, Jackie. What?" Victor replied.

"Why were you in bed with your tux on? Now it's all wrinkled."

Margie turned around to Jackie. "And *that* was worth bellowing in my ear?"

"Yes, yes it was."

Victor disappeared into the bathroom, while the two cousins continued to argue. The sound of the shower turning on silenced the bickering and all three ran to the door.

Jack shoved the door open. "What are you doing? We must go now. You don't have time to take another half an hour shower."

"I'm just letting the steam get some of the wrinkles out before we go."

"Oh," Jack replied. "Oops."

After a brief awkward silence, Victor looked at his cousins and sister standing in an open door and barked, "Will you close the door? You're letting out the steam."

"Sorry," they all said as they retreated and closed the door.

Margie looked at Jackie. "Does he seem depressed to you?"

"I'm — not — depressed!" Victor called out from the bathroom.

"Shut up and de-wrinkle," Jackie bellowed back through the door, making her two cousins wince. Then she continued in a normal voice, "Yes."

"He is not depressed. He's just stressed."

Jackie and Margie both stopped and looked at Jack with a dumbfounded look and then continued their conversation to each other. "He's dealing with a lot right now — a lot of pressure."

"Yeah, that would be an understatement. He's stronger than I am because I would have said never mind by now."

"How is your mom dealing?"

"She's been talking to your mom way more than before," Jackie replied.

"I noticed that too. They rarely fight anymore."

"I don't know if that's a good thing or a bad thing and I really don't want to find out."

Jack spoke softly so Victor couldn't hear, "What can we do to help him?"

"I don't know," Margie replied. "I guess we try and make sure that Victor actually has fun tonight. Like, a really good time."

"No shop talk."

"Agreed."

The shower turned off and about a minute later, Victor emerged 50% less wrinkled. "Let's go."

The four left the room and made their way down the hall, down the Residential Foyer stairs and throughout the palace. About halfway through the palace, Seth filed into formation with Victor leading. They could hear the voices of the guests grow louder as they approached the Main Dining Room. It was half the size of the State Dining Room, but about four times larger than the Private Dining Room. They turned the corner and stopped as the announcer presented them.

The doors opened to the dining room and the guests burst into applause. About 50 people were in attendance, a relatively small size for a celebration at the palace. *Vince must have enjoyed the easy workload for this event rather than a 250-guest state dinner,* Victor thought to himself.

They filed in and took their places seated next to each other. Victor painted his diplomatic smile on his face as he stood and greeted his guests. "Thank you so much for coming tonight to celebrate my birthday. This past year has been the most trying but the most wonderful. I've learned so much, met many new faces - some of whom are here tonight - and finally came out of my shell and into the world." Victor's eyes scanned the room as he spoke. The table was surrounded by some of the people he'd gotten to know since he began his public work: famous entertainers, diplomats, influential people in the community, etc.

He continued, "This birthday is very special for more reasons than you'll ever know but what I will say is that 24 feels very different. I'm in a very different place in my life and I like it." The guests chuckled. "Every person here helped get me to this mark over the past year, all but one. Her Majesty couldn't join us this evening, but I still want to say, Thank You, to all of you. So, enjoy, eat, and have fun."

As Victor sat, his eyes locked on a face he didn't expect nor want to see down near the other end of the table. *How did he get in here?* Part of him wanted to kick him out but then again, he didn't want to make a scene. He leaned over to Jack who sat on his right, "Is that Marcus Frazier?"

Jack's head snapped to his right until his eyes found the unwanted guest. After confirming his suspicions, he turned back to Victor and placed a hand on Victor's clenched fist. "Are you ok?"

195

Victor once again smiled the deceiving smile, "Yup. I'm fine."

Jack leaned in close to Victor, "Do you want me to call security?"

Victor thought for a moment. To be honest, he liked the idea but he decided to leave it be for now. "I'll just have a conversation with Ms. Zhang tomorrow." Jack smirked at the thought of Victor ripping into people. It rarely happened but when it did, it tended to be brutal.

The servers entered with platters of appetizers and Victor actively ignored Marcus' presence. The evening continued without a glitch. The conversation was pleasant, the music was mellow, and the food delicious. Throughout the night, the random thought of Vince preparing the very food he was eating pulled at his heart, but he just continued to force himself to enjoy his evening.

About halfway through the dinner, Jack stood up and kicked off the gift-giving portion of the evening. It wasn't required but the guests seemed to bring them anyway. As tradition said, they piled them neatly in the corner of the room to be opened by the prince later. The only ones announced were from the Royal Family. Jack went first, presenting Victor with the newest diamond Cartier watch. Jackie and Margie gave him a collection of new suits. Seth decided to give Victor the latest iPad.

Finally, Victor stood once again at the head of the table. "I know it's not tradition but I wanted to give a few gifts in honor of my birthday." The guests looked around at each other, confused. The servers entered with white gift bags and placed them in front of each person at the table. "Inside, you will find a VISA gift card, €50 gift cards to various local venues such as restaurants, events, and museums, a small gold plated plaque with my crest on it and your name, and a pair of earphones with Her Majesty's crest engraved on the sides, among other goodies." The guests all went digging into the bags, excited, showing each other their gifts.

Finally, I have one more gift. One of the servers gave him an envelope. He opened it and turned the certificate around. "In honor of my 24th birthday, I hereby gift €24,000 to the Parados High School of Performing Arts." Everyone in the room gasped, including his family members, and jumped to their feet in applause.

The rest of the evening was filled with dancing, conversation, and avoiding Marcus, or so he thought. As the guests began leaving, Victor decided to turn in and snuck down the hallway. He rubbed his cheeks that ached from smiling the whole night. He turned a corner and on a bench sat Marcus. He stood and blocked Victor from walking past. "Four hours and you couldn't even say, 'Hello?'"

"How did you even get in? You weren't invited."

"Yes, I noticed. Thanks for that. I came as a plus one for my best friend."

Victor shook his head. "I'll remember to alert security too, next time."

"Really? What did I do wrong?"

"Why are you here, Marcus?"

"I told you, I miss you."

Victor sighed and took a small step back.

"And I know you miss me too," Marcus said, grabbing Victor's hand. "You may have been able to fool all of those people in there, but I know you. You need a friend."

Victor snatched his hand away, "I have a room full of friends, thank you!"

"Come on! They are not your friends."

"You c'mon! You and I both know you want to be more than friends," Victor growled quietly so his voice wouldn't echo.

"What's wrong with that?"

"I'm in love with someone else, Marcus."

The singer stopped and his jaw hit the floor. He wasn't expecting that response from Victor. "Who? That cook?"

Victor rolled his eyes and walked past him. Marcus grabbed him by the arm and spun him around. "Get off," Victor warned.

Marcus pulled his arm, grabbed the prince by the back of the head and tried to kiss him. Without thinking, Victor struck him in the chest with his palm-heel, and then added an elbow strike to the face. Still in a fighting stance, Victor watched Marcus stumble back, trip over his feet, and fall to the floor. With perfect timing, Jack came running down the hall.

"What the hell just happened?"

197

Victor stood up straight and covered his mouth in shock. Marcus held his face and gasped for air. "Oh, my gosh!"

"Victor, talk!"

"I don't know what happened. He tried to kiss me and -"

"And what? You decide to use him as a sparring partner? Did he hurt you?"

Victor shook his head, ashamed.

Jack knelt to Marcus, checking him out. Marcus' breath was coming easier, so there was no damage to his ribs. "Are you okay?"

"Yeah. I'm sorry, Victor."

Jack's face contorted, confused. "*You're* sorry?"

"Yes," Marcus spoke through labored breathing. "I caught him off guard and got a little too rough."

Jack didn't know with whom to be upset. "Marcus, I think you'd better go."

Marcus nodded, struggled to his feet still holding his chest. "I'm sorry, Victor. Happy Birthday!" With that, he headed back down the hall.

"Victor, I know you're going through a lot but you can't go around attacking people."

"It was a reflex."

"A reflex? To a kiss?"

"I'm sorry. Ok? I don't know what else you want me to say," Victor yelled. He turned and marched down the hall to his room.

Jack pulled out his phone and dialed Margie's number.

"Hello?"

"It's worse than we thought."

* * * * *

Margaret flipped through the channels studying the news headlines of the day. US President Taylor says something else crazy, European elections fear foreign interference: same old stuff, different day. A knock on the door pulled her out of TV land. "You may enter."

"Your Majesty," Mo Li said. "Sorry for the interruption. The Duke of Spiti is here."

"Thank you. Let him in." Margaret sat up in her bed and adjusted herself to be more presentable.

The Duke entered, walked over to the bed, and bowed at the neck. "You summoned me, Your Majesty."

"Hello, dear. Yes, I d-did." She gestured to a chair on the other side of the room. "Pull up a chair. I would like to talk with you."

He obeyed and retrieved the chair. He sat down and folded his hands in his lap.

"The last time w-we spoke like this was just after the w-wedding."

"Yes, ma'am."

Margaret smiled at him to put him at ease. "This conversation should be a lot more pleasant."

He let off a stoic chuckle but his nervousness remained.

"I-I-I'm sure my daughter knows that you're here."

"Yes."

"And did she try to warn you? Prepare you?"

Christopher nodded his head slowly.

"I promise, there is nothing to fear," she reassured him. She spoke slowly to avoid stumbling. "When one's Earthly life will soon come to an end, one finds solace in finally saying the things they've kept hidden for years. You and I have not had many conversations together. Our relationship has been infected with politics and family drama that came before you. So, I'd like to talk to you, and only you, if that's ok?"

Christopher sat with a puzzled expression on his face. "Sure. What would you like to talk about?"

"Well, first," she began, "I wanted to say, 'Thank you.'"

"Thank you?"

"Yes, thank you. I'm not sure how much you know about the man who previously held your title, but when he left, my daughter had a rough time. It was a dark season for her and you have brought joy back into her life. Though I didn't approve of the marriage, I've watched you stay firm in your position as a duke and a husband during this trying time. It would be easy for one to run from the responsibilities of being a member of this family. In fact, others before you have, but not you. You're sticking beside her and that reassures me that I don't have to worry about her when I'm gone."

Christopher hadn't realized that he'd begun to blush. He was pleasantly taken aback by her words but still listened to her take her time.

The Queen continued, "Now, the next few months are going to be even harder on your marriage than before, if you can believe it. I have a tremendously difficult, historic, and seemingly impossible decision to make. Whichever outcome I choose, it will affect our country, this family, and your marriage greatly. It *will* change the dynamics and circumstances of your marriage. I don't say this to scare you, I say this because I need to know that you will remain supportive and steady for my daughter, whether a Queen or a Duchess."

"Yes, ma'am," he replied. "I love your daughter for who she is and I'm not going anywhere."

Margaret smiled at him and reached out a hand. The Duke took it and held it as she rested it on the side of her bed. "I, also, need you to do something else for me."

"Anything, Your Majesty."

"I need you to…" Margaret stopped with her mouth open and her eyes fixed forward. Christopher followed her gaze but found a television turned off. He looked back at her but could only see the whites of her eyes.

"Your Majesty?" He shook her hand but she didn't respond. Suddenly, Margaret's body began convulsing and thrashing violently from head to toe. Christopher sprang into action, picking the flailing Queen up from the bed and placing her on the floor in front of him. He rolled her to her side and held her head. Then he called out as loudly as he could. "HELP! SOMEONE!"

One of the ladies-maids came running in. "Sir, is everything…" She gasped at the sight, clutching her pearls.

"DON'T JUST STAND THERE. GET THE DOCTOR! NOW!!!"

April

<u>Chapter 21</u>

The low hiss of the nasal cannula and the deep hum of the attached tank sang a lullaby to Victor as he rested his head on the side of his grandmother's bed. Since the Queen was finally resting, he could try and rest too, until the next vital check from the nurse. He just didn't expect it to come so quickly. In walked the young African-Iakon nurse from Dr. Ryan's practice.

"Already? She just got to sleep," Victor pleaded.

"I'm sorry. I'll try not to wake Her Majesty." She gently lifted Margaret's arm and wrapped the blood pressure cuff around it. Victor laid his forehead back down on the bed, praying that his grandmother would not wake up. But, of course, his prayers were in vain. She slowly fidgeted, wincing under the pressure of the cuff. "I'm sorry, Your Majesty," the nurse whispered. "I'm almost finished." The automated monitor released the air slowly and then numbers lit up next to the monitor hanging above her bed.

"Ah, Nurse Stacy," the Queen mumbled, still half-asleep. "Are you pleased with your room here?"

Stacy whispered, "Yes, ma'am. Everything at the palace is beautiful. Thank you."

"Did that boy finally ask you out yet?"

Victor's head shot up and his face erupted in heat. "Grandmother, leave the woman alone."

"It's fine," Stacey smirked. "It's perfectly fine. And no, he didn't."

"Shameful. Just shameful! I could have him arrested if you want."

Her smirk grew to a full-blown chuckle. "That won't be necessary, but I appreciate the backup."

"We, women, have to stick together. Can't let the men run everything, now can we?"

"I hear that," Stacey practically gushed, although her face never seemed to show much emotion unless one was looking closely. She simply wore a pleasant and reassuring smile. She continued writing down the information onto a clipboard, took Margaret's temperature, and then turned to leave. "The doctor will be here within the hour to talk to you."

"Thank you, dear."

The nurse curtsied and began to walk out. She then stopped for a moment, "Oh, and your daughter is here."

"Which one?" Victor asked before Margaret could open her mouth.

"Princess Rose."

"Oh."

She then turned and just as she opened the door, Rose came rushing in the room. "Mother, are you ok? I'm sorry that I was out of town."

"It's all right, it's all right. I know, fashion week. Calm down."

"Victor."

"Aunt Rose."

"What is the doctor saying?"

"No changes so far."

"Ok? What caused the seizure?"

"The tumor in her brain."

"No shit, smart ass. You want to try answering me like you are intelligent this time?"

Margaret pointed her finger at Rose, "L-l-language."

"The doctor said it might have grown even larger. He comes today with the scans to give us the full picture and a new prognosis. Is that intelligent enough for you?"

"See, was that so hard?"

Victor fought the urge to flip her the middle finger with everything in him. "Is Jack and Margie here?"

"*Are* they here?" She corrected him. "Yes, they are."

Margaret adjusted herself on the bed. "Rose, stop it," she demanded through her teeth.

Victor stood up kissed his grandmother on the forehead. "I'll be right back."

"Victor, I want you here when the doctors come," Margaret said.

"I'm just going out into the hall." With that, he left to find his cousins.

As he entered the lounge area across the hall within the Crown Suite, two uncharacteristically concerned faces met him. They both ran up to him and started rattling off a long list of questions. Victor threw up his hands to stop them. "Slow down, please."

Jack started, "How is she?"

"She's as well as to be expected," Victor replied.

Margie chimed in. "Do they know what caused it?"

"They assume the tumor. The doctor will be here shortly."

"What do we know?"

"There was no damage from the seizure, but it's a sign that things are getting worse." Margie's head sagged as she began to sob. Victor and Jack both rubbed her back and tried to console her. "You knew this was going to happen sooner or later," Victor said.

Margie sucked in a hyperventilated breath. "Yes, but I didn't expect it to happen so soon. I guess I hoped for a miracle. Maybe she'd get better."

"I know," Victor replied, resting his head on her shoulder. He pulled her into a tight hug. "I did too."

The three royal cousins stood hugging each other for a few moments until Dr. Ryan, Dr. Bennett, and Nurse Stacy came around the corner. The three bowed to the princes and princess and entered the Queen's bedroom. Victor, Jack, and Margie followed.

Dr. Bennett spoke first, "Good morning, Your Majesty, Your Royal Highnesses. How are you feeling this morning?"

Margaret propped herself up on the bed and painted a smile on her face as best she could. "I'm feeling just fine, thank you."

"Mother, you are not feeling fine. You just said that your head was hurting and your legs felt weak," Rose interjected.

"My head always hurts and my legs always feel weak. So, hush."

Rose bent down and whispered into her ear, "I know you want to feel better — to get better for that matter — but pretending you are better to get the doctors to *think* you are isn't going to change anything. They need to know so they can treat you."

Margaret lifted her daughter's head with both hands affectionately, "It's rude to whisper." She turned to the doctor. "Tell us about this seizure, doctor?"

"Unfortunately, it's common with this kind of tumor. We can treat the symptoms but things will only get worse."

Rose turned to her mother and placed a hand on her shoulder to try and comfort her. "Well, at least we have a few more months with you."

"Actually, Your Royal Highness, that isn't accurate anymore," Dr. Ryan interjected.

"What do you mean?" Margie asked.

"Well, we didn't expect things to progress as quickly as they have."

The room fell silent as the Royal Family's minds raced trying to digest what was being said, or not said. Jack finally stepped up and asked what no one had the heart to ask. "How long does Her Majesty have?"

"I'd predict another month or so, but I doubt Your Majesty will make it to your 80th birthday."

Victor's vision became blurry as his mind raced. He wanted to run over and hug his grandmother, but also run out of the room and hide. His face felt cold. When he touched his cheek, he realized that it was wet. Jack stepped over and hugged him tightly before he could resist. Margie and Rose climbed up on either side of the bed and hugged the Queen. Shocked by the emotion erupting in the room by people who rarely showed it, the physicians bowed and left the room and Nurse Stacy sat in the chair in the corner with her eyes glued to the floor. The family openly grieved in a way that the world had never seen.

After what seemed like half an hour, the wailing had stopped and the hyperventilation had calmed, they all sat and stood very still. The occasional sniffle kept them grounded in reality, though no one was present in that room.

Nurse Stacy stood up and quietly stepped over to the bed. "Your Majesty, it's time to check your vitals."

Rose climbed off the bed and walked out of the room. The Queen grabbed the nurse's hand as she tried to put on the blood pressure cuff. "What about the Easter service this month?"

"I'm sorry, ma'am."

* * * * *

Victor's eyes opened to a loud beeping sound. He looked out of the window to check the time. The sun was still high but the horns honking and busses hissing sang the song of evening rush hour. He stood and walked to the IV drip that towered next to the head of the bed. A red light glowed above the picture of a battery. Victor grabbed the plug that was hanging on a hook attached to the back of the machine and plugged it into an outlet just behind the bed. He then returned to his comfy chair, sitting on his feet this time.

He heard a barely audible knock on the door.
"Come in," he whispered loud enough that it almost couldn't be a whisper.

The door creaked open and in walked Chef Vincent with a tray. "Hello, Your Royal Highness. I have Her Majesty's dinner."

A cold chill rushed down Victor's spine. Normally, that duty was carried out by a footman, but clearly the chef volunteered for a reason. "Hi. You can set it down on the table over there. I'll give it to her when she wakes."

Vince obeyed and quietly placed the tray on the side table next to her bed. He looked at the IV, the oxygen tank, and then stared at Victor.

Victor began to shrink under the man's gaze. "What?"

"How are you dealing?"

"I'm fine. We're all fine."

Vince shot him a look as if to say, *Don't lie to me?* "Is that why your eyes are red and puffy?"

Victor stood up and walked around the bed. He walked by Vince, grabbing him by the arm as he passed, and dragged him out of the room.

The nurse was sitting in a chair reading. "Nurse Stacy, would you mind sitting with the Queen for a moment?"

"Is she awake?"

"No, but if you could just sit with her..." He raised his eyebrows and gestured to the door with his eyes. She smiled and entered the bedroom, closing the door behind her. Victor sat in the chair where she sat.

"Whoa."

"Whoa what?" Victor asked.

"I've never seen that side of you."

"What side?"

"The authoritative side."

"Well, you better get used to it."

Vince stopped the witty repartee and stared at Victor. "What does that mean?" Victor didn't respond nor look at him. Vince squatted down in front of Victor and grabbed him by the hands gently. "Talk to me. What's going on?"

The prince turned his head and locked eyes with Vince. "Aren't you tired of asking me that?"

"Never."

"Well, I can't tell you."

"Why not? Is Her Majesty dying?"

Victor just stared at him, trying hard not to give him too much information. Chef Vince rose to his feet and turned away from Victor. The prince watched him and the thought of him leaving made his stomach plummet to the floor. But then, something he didn't expect to happen, happened. Vince sat in the chair on the other side of the coffee table and pulled out his phone. "Yes, I'm going to be up here for a while so you can finish dinner for the rest of the family. Thanks." Vince hung up the phone and turned to Victor. "I'll wait here all night if I have to. I'm not going anywhere. Talk."

Inside, Victor was cheesing from ear to ear, but on the outside, he could only muster a smirk. *You'll be sitting there for a while.*

Chapter 22

The sound of American crime dramas filled the room as Victor and Margaret slept. The day was a bit rough with the headaches and aphasia getting the best of the Queen. If Chef Vince hadn't been coming up to visit every day, everything would be getting the best of Victor too. A low hum came from the pocket of Victor's pajama trousers as the vibration tickled his leg. Without opening his eyes, he reached into his pocket, retrieved the phone, tapped the screen with his thumb, and put it to his ear.

"Hello?"

"Prince Victor?"

"Yes?"

"It's Mo Li."

"What's wrong?"

"Are you near a television?"

"Yes, though I was kind of asleep."

"Well, then wake up," she barked. "Turn on the television and switch to ICNN now."

Victor sighed in frustration. "You know, I'm beginning to dislike seeing your number on my caller ID."

"Trust me. I'm tired of having to call you with situations like this."

Victor chuckled, "Well you better get used to it. I may be king one day."

"You'd better turn on ICNN before you say that..."

He defiantly grabbed the remote from the windowsill and channeled up until he reached ICNN. The screen read:

"BREAKING NEWS: PRINCE VICTOR MAY BECOME FIRST LGBTQ+ IAKON MONARCH".

Victor gasped in shock.

"I told you that you'd want to see it," Mo Li sang with panic in her voice.

"What the hell is this?" he said. He tried to read the subtitles because he didn't want to turn up the TV and disturb the Queen, though he hadn't realized that his voice and choice of language had already awakened her.

"V-v-volume!" She tried to yell.

Startled by the Queen, Victor's fingers couldn't turn up the volume fast enough. The middle-aged woman with a short haircut and what appeared to be a pants suit spoke quickly but deliberately. "Our sources say that the prince is quote 'openly gay but private about his life'. The same source has cited two separate relationships in which Prince Victor has been involved within the last year: one of which with the State Palace head chef, Nathan Vincent Grant, and another with Iakos pop star, Marcus Frazier. Now, Frazier has been suggestive about the fluidity of his sexuality for years but this is the first time we have confirmation…"

Victor dropped the remote, along with his jaw.

"WHAT?" The Queen bellowed over top of the television. "YOU DAMN JACKASS! YOU COULDN'T KEEP IT IN YOUR PANTS, COULD YOU? YOU HAD TO GO SCREW THE WHOLE TOWN, AGAIN?"

"This was before you got really sick," Victor replied. "And you know that I'm celibate. I'm not sleeping with anyone."

"RIGHT," she retorted, like a sarcasm dart straight into his heart.

"Is that the Queen?" Mo Li asked through the phone.

"Yes!" He replied. His face felt a thousand degrees while his head pulsed. It was like the naked dream that plagued every teenager, but in real life and on international news.

The television could be heard briefly between the Queen yelling and Mo Li talking. "Neither the State Palace nor the spokesperson for the pop star have been willing to comment, but it is still early in the morning, so that could change later in the day."

Victor flopped onto the foot of the bed. Both royals sat in silence studying the panel of commentators dissect his alleged dating life.

"I'm on my way!"

It only took 15 minutes for Mo Li to get from her home in downtown Parados to the State Palace. She came through the door panting as the television played, muted. Victor's head was hanging low as the Queen ripped into him. Somehow, she didn't stutter once. "I cannot believe you could be this stupid! You had put *everything* at risk."

Mo Li curtsied quickly and then threw her hands up, "Alright! Your Majesty, with all due respect, this isn't helping. Whatever happened, it's out there now."

"How many times is this family going to have to cover up for your sexual escapades?"

"They weren't sexual. I'm celibate; Marcus and I were just friends. And *that* was long ago, and above top secret. How would they even know?"

Mo Li sat in her chair and opened her iPad. "Maybe your 'friend' has a big mouth. Maybe he needs publicity for an upcoming record or something."

Victor turned to Mo Li.

"He's not my friend anymore," he spat.

"And the chef?" the Queen added.

"He and I *were* together, but not since you told me to stop. I ended it … I chose country."

The Queen turned to Mo Li. "Get - ow - get that chef in here." She held her head, wincing. "He wants to be part of this? Well, he's a part of this now."

Victor was worried about Vince's fate considering what happened to the last person with whom he'd become intimate. But honestly, he did want to see him. The prince looked up at his wincing grandmother and ran over to her. "Are you ok?"

"Yes, I'm fine." She breathed deeply and then looked up at Mo Li. "Find that 'source.'"

"How? The law prevents us from interrogating journalists unless he or she commits a crime himself or herself," she pleaded. "And even then, the questioning cannot pertain to their work."

Margaret practically growled into her hands. "Then get me the Director of the National Investigation Bureau. I want to know from where they got this. Who the hell is their source? Considering the past, I want this to be classified as a national security matter. Victor's relationship history cannot be dissected any further."

Victor rubbed the Queen's back, trying to calm her but it didn't seem to help. He turned to Mo Li, "What do I do? Do I deny it?"

"No, you can't refute it. We don't know what evidence they have," she replied, typing back and forth between her phone and her iPad. She then put the phone to her ear, "Hello. Her Majesty would like to see Chef Vincent. Bring him to the palace at once."

"Who was that?"

"The head of security."

Victor's eyes practically bulged. "You're having him dragged here? Why not just summon him?"

Margaret punched the bed in anger. "DO YOU REALLY THINK YOU HAVE A SAY IN HOW ANY OF THIS IS HANDLED?"

Mo Li lifted the phone to her ear again.

"Who are you calling now?" Victor asked.

"The NIB Director."

Victor swallowed hard, for he knew to what lengths the Queen was willing to go to protect the Crown and now so did Vince. "Why are we wasting time and resources on an investigation when we all know who is responsible?"

Margaret and Mo Li waited for him to continue, but when no answer came, they both asked in unison, "Who?"

"My mother."

"Do you really think she'd be that crazy?" Mo Li asked, genuinely.

Victor nodded, "At this point, I honestly don't know anymore. I mean, she has violated how many laws within the last year, one of which being divulging *supremely* secret information about your health."

"Well, either way, this is now on the public stage so proper channels have to be taken," Mo Li replied, pulling the phone from her ear. "No answer. We need to put out a statement in the morning."

"If my mother did leak this 'story,' then that should be addressed in that statement once and for all."

Mo Li froze, staring at Victor for several seconds. "And if you stand on that podium and blame the Princess for this and she's *not*, that would be catastrophic in more ways than one. Your credibility would be shot."

Victor sighed in frustration. "So, what do we do? We can't just put out a cookie cutter, pre-prepared statement."

Mo Li's eyes shifted rapidly back and forth as she calculated a game plan. "We wait."

"What?" Victor asked in an elevated voice. "You just -"

"We wait to see how the public is reacting in the morning. It could blow over."

Margaret finally emerged from her hands, "Or Parliament could freak out and call for your renunciation."

"Why would they do that? They have no say now. It's not up to them anymore. Their decision has been made. Besides, I think you two are missing a third option."

"And what would that be?" Margaret snapped.

Victor began to pace. "Considering it was an overwhelming public petition that led Parliament and Your Majesty to pass legislation legalizing 'same-sex marriage' and outlawing discrimination against the LGBT community, I think that the public may support me."

"As long as they don't try and dig up the past," Mo Li suggested into her iPad.

"They don't know that there is anything to dig up in the first place. Wait, how do *you* know about that?" Victor asked. "You were only the 1st Assistant Private Secretary to the Sovereign at the time."

"I make it my business to know every decision and event of current, previous, and future monarchs that could be dangerous in any way to the monarchy," Mo Li replied.

The Queen looked at Mo Li, "Did you summon the Director?"

"Yes, ma'am. He just responded to my text saying that he just saw the breaking news and is on his way. He is up in Makria."

"S-send the cho-opper then. I want him here A-S-P-A," the Queen barked.

"A-S-A-P, got it."

"And the chef?"

Mo Li looked at Victor who stared back at her eager for her response, and then to the Queen. "They are bringing him as we speak. It shouldn't be long."

I hope they aren't hurting him.

* * * * *

Margaret opened her eyes in a haze. She looked around to find her room filled with Mo Li, Victor, Chef Vincent, and the 2nd Assistant Private Secretary to the Sovereign, Nicholai. She realized that she'd fallen asleep. *Damn medication!* The room was silent, except for the news report going over the same story from a few hours prior.

"Mo Li?"

"Yes, ma'am!" She put her iPad on the foot of the bed next and came to the bedside.

"Is the D-Director here?" She asked.

Mo Li nodded. "He arrived about 20 minutes ago. He's waiting out in the hall."

"Well, then bring him in." Mo Li turned and left the room to get the Director. Margaret then turned to Vincent. "Chef."

Chef Vincent stood and bowed. "Yes, Your Majesty."

"I'm going to have to ask you to step out, due to the discussion of classified information," she said.

He turned to Victor as if to make sure that he was okay. Victor nodded and smiled slightly, granting him permission to comply. He acknowledged the Queen and left the room. Margaret sat up in her bed as Victor noticed that her hair was lopsided. He walked over to his grandmother and subtly adjusted the wig on her head. "Thank you. Now go sit back down," she told him. He obeyed and walked back to his seat.

Mo Li entered with a tall, elderly yet fit African-Iakon man with white hair and a custom-tailored suit. He snapped to attention and bowed twice, once to the Queen and another to Prince Victor. "Your Majesty, Your Royal Highness."

"Director Townsend, it is lovely to see you again," Margaret said as she made sure to sit up in the bed. She outstretched the hand that didn't have the IV needle imbedded in it and he willingly kissed it.

"Yes, ma'am. I wish it were under better circumstances."

"As do I," Margaret said, shooting a look at Victor. "Any word on the source of these leaks?"

"Your Majesty, as you know, we are dancing a fine line with investigating reporters and their sources. We cannot legally force them to give up their sources. However, we were able to confirm through digital intelligence that the information *did* come from within the family or someone extremely close to the family."

Victor leaned forward, "Is there any info about from which palace it came?"

"No, sir."

The Queen looked at him confused. "If this is a national threat, doesn't this surpass the limitations of press protection?"

"Ma'am, I can say with certainty that your grandson's alleged sexuality is not a threat to national security. Now if they were alleging that he was involved with a foreign operative or someone of an adversarial nation, then maybe. But chefs and pop stars are not a danger to this country."

"I'd argue that any leaks from the Palace would constitute a national security matter, no matter the subject."

The Director thought for a moment. "We could investigate the leak as the main subject in question rather than the news report."

Margaret nodded her head. "Then let's do that."

"Yes, ma'am."

"And Mo Li, I want you to call Princess Mary and summon her to the palace. I want her to look me in the eye and tell me that it wasn't her."

Mo Li's eyebrows read exactly what was on her mind. *It's about to go down.*

* * * * *

"How are you feeling?" Vincent asked, holding a cup of tea to Victor. His head hung low in his lap.

"How do you think I'm feeling? What if the country turns against me?"

Vince placed a gentle hand on his shoulder. "Why would they? They love you. This country loves you, certainly more than your mother." Victor chuckled softly, as his lover continued. "Everything will work out fine. You didn't do anything wrong."

"Then why do I feel guilty?"

Vince paused a moment to tame his response. Roasting Victor's mother and the way he was raised would not help him at that moment. "You didn't do anything illegal. You didn't hurt anyone. All you did was make one friend and fall in love with the help."

Victor turned his head sharply with a playful smile painted across his face. "Hey, I told you about that 'help' stuff. You are so much more to me than that."

"I know that, I just wanted to get that beautiful smile to show again."

Victor blushed hard for a moment, and then the smile melted off his face again. "How do you know everything is going to work out?"

"Because I'm older than you. I know these things." Vince smirked and began to sing off key, "You are 24 going on 25, baby it's time to think. Better beware be canny and careful…"

Victor practically exploded in laughter and threw his hands over Vince's mouth. "Oh, please," he gasped, "Please stop. Don't do that to my favorite movie."

They both sat on Victor's bed, laughing for about a minute until Victor settled his head onto Vince's shoulder. Vince capitalized on the proximity and planted an affectionate kiss on Victor's forehead. Victor leaned into the gesture and sighed as if his whole world was at peace for that moment. But, of course, it wouldn't last long.

Assistant Secretary Nicky came running into the room, "Your Royal Highness." Victor jumped up to his feet as if he'd been caught with his hand in the cookie jar.

"What? What is it? What's wrong?"

Nikolai looked at the two and his face looked like a teenager who'd just heard a that's-what-she-said joke. "I'm sorry. Am I interrupting?"

"Nicky, speak."

"Her Majesty and the Director would like to see you. Both."

Victor began hyperventilating slightly, but soon stopped as Vince's hand caressed on his shoulder. "Let's go," Vince said and they marched off to the Crown Suite.

Down the whole hallway, Nikolai looked like he was singing in his head, "Victor and Vincent, sitting in a tree…" When they finally entered the Queen's bedroom, that look quickly fell away as the energy of the room seemed very serious.

Vince looked around and said, "I will be just outside."

"No, it's ok," Queen Margaret said. "The Director has advised to raise your security clearance for this matter." Victor was pleasantly surprised, but he dared not show it on his face. "Director, please share with the prince what you shared with me."

"Well, sir. My staff has traced the leak to an anonymous email. We have traced this email to Washington, DC."

"America? What? President Taylor? We only met once."

The Director continued in his deep voice. "Though according to my agents, it was made to look like it was from there. It was bounced from all around the world, but it seems to have originated from a server in Rousel Palace."

Victor's mouth fell open yet again. He knew that it was a possibility, but it being a reality felt ten times worse than it being a bitter conjecture. "So, it *was* my mother?"

"Or someone in the palace, yes."

Victor turned to his grandmother, "So we got her."

"No, sir," the Director told him. "It is all circumstantial. We cannot put the email in her hands, so to speak. It wouldn't be enough to convict."

Victor turned back to his grandmother, "But it does give you reason enough to remove her from the succession."

"Let's not jump there," she said, holding her hands up for emphasis. "First, you should address the nation."

"Me?"

"Yes, you," Mo Li said. "The statement should come from you."

"What should I say?"

Mo Li lifted her iPad, "I have a draft that we can tweak while you get dressed."

"Where is the Princess, anyway?" Nikolai asked, bashfully.

Everyone in the room began looking back and forth between each other waiting for someone to answer. When it was clear that no one knew where she was, the Queen turned to Mo Li, "Find her."

Chapter 23

Listen, you can do this. Take your time and just read the teleprompter. You will be fine. Nikolai frantically ran up and down the room coordinating with the press. Victor tried to ignore the Assistant Secretary's nervous energy because it just compounded on his own. He looked around the room in search for an anchor, but the chef was nowhere to be found. Victor wondered what would become of Vincent. Would he keep his job as the chef, or even better, could they get married?

Victor got so distracted that the Press Secretary's booming voice made him jump out of his skin. "His Royal Highness, Prince Victor II."

Let's go. Victor took a deep breath and walked into the room. The flashes of the cameras came so rapidly that he had to turn away from them and looked down at the bottom of the podium. The snaps of the cameras were like rapid-fire raindrops on a glass window. But louder than the clicks were the hundreds of questions being thrown his way.

After a few moments, he leaned forward into the microphone. "I will make a brief statement and then take a few questions." Finally, the press corps settled and he began to read from the glass stands in front of him. "The Palace, including the entire Royal Family, is saddened by the invasion of privacy that has taken place and has continued over the last few months. These so-called leaks ultimately distract from the important work that we do and intend to do for the nation and people of Iakos. If we condone leaks of this nature, then the sharing of more sensitive information becomes at risk too and this cannot be allowed. As we move forward, we ask that you remain respectful of our privacy and of legal confidentiality as we maintain to have an appropriate openness with the Iakon people, as we always have. Now, any questions?"

The vultures jumped to their feet and began squawking louder and louder. The prince pointed to one reporter who yelled above the rest, "Your Royal Highness, what do you say to the

217

unconfirmed reports that the leaks about your alleged relationships came from inside the Royal Family?"

Victor paused as he quickly considered how to approach this answer. He didn't want to go flying off the handle with an incoherent rant. He settled on a short and simple sentence. "I'd hope that they aren't true."

"And if they are?"

"Well, then whomever has been sharing private information about the Royal Family should be ashamed of himself or herself, especially if it came from the primary family. A snake leads from the head, but if not careful, it can also rot from the head."

The reporters all began shouting questions again, and Victor chose one from the other side of the room. "Sir, are the reports true that you dated singer, Marcus Frazier, and the palace cook? And are they the only relationships you've had."

"While I'm not going to get into confirming and/or denying specific claims about my personal life and relationships, I will say that I am a young man and have dated in the past." He quickly chose one young reporter before they all could shout again.

They called, "Sir, wouldn't it be fair to say that your relationships are not private because she, or he, could potentially become your consort?"

"Once one becomes serious enough for that kind of consideration, it will be made public," Victor replied. He immediately thought of Vince becoming his consort and it warmed his heart a bit.

"Sir, can you confirm your sexuality?"

Victor froze and even the other reporters gasped at the bluntness of the man. He figured he'd answer the same way he did with his grandmother and mother when they asked him years ago. "I prefer not to label myself with categorizations."

"And what does that mean?" another reporter blurted out.

"I am attracted to the person. Who they are is most important to me — their personality."

The young reporter yelled out quickly, "Do you prefer one over the other?"

Victor chuckled wryly and said, "History has shown a preference, yes."

Finally, a female reporter stood up and called out the question everyone seemed to want to know. "Are you single now?

"Life as your prince, though an honor, is not the easiest for a dating life." The prince decided in that moment not to grant the reporter the follow up. He knew they would hound him because of that vague, politician answer. "Thank you!" He stepped off the podium with a wave and walked out of the room while the wolves went crazy. Victor, Nicky, and his security team walked down the hall and into the corridor.

As they walked, Mo Li joined them and grabbed Victor by the arm. Before she could talk, Victor quickly asked, "How did it go?"

"Honestly, we will see. In my opinion, you were dignified yet witty, without giving too much away."

"So that's good?"

"We shall see. Oh, by the way, your mother is here."

"Great," he whined sarcastically as he began to drag his feet.

The entourage made their way through the palace to the Crown Suite. Victor was nervous at how the public was going to receive it, and maybe more importantly, how the Queen will take it. When they finally arrived, Vince was sitting beside the bed feeding Margaret some ice cream. They were enjoying a nice conversation, though she kept herself at a distance that only Victor's closeness could recognize.

"Grandmother, what are you doing? Why do you have Chef Vincent feeding you like you can't do it yourself? You're not *that* sick."

"Because I asked him to," she replied, very matter-of-factly.

Everyone in the room laughed, ranging from a snicker to a witch's cackle. Princess Mary was sitting in the armchair next to the window, glaring at Victor.

"What?" Victor asked.

"Snake rots from the head? For whom was that intended?"

Victor looked her square in the eye and mocked her, "It was intended for you-m, that's whom!"

"How dare you insult me? I am your mother."

219

"How dare I? You, with more leaks than a rusty pipe, have the nerve to ask me, 'how dare I?' Why would you put my business on blast like that?"

At this point, the whole room got quiet and watched the battle ensue. Mary stood up and stepped toward him. "Because you don't deserve the crown! You walk around here as if you're the heir apparent. Well, guess what, you're not."

"How do I not deserve it?"

"Just look at your track record?"

Victor's face twisted. "My track record? I have yet to make one negative news headline up until now, and even that is debatable."

"Your track record in life. Your sister, your brother, and even your cousins have all made names for themselves. But what have you done, other than ruin everyone's lives?"

Victor practically bellowed, "Whose life did I ruin?"

"MINE!"

"WHAT? HOW?"

"Where's your father?"

Victor stopped, stunned. He couldn't believe she went there. "That was NOT my fault."

"Oh, it wasn't? If you had been focusing on your studies instead of letting everyone and their brother in your pants, he would still be here?"

Victor turned to find the Duke sitting in the corner looking at his wife with a facial expression Victor couldn't read. He looked back at this mother, "What does it matter? You are remarried now! Newly and illegally, I might add. And did I 'out' you to the world that your claim was in question? No! Did I try to publicly humiliate you? No! Why? Because, contrary to popular belief, I don't wish you harm. You've been the one playing all these games and humiliating yourself in the process."

"ENOUGH," Margaret shouted. Mary was seething with her eyes locked on Victor. He returned the gaze on the other side of the bed, his knuckles white as he clutched the rail to the Queen's hospital bed. "Look at me!" she said, but neither heard her, so she shouted again, "LOOK AT ME!" Both of their heads snapped to her. She pushed the button on the side of her bed and sat herself all the way up, "This has got to stop. You were both raised that we are a family first and somehow you have lost that. Neither one of you wants me to make a decision on who will succeed me at this moment, because it would be neither of you. Until you two can come to peaceful ground, I will make my decision and leave it in my will. No one will know before then, understood? No more lobbying, political games, none of it! Absolutely no more!"

"Yes, ma'am," Victor replied.

"Yes, ma'am," Mary mimicked mockingly and childishly.

One royal hand shot up and the back of it landed with full force on the princess' mouth. "GROW UP!" the Queen barked.

No one in the room knew what to do, not even Victor. Vince wanted to grab the prince's hand but he dared not move. The Duke wanted to reach for his wife, whose hands now squeezed her mouth and chin, but he was frozen in shock. Mo Li held on tightly to her iPad as she turned her side to the family as if to say she hadn't seen anything. Nicky held his breath in fear of bursting into hysterical laughter and slowly stepped out of the room. It was official. Victor was scared.

Margaret held her hand to her head and continued. "I am not getting better anytime soon, so it is time for *both of you* to receive Regent security clearance. You will go to briefings in my name, together. You will attend Royal Court meetings with the Cabinet members. You will make decisions in my name and you will deputize for me in the event of my incapacity. *Together!* Are we clear?"

Both Mary and Victor replied, "Yes, ma'am!"

"Now get out of my sight. Mo Li?" Mo Li was too afraid to answer. "MO LI!"

"Yes, Your Majesty," she said, her voice shaking.

"Have Nurse Stacey come in here and check my blood pressure," she said as she laid her head back and began to take slow, deep breaths.

Victor turned and left the room with Vincent following close behind. When they got to the doorway of his bedroom, he looked up at Vince's brown eyes and strong jawline and all he could say was, "What the hell just happened?"

* * * * *

221

The brightness of the ceiling projection screen burned Victor's eyes. Images of crowds of crying people and diagrams danced across the screen as Victor struggled to see. Princess Mary sat across the table opposite Victor, her eyes fixed forward. Victor scanned the room and the light reflected off the faces of the Head of Royal Security, various Cabinet secretaries, the Private Secretary to the Sovereign, and the Director of the NIB. The Parliamentary Speaker sat at the head of the table with the pointer in hand. "Your Royal Highnesses? Any questions?"

"This plan will take effect at the announcement of Her Majesty's death or in the event of her actual death?" Princess Mary asked.

"Well, since the announcement is stage 4 of the plan, then I would say at the event, ma'am."

Victor snickered louder than he expected. He looked around and everyone was looking at him. He quickly cleared his throat to replace the awkwardness with a question. "So, if we don't know who will be Sovereign until after the will is unsealed and read, then how will this plan work?"

Mo Li replied, "Her Majesty's Counsel will hopefully arrive quickly to read it. Then begin stage one with alerting the new Sovereign and the Family."

Victor sat puzzled. He saw a major flaw in that moment. "Well, what if he can't?"

"I'm sorry?" the Parliamentary Speaker asked.

"What if he can't arrive quickly? Our country will be without a monarch. The Princess and I would just sit there waiting to hear our nation's fate?"

The NIB Director leaned onto the table and spoke in his deep, powerful voice. "Well, I'd hope you two would be focused on the death of your mother and grandmother rather than acting beneath the dignity of your titles."

Princess Mary turned to him, "And just to whom do you think your talking?"

"No, no!" Victor tapped the table to grab his mother's attention. "He's right! We have to make an agreement, right here, right now, that when Her Majesty passes, it will invoke a ceasefire until the will is read and we know for sure what the decision is."

"And then what? We dual for the Crown?" Mary half-mocked, half-considered.

Victor paused, trying to keep his irritation from getting the better of him. "No. Then, that's it. The feud will be over. The other will bow to the Crown as we all must do."

"And just let you walk off with my crown?"

"That's assuming I'll be given the crown," Victor replied.

Speaker Michaels looked back and forth between the two Royals. "I don't think this is the best time to have this conversation."

"I'd argue that this is precisely the time for this conversation. We need to come to an agreement," Victor replied.

A knock rapped on the door. Just as one of the security guards opened the door, the projection screen shut off and the lights sprang on which made everyone in the room squint. A palace staffer ran into the room, panting. "Madam Private Secretary."

"Yes, what is it?" Mo Li replied jumping to her feet.

"You have an emergency phone call. It's about Her Majesty."

Victor and Mary looked at each other with a mutual worry. Mo Li took the phone and walked out of the room with the staffer. The room sat in silence as every worst-case scenario leapt through everyone's mind. Finally, Mo Li returned and grabbed her purse from the back of the chair and began out the door.

"What?" Victor thought he'd simply spoke, but instead he'd almost yelled at her.

"Her Majesty is being rushed to the hospital."

Victor and Mary scrambled to their feet, while everyone else gasped. They took off running following Mo Li. Victor could only think two words over and over. *Not yet! Not yet!*

May

Chapter 24

The repetitive hiss of the tube protruding from his grandmother's mouth and the beep on the screen that indicated life chipped away at Victor's sanity. He rested his head on his grandmother's still hand. It had been so long since he'd prayed last, but he tried repeatedly. He begged and pleaded for one last laugh, conversation, even moment, but all the Earthly evidence showed the contrary.

A knock on the door stole Victor out of his inner hurricane and he spoke out in a broken, monotone voice, "Come in."

The door creaked open and Nurse Stacy emerged. She curtsied to Victor and then walked over to the IV drip above the hospital bed. Victor rested his head back down and tried to breathe deeply. The sounds of Stacy adjusting the machine barely entered his psyche. In fact, he didn't hear the word she spoke to him at first. "Sir," she repeated.

"Yes?" he replied, without lifting his head.

"Would you like me to bring you anything? A pillow or a warm blanket?"

"No, thanks. I'm fine." Victor then felt a warm pressure on his shoulder that he recognized to be a hand.

"Are you sure? You've been here a week and have barely slept — and in that recliner," Stacy pleaded.

Victor chose to ignore the breech of royal protocol and be appreciative for the gesture. "No, thank you! I am fine."

"Ok. If you need anything, you know to push the button."
And with that, the young woman fixed her natural curls and backed out.

Victor then thought he'd ask her the question that had been pinballing around in his brain. He lifted his head as he spoke, "May I ask you a question?"

She stopped and looked at the prince. "Sure, anything."

"My grandmother isn't going to wake up anytime soon, is she?"

Her genuine smile morphed into an awkward one that indicated her true answer. Instead, she towed the party line. "You should ask Dr. Ryan about that, sir. He should be coming in a little later."

"Please, just answer. You must have seen cases like this one before. In your professional opinion, will she regain consciousness or..."

Stacy looked down at her shoes and awkwardly kicked her feet but didn't answer for a moment. In the month or so that he'd known her, he'd never seen her look like a kid in school who didn't want to answer because she knew the class bully would tease her later. Then suddenly, her whole posture changed. Her back straightened with her head falling into alignment. Her hands folded tightly in front of her abdomen and her face sat cold. "In my experience, it is rare for someone to come back from a brain bleed of that size. The tumor has caused a lot of damage and the bleeding caused Her Majesty's brain to swell."

"So, what are you saying? She's brain dead?"

"No," Stacy replied. "Her Majesty is in a coma."

"What's the difference?" he replied, his voice dripping of frustration.

Stacy patiently explained, "Brain death means one is no longer alive — no activity in the brain or brain stem. Only the machines would be maintaining life. A coma means one is alive but cannot be awakened from their depressed state of consciousness."

"So, then she could become brain dead," Victor looked at her with his red, puffy eyes.

The nurse tried to console him. "Or she could regain consciousness. We just have to wait and see." Her tone said that she knew it was unlikely, but she felt he needed to cling to some hope, even if it was false.

The door behind Stacy clicked open and all Victor could see was Prince Jack's head. "Hi, you guys."

"Hey," Victor said softly with a weak smile. Jack came into the room and gave Victor a tight hug. He kept his eyes closed until he let Victor go. Margie followed into the room and froze at the sight of her grandmother. Victor could see her eyes welling up and he let go of Jack with one arm and stretched it out toward Margie. She was stuck in her cognitive dissonance. She studied the Queen's body and the monitor at the head of the bed. Victor pulled Jack closer and grabbed Margie. Jack and Victor squeezed her as her gasps for air burst into loud sobs.

Nurse Stacy quietly stepped out of the room and closed the door. The three stood at the foot of the bed holding each other. Victor joined in on the waterfall but Jack held firm. He simply squeezed his eyes shut and his arms around them. A few minutes passed as they swayed and released what had been building up. Once they finally felt stable enough, Victor released the group hug and grabbed Margie's face. He wiped the running mascara from her cheeks with his thumbs and chuckled. "Girl, we need to get you some better makeup. What is this?" All three began to laugh softly.

Jack stepped over to the wall and sat in the chair next to Victor's. After Victor finished wiping her face, Margie walked over to the other side of the bed and sat down next to it. She placed a hand on the back of the Queen's hand and looked at her face. Victor returned to his seat and watched Margie come to terms, at least, with the Queen's current condition.

"This is the quietest she's been in months," Jack said. Victor chuckled but Margie didn't react, stuck in her trance. In true fashion, Jack's inappropriate sense of humor had once again lightened Victor's mood a bit.

Another knock on the door gave birth to the Duke and Duchess of Makria. Rose walked toward Victor and smiled at him, something he wasn't expected but embraced for as short of a time as it would last. "Hiiiiiiiii. How is she?"

"She and I are fine." He couldn't let that slight go.

Rose's fake smile remained porcelain as she patted his hand and sang, "It's not always about you."

Victor turned on an unnaturally big smile and patted her hand back, "But you wish it were about you."

Jack let out one loud "HA!" and then covered his face as he finished his laugh. Margie turned her head and threw her arms up, imitating a child. At least, Victor hoped it was an imitation. John reached out his arms as she practically ran to him and hugged him erupting into tears again. Victor turned to Jack as they shared a look of disgust.

"Why are you so dramatic? We just went through this," Jack taunted.

John turned to his son, still holding his daughter, "Hey, don't do that. This is hard on everyone."

Jack lit up in a smirk and turned to Victor and mouthed, "That's what she said."

Victor smirked and stood up. "You're a nut. Do you want to go to the cafeteria with me?"

"What's down there?" Jack asked.

"I don't know but I want some coffee."

"Cool." With that Jack and Victor began out the door.

"Wait," Rose called out. They stopped and turned around. "Can you bring me a nonfat triple iced grande Caramel Macchiato in a venti cup with one pump Classic, one pump vanilla, with two Splenda on the bottom, and a raw sprinkled atop? Thanks! You're a prince."

Victor looked at her with a straight face. "No." They turned around and left with Jack filling the hall with loud laughter.

They walked down the hall and two security guards followed them out of the secure wing of the hospital, through a maze of corridors and stopped at the elevators. Victor pushed the down button. Jack went on and on about this girl he met back in Makria as they got on and went down seven floors. Victor tried hard to listen but his mind jumped back and forth between Jack's story and the Queen. All he wanted were some answers. The bell dinged and the doors opened. Three young women were standing in front waiting to get on. Three gasps made Jack smirk as he nodded his head as if to say hello. The three dipped into a curtsy as they squealed quietly to themselves. Victor simply walked off the elevator. As Jack passed, he winked at one and all three girls practically swooned. Jack laughed and picked up his speed to catch up to Victor.

Victor entered the cafeteria and noticed a security guard at each entrance of the room. He ignored the other people in the room bowing and gawking, and walked right to the coffee station. He picked up a cup and poured the coffee. He added the creamer and sugar, and then turned to find Jack on the other side of the room with the phone to his ear. Jack's face was more serious than normal, so he walked over.

"Yes, mother. We're coming up now," Jack spoke into the phone and then tapped the screen to disconnect the call.

"What?" Victor asked, sipping his coffee.

"The doctors are in the room."

Victor turned to the guard, pulled out €20 from his pocket and handed it to him. "Please pay for this. Thank you."

Before the guard could protest, the two princes took off for the elevator with one guard following. They ran into an open elevator with a young nurse and an old man in a wheelchair. The guard positioned the princes against the opposite wall and placed himself in the middle. They rode up to the 7th floor and then took off again for the secure suite. Through the maze of white walls, they finally ended at the room door. Victor stopped just before the door as Jack slid trying to avoid colliding with his cousin. They gathered themselves and entered the room calmly.

Dr. Ryan and Dr. Bennett both turned to the princes and bowed. "Your Royal Highnesses."

"Doctors," Victor said. He looked at Rose who was almost in tears, which was a shock, even to Victor. Mo Li was standing at the foot of the bed.

"I was just telling your aunt and uncle that the results of the EEG test have confirmed the worst-case scenario."

Victor looked confused. "Dr. Ryan, please don't speak in code. I need you to tell me in plain English." Jack placed a hand on Victor's back meant to comfort him but he simply shrugged it off and focused on the words of the middle-aged man in front of him.

Dr. Ryan began again, choosing his words carefully. "Sir, Her Majesty is in a persistent vegetative state. There was very little activity on the tests. I'm sorry. You should make preparations for the remainder of the Royal Family to come and say their last goodbyes over the next month."

At that point, Victor's mind was stuck on the word "Coma". Nurse Stacy had explained it before but he didn't want to believe it. Rose's voice sucked Victor out of his fog.

"The next month? Why the next month?" she asked.

Mo Li turned to her and explained that the Royal medical directives for the Sovereign determine that 30 days of no improvement or sign of life must pass before a monarch can be taken off life support.

"It's also meant to allow for a medical miracle," Dr. Bennett added.

"My father didn't have to wait 30 days," Rose argued with her eyes spilling over onto her face.

"He wasn't a monarch, ma'am. He was a prince consort," Mo Li replied.

Victor looked at his watch. "It's the second. We have to wait until the first of June?"

"Yes, sir."

Mo Li looked at Victor with laser focus. "Since no one knows what Her Majesty's decision is yet for heir apparent, Princess Mary, the Duchess of Spiti, has been officially named Acting Regent until Her Majesty's official time of death." Victor froze. A myriad of questions came racing through his brain so fast that his mouth couldn't pick one. Indecipherable nonsense noises came blurting from his mouth and Mo Li moved swiftly over to him to clarify. "It's in name only. The current roles still stand. Princess Mary will continue getting the country prepared for the peaceful transition and you will be making public appearances."

"What?" Victor finally could say. "I'm not marching in the national parade next week knowing that my grandmother, for all intents and purposes, has just died. The parade is in her honor for crying out loud."

"Exactly!" Rose blurted. "All you're doing is whining out loud. The parade marks the signing of our country's constitution, not one monarch."

"I will be the first royal to have to deputize the parade."

"It could also be your parade next year," Jack sat, calmly from behind him. Rose practically snarled at Jack. Victor wanted to crawl into a corner but instead he was being asked to step out in front of the nation.

Rose then spoke words that no one in the room expected. "Your mother actually said it's ok."

"It wasn't up to her approval but thanks," Mo Li snapped back.

"Wait, what? My mother knows about Grandmother already? How? Where is she?" Victor asked.

Dr. Bennett turned around to Victor. "Her Royal Highness is at Rousel Palace, so we spoke to her on the phone just before we came here to speak with you."

"Victor, we will be there to support you. Jackie, Seth, and myself will all be in the parade if you want us," Jack said.

Victor smiled what little smile he could muster. "Thank you!"

* * * * *

Jackie studied the tiara with such determination that she didn't notice that Seth had walked in. She moved it around to get the full effect of the stones. Seth watched lights dance across her face and got a mischievous idea. He walked past her and without batting an eye, snatched the white gold, diamond tiara from her hands. "Hey," Jackie bellowed as Seth leapt out of her reach and took off out the door. Jackie kicked off her stiletto heels, hiked up her dress, and raced after him. He only made it about 50 yards down before Victor came out into the hallway to inspect the noise. Victor stood in full military regalia with his arms folded and a look on his face like a scolding father.

"Oh, hi Victor. Umph!" Jackie tackled him to the floor and reached for his extended arm that held the tiara out of reach.

"Give that back, it's worth a million euro and it's grandma's!" Jackie shouted.

"You didn't ask her for it," Seth teased.

Jackie stopped her attack and looked at him with face that read, *You idiot*! "What? That doesn't even make sense."

Seth stammered, trying to recover from his faux pas. "Then, then, you didn't ask mother. She's acting regent."

"Seth!" Jackie gritted through her teeth.

With his sister still on top of him, he turned to Victor, Sorry, Victor!

231

"It's fine, Seth. Just give her back the tiara so we can go." With that, Victor returned to his room.

Seth slowly handed her the tiara. Jackie snatched it away, landed a smack on the top of his head that echoed down the halls, and then went in after Victor. As she entered the bedroom, she found Chef Vince sitting on the bed. "Why, hello Vincent."

Vince chuckled and bowed while still seated. "Hello, Your Royal Highness."

"Oh, stop. You can call me Jackie."

"I'm not sure I should."

"I look like an early 20th-century painting," Victor called out from the bathroom.

"Will you stop it? You look fine," Vince replied.

Victor appeared in the doorway and leaned up against the doorpost. "But what if they don't like me. What if they boo and jeer, but the Queen makes me King. It would cause a revolution."

Vince got up from the bed and walked over to his lover. Victor rested his head on Vince's chef coat as he embraced Victor.

"Stop that now," he said sweetly. "You read those newspapers and saw the news. The people are supporting you. You will be fine." Seth came limping into the room. Vince turned to him, "What happened to you?"

All Seth could do was point to Jackie who had placed the tiara back in its velvet box, and walked over to the mirror to fix a fascinator hat onto her head.

"Ah," Vince replied.

"Here you all are," Mo Li said at the door with Jack standing behind her. "Come on. Let's go."

Vince held Victor by his cheeks and gave him a deep, reassuring kiss. When the two separated, he looked the prince in the eyes and said, "It will be great, babe." He placed one last kiss on Victor's forehead and said, "Go. Be great!"

Man, it's nice to be back with him and not have to hide it. Victor smiled as he left the room. All of the royals followed Mo Li out the door. Once outside, Jackie, Seth, and Jack climbed into the horse-drawn carriage. Victor stopped and turned to Mo Li. "Are you serious?"

"What?"

"A horse drawn carriage?"

Mo Li sighed. "Well, you can't ride in the state coach yet."

"What about a limousine or a town car? And an open top carriage at that? Have you ever heard of a man named President John F. Kennedy?" Victor argued.

Mo Li turned to him in frustration and pushed him into the car. "We have secured the route. You are perfectly safe."

Victor climbed into the carriage and continued pleading. "You and I both know that it's impossible to eliminate every threat."

Jack wrapped his arm around Victor. "Cousin, you will be fine. Just sit back and enjoy the praise."

Victor leaned back in the seat and closed his eyes. *Deep breaths, deeeeeep breaths.*

The carriage pulled off and Victor kept his eyes closed until he heard the crowd outside the palace almost sound like a jet engine. The squeals of little girls, the shouts of men, and the thunder of applause all compelled Victor to open his eyes. The motorcade traveled down the road that was lined with thousands upon thousands of people. Jackie and Jack waved back and forth on either side of them. Seth gave his smolder to the passing girls and Victor simply rolled his eyes. He kept his eyes down on the floor.

"Look, read the signs," Jack shouted over the crowd. "I promise you'll want to read them."

Victor looked up and people held up signs. Some had rainbows on them, others had drawings, but one caught his eye. It was a huge yellow sign that read, PRINCE VICTOR, WE LOVE YOU! Another a half a block away was littered with silver glitter hearts that glinted in the sunlight and said, OUR FIRST GAY KING! Another, THE PRINCE + THE CHEF! Victor chuckled to himself. He turned to Jack and pointed to the last sign he'd read, "A new Iakos children's book." Jack threw his head back in boisterous laughter.

Victor's whole body tingled as the shouts of adoration and support continued from block to block. He couldn't believe that the country was supporting him to such an extent. The sidewalks were packed to the inch. National flags, along with rainbow flags, waved vigorously. A woman held up her baby who seemed to be smiling just as hard as she was. Victor chuckled to himself and waved back to the woman and her baby. The entire crowd around grew even louder, making Victor wince as his eardrums reacted to the volume.

About ten minutes had passed as they slowly traveled from street to street. There was no break in applause and cheers until the procession passed one man who wore a white button up shirt and black slacks. Though his shirt glowed from the sun, there was a darkness around him that pulled Victor's smile off his face. He watched as the man slowly passed and disappeared into the crowd. Suddenly, there was a loud pop. Victor looked up to see if it was a firecracker. Then two more pops rang out followed by a high-pitched whiz. Finally, someone screamed loudly as one more pop rang out and sharp pain erupted from his right shoulder. Victor fell to the floor and grabbing his arm.

Five security guards dressed in all black including black shades piled into the carriage from all sides, tackling all the royals to the ground and spreading out on top of them. With Victor at the bottom, he could barely breathe under the weight of the guards and his arm seemed to radiate pain. Suddenly, the ambience of screaming crowds grew quiet as the emergency roof to the carriage sprang closed. The carriage picked up speed.

"Sir, are you hit?" One guard shouted out. Victor couldn't take in the breath to reply. His head felt like it was going to explode. His neck and cheek were beginning to grow wet. With the lid closed, the men lifted off the royals and they spread around to the edges of the carriages, clearly jarred by what had just happened. Victor, however, stayed on the ground with Jack kneeling next to him.

"Oh, my God," Jack spoke in pure shock.

The guard on top of the prince lifted Victor's hand from across his arm to see it covered in blood. "Prince, can you hear me?"

Victor inhaled to talk, but pain ripped through his side with every deep breath he tried to take. He settled on quick, shallow breaths. Weakly, he could only make out one word, "Help."

"Driver," one of the guards bellowed at the top of his lungs. "To the hospital, NOW!"

Chapter 25

"Victor, you need to get up! Victor - get - up, please! Don't give them the satisfaction. You need to fight and wake up." He could hear the sound of the voice above his head whispering with intensity and strength. "You can do it. I'm telling you that you are strong enough. Just open your eyes."

Victor tried to talk but couldn't move. In fact, his body felt so heavy that he just lay there. *Just my eyes,* he thought to himself. Over and over again, he tried to open his 10-ton eyes until they finally fluttered open. The figure before him was blurry, but even so, it was unmistakable.

"Vvvvvince," Victor muttered, trying to say the name of his lover who continued to urge him to consciousness.

"That's it," Vince softly cheered. "You can do it. Keep going."

One last push and, finally, Victor became aware of everything around him. He looked around to see an almost identical room to his grandmother's, with some additional security measures. There was a guard with a large gun at the door and the window shades were pulled shut.

Vince pushed the red button on the remote and a voice called out over the speaker. "Can I help you?"

"He's awake. Prince Victor is awake!" Vince called out and then returned his attention to Victor. "Hi. How are you feeling?"

"Tired," Victor replied, barely audibly.

"I know. It's just the painkillers. We asked the doctors to lighten up on them so you can wake up."

"We?"

"Princess Mary and myself."

Victor's face contorted in confusion. "Mum?"

"Yes. She's been going back and forth between yours and Her Majesty's rooms. Do you remember what happened?" Vince asked, stroking Victor's head.

Victor shrugged his shoulder to make sure it really happened and the pain that leapt from his arm validated the events. "I was shot."

Vince nodded. "Yes, but you are ok. The NIB got the person responsible."

"My mum," Victor said with a straight face.

"Your mum? What about her?"

Victor rested his head into the chef's hand and peered into his eyes with as much fury as his sedated mind could muster. "She did this."

Vince shook his head. "No, babe. I doubt that she was involved. She's been crazy worried about you."

"She did this," he repeated.

And just like that, Princess Mary burst into the room with Dr. Bennett and Nurse Stacy. The doctor and nurse bowed and walked over to the bed. "Your Royal Highness, how do you feel?"

"Tired."

Dr. Bennett replied, "Yes, we can lighten up some more on the pain medications if you'd like."

"Yes, please. Thank you."

Dr. Bennett indicated with his head to the nurse and she walked over to the IV drip above his head and adjusted it accordingly.

"Why does my side hurt too, if I was shot in the arm?" Victor asked softly.

"Because when the security team tackled you, you suffered a cracked rib. It will heal on its own in about 4-6 weeks, but in the meantime, I'd recommend staying away from strenuous activity — twisting, bending, that sort of thing."

"Son, oh, thank God you're ok," the princess said as she moved over to the bed and grabbed Victor's hand.

He ripped his hand from his mother's grasp and looked her square in the eye. "You did this."

"Pardon?" Mary asked, as her face displayed what seemed to be genuine shock. "I did what?"

"Shot me!"

Hurt, she motioned for everyone to leave. The doctor and nurse bowed and obeyed. Vince took a longer look at Victor and then got up from the bed. As he passed the guard, he whispered, "Do not leave this room." The guard nodded and closed the door behind Vince.

"I know we've had our issues over the years," Mary began, "You are my *son* first. I would never. The guy was a lone gunman with no political or radical affiliations; just a homophobe who hated that you are gay."

Victor sat staring her in the eyes before he spoke. "How'd he know?" Mary simply stared at him. "I've never publicly confirmed my sexuality, but someone did and I think we both know who it was."

"Ok," Mary pulled the chair next to the bed and sat with her arms resting on the bed. "Yes, I was the one who leaked your sexuality to the press. I figured Parliament would call for your abdication or renunciation. But when I saw that the country supported you, I realized that it was pointless."

"You hired someone to kill me."

"No, I didn't."

"And how do I know that?"

Mary's voice began to quiver. "How can you say that? I've lost my baby sister, my father, a husband, and soon my mother. I wouldn't survive losing one of my three babies too, Crown or not. As much as you are a pain in my ass at times, you are my son - my eldest son - and I would never want to see you hurt. I was terrified when I saw my son shot live on television." Victor looked her in the eye, not believing a word that she said and she read that on his face. His right eyebrow raised high and his lips pursed at her. "Victor, killing you wouldn't get me closer to the throne at all. In fact, if Her Majesty passes me over for the Crown and you were dead, then Seth would become king." Victor looked at her realizing that she'd considered this before but found it wasn't politically beneficial to her. He turned away from her and adjusted painfully on the bed. She placed a hand on his side. "Son, what do you want me to say? I would never knowingly endanger your life."

"You outed me to the world and caused me to be shot," Victor spat at her.

Mary's head hung and something small and cold hit his arm. He looked over to find tears streaming down his mother's face. "I will regret that for the rest of my life."

"No, you won't. You don't regret anything, never have. As long as you get what you want."

Mary sobbed. "Please, son. Forgive me."

He turned to her with pointed eyes and said definitively, "I don't." The princess laid her head on his lap and began to cry harder than he'd ever seen her cry before. Even when his father left, it didn't compare to this hysteria. "Did you have my father killed too? Is that why we've been prohibited from seeking him out?"

Mary's head shot up with her face soaked with sadness, and yet her eyes glared at him. "What did you just say?"

Victor got the sense he'd gone too far but then again, he was in a hospital bed with a through-and-through gunshot wound and a broken rib. *The gloves are off.*

"Your father is alive and well, thank you!"

Victor looked at her, shocked. He expected her to be angry and defensive. Instead, she genuinely seemed hurt by the implication. She hung her head and began to cry harder in his lap. He let her put on her show for a few more minutes until it was clear that she was prolonging her distress in theatre. Finally, Victor carefully adjusted himself from under her and told his mother, "You may go."

"What?"

"I said, 'You may go!'" Victor repeated.

Mary stood up prideful, swallowing her sobs and wiping her tears. "No matter what happens, I want you to know that I love you and will regret this day for the rest of my life." And with that, the princess turned and left.

Vince slowly appeared at the door. "Do I have permission to enter?"

Victor nodded, wincing at the stabbing in his side. He gestured for Vince to enter and patted the bed next to himself. Vince closed the door behind him and carefully climbed onto the bed beside the prince. "Thank you for not dying, babe."

Victor sighed deeply and leaning onto the comforting chest of his lover. "Thank you for not wishing me dead!"

June

Chapter 26

Beep. Beep. Beep. So many royals hadn't been in one room since the death of his grandfather. The news vans outside were surrounding the hospital and crowds had gathered outside. The world knew something was going on because of the arrival of so many members of the extended royal family, but thankfully no one had leaked anything. The body of Her Majesty, Queen Margaret I lied on the hospital bed, which was surrounded by her family members:

HRH Christopher, Duke of Spiti - son-in-law

HRH Princess Regent Mary, Duchess of Spiti and Princess - daughter

HRH Princess Jacqueline "Jackie" of Spiti - granddaughter

HRH Prince Victor II of Spiti - grandson

HRH Prince Seth of Spiti - grandson

HRH Princess Rose, Duchess of Makria - daughter

HRH John, Duke of Makria - son-in-law

HRH Princess Margaret "Margie" of Makria - granddaughter

HRH Prince John "Jack" of Makria - granddaughter

HRH Princess Eleanor, Duchess of Voreios - sister

HG Sir Edwin, Duke of Voreios - brother-in-law

HRH Prince Apollo of Voreios - nephew

HRH Prince Artemis of Voreios - nephew

Lady Gemma Rousel - niece

HRH Prince David - brother
Lady Aramat Rousel - niece

Victor looked around the room squeezing Vince's hand as everyone sat quietly. Vince's eyes shifted from one television character come to life to another. "Relax," Victor whispered. Victor rubbed the bandage on his arm as it ached.

"There is so much blue blood in this room, one could make an ocean," Vince whispered.

Victor simply patted his hand to comfort him but he couldn't calm himself. The door opened to reveal Dr. Bennett and Private Secretary Mo Li Zhang. Several of the women in the room began to sob at the indication. Victor, himself, fought to hold back his tears, a war he was winning so far. Dr. Bennett and Mo Li stood at the foot of the bed. "Your Royal Highnesses, Your Grace, Ladies, Mr. Grant, I fear that the time has come. It has been 30 days since any signal of improvement or any sign of life. Her Majesty has remained in a coma for the past 30 days and has needed extensive medical intervention for the duration of such time. Therefore, in accordance with the Royal Medical Directives for the Sovereign Act of 1982, it is my duty to release Her Majesty to the will of God."

Everyone in the room rose to their feet as the doctor stepped to the head of the bed. He pulled out a syringe, pushed what Victor knew from his interrogation this morning to be a sedative directly into the Queen's IV and then turned off the IV machine itself. Then, he turned to the breathing ventilator and clicked the switch. Victor's eyes began to fill has he watched the man pull the tube from his grandmother's mouth. The beeps from the heart monitor began to slow and the number decreased. Victor remembered that the doctor told him that morning that it may take some time for his grandmother to pass, but as fast as that number on the monitor dropped, it seemed she only had seconds. He snapped to attention and saluted his Sovereign one last time. The Duke saw Victor and joined in the salute, along with the Queen's brother, HRH Prince David, a retired Royal Air Force colonel. The rest of the Royal Family bowed or curtsied.

Victor closed his eyes to avoid the tears but his defenses were assaulted by the sound of one tone that rang out which indicated the end of a life, a reign, a relationship. He lowered his salute and grabbed Vince and squeezed him as hard as he could. Everyone in the room including Mo Li began crying loudly as the doctor covered the Queen's face with the white blanket. Minutes passed filled with hysterical weeping, which finally subsided to sporadic sniffles and sobs. The family held each other and mourned together. Prince Apollo looked at Victor and gave him a reassuring and supportive smile. He lifted his head and began to sing, "I've got my mind made up, And I won't turn back, Because I want to see my Jesus someday…"

Princess Eleanor, Her late Majesty's sister and Prince Apollo's mother, joined in, "I've got my mind made up, And I won't turn back because I want to see my Jesus someday." Some more members of the family began to sing, but not Victor. He could barely breathe, let alone sing. All he wanted was to talk to his grandmother again.

After about 15 minutes of singing and fellowship, the Sovereign Chief Counsel, Sir Abioye Kouyate, entered the room and bowed at the neck. "I am deeply sorry for your loss and the loss for our country. Her late Majesty was an amazing woman and monarch."

"Thank you," Princess Mary replied.

"Despite the immense grief we all feel, Iakos must have a Sovereign. So, may I have the Princess Regent, Prince Victor, your respective consorts, and all members of the primary royal family follow me, please?"

Mary and Christopher stepped forward, along with Jackie, Seth, Jack, and Margie. Rose wiped the tears from her face and stood with her husband. They all filed out of the room after Counselor Kouyate. Victor took Vince's hand and began walking dragging Vince along. In the hallway, Rose turned to see Vince and stopped with her hand in the air. "No."

"What?" Victor challenged.

"He is no one's official consort nor a member of this family."

Victor looked at her with a deadly stare. "He's coming with me. Do you really want to have this out right now?"

Mary grabbed Rose and turned her violently around to face her. With her pointer finger in her face, Mary threatened, "Leave him alone."

241

Victor's jaw dropped open, along with everyone else in the hall. Rose dared not protest considering one of them was king or queen. They continued again down the hall and into a conference room with a long ovular table in the middle. Victor, Vince, Jack, Seth, and Jackie sat on one side, while the others sat at the other side of the table. Mo Li entered the room last and closed the door behind her. They all sat except Counselor Kouyate who stood at the head of the table.

The man said, "Before I start, I need everyone here to understand that this document is legally binding and is to remain sealed at the highest level of top secrecy. Are we clear?" the man said with a stern, straight face.

Victor to his left and Mary to his right both nodded. Victor and his mother stared at each other across the table as the Last Will and Testament was read, bequeathing valuables, jewelry, money, and other possessions to different family members, charities, organizations, etc. After about 9 pages of reading, the final clause was read.

"AS MY LAST EARTHLY ACT, I HEREBY PARDON MY DAUGHTER, HRH PRINCESS MARY, THE DUCHESS OF SPITI, OF ALL CHARGES REGARDING HER MARRIAGE TO CHRISTOPHER SCHAEFFER, NOW KNOWN AS HRH CHRISTOPHER, THE DUKE OF SPITI. HOWEVER, IN ORDER TO MAINTAIN AND PRESERVE SUCH MARRIAGE, I HEREBY REMOVE THE HONOR AND TITULAR DIGNITY OF HEIR PRESUMPTIVE FROM HRH PRINCESS MARY, THE DUCHESS OF SPITI. LOVE IS THE GREATEST JOY ONE HAS ON EARTH AND I WISH ALL MY DESCENDANTS TO ENJOY THE BENEFITS AND STRUGGLES OF LOVE.

TO MY DAUGHTER, HRH PRINCESS MARY, THE DUCHESS OF SPITI, I LEAVE YOU YOUR TRUE LOVE. TO MY DEAR AND LOVING GRANDSON, HRH PRINCE VICTOR II OF

SPITI, I LEAVE *MY* TRUE LOVE - MY COUNTRY."

Everyone in the room gasped in shock. Mary snapped to her feet swiftly as if to protest, but instead she did the unthinkable. She bent in a floor-deep curtsy and said four words no one expected to hear from her, "Long live the King."

Epilogue

October - 4 months later

The motorcade moved slowly through the streets of the nation's capital toward Parados Church of Christ. The newly invested prince consort, HRH Prince Vincent, sat opposite Iakos' new king, His Majesty King Victor I. The armored limousine dampened the roar of the projected millions who lined the streets. However, the king tried not to look up to avoid a similar panic attack to the one that swept over him at his predecessor's funeral. He just focused his attention on the love of his life.

"Are you happy?"

"Yes, I am," Victor replied without hesitation.

"Are you nervous," Vince asked.

"Terrified," the new monarch admitted.

Vince leaned forward and placed his hands onto Victor's knees. "You will be fine." He looked into his husband's eyes to find something deeper than he'd expected. "What's on your mind?"

Victor looked up at Vince. "A year ago today, Grandmother was telling me she's sick, I was single, and second in line for the throne. Now…"

"Now, you are married and are on your way to be coronated as King of Iakos?"

Victor nodded. "Why do I feel guilty?"

"Beats me," Vince teased, poking the tip of Victor's nose.

Vincent's phone began to chirp. He put it to her ear. "Hello? Yes. Now?" He held the phone to Victor. "It's for you, Your Majesty! I think you may want to take this call."

"Now? Do you think that's a good idea?" Victor asked.

Vince patted Victor's hand. "It's ok."

Victor took the phone. "Yes?"

A man's voice spoke, "You have a call, Your Majesty. Putting you through." The phone beeped and a familiar woman's voice called out to him.

"Mother?"

"Yes, Your Majesty. It's me."

"Mother, you don't have to call me that. What's the matter?"

"Yes, I do! I need you to do something for me," Princess Mary said.

Victor rolled his eyes. "What is it? I let you keep your title and style, your land, and I allowed you absence from the coronation to spare you the embarrassment. What is it now?"

"Actually, I've just arrived at the church."

"Why? I thought you were going out of the country."

Mary leaned close to the phone to hear over the trumpets echoing fanfare in the church. "I don't care if I'm bleeding to death. I *will* be attending the coronation of my son. After the ceremony, I will leave for 3 months. But before you arrive and you are invested, I want you to know that I truly apologize for everything, son. You have grown into a fine young man and a loving human being. You will be an excellent king and this country — this world — is blessed to have someone like you as a leader." Victor began to tear up.

"Mother, why are you telling me this?"

"Because I wanted to remind you that you come from good stock and you are loved by your country, but mostly by me."

"Thank you, Mother," Victor said, half-sarcastically as the healing wound in his shoulder sent an ache through him. He was truly amazed that this one call had more affection from her than all the conversations throughout his life put together. "We are about to arrive so I have to go."

"Wait, one more thing."

"Yes?" Victor waited for the response but silence came for several seconds until finally she spoke.

"A king needs wise counsel and there's one man I think would help you greatly. His name is Dr. Michael Buchannan, now. He lives in Voreios, in the north."

Victor looked confused. *She chooses now to give me advice on possible courtiers and advisors?* He thought to himself. "Who is this Buchannan?"

"Your father."